D. R.

BAR-20 DAYS

**Center Point
Large Print**

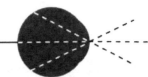

**This Large Print Book carries the
Seal of Approval of N.A.V.H.**

BAR-20 DAYS

• • • • • • • • • • • •

A *HOPALONG CASSIDY* NOVEL

CLARENCE E. MULFORD

CENTER POINT PUBLISHING
THORNDIKE, MAINE

This Center Point Large Print edition
is published in the year 2011.

Originally published in the U.S.
in 1911 by A. C. McClurg & Co.

The text of this Large Print edition is unabridged.
In other aspects, this book may vary
from the original edition.
Printed in the United States of America
on permanent paper.
Set in 16-point Times New Roman type.

ISBN: 978-1-61173-041-8

Library of Congress Cataloging-in-Publication Data

Mulford, Clarence Edward, 1883-1956.
  Bar-20 days : a Hopalong Cassidy novel / Clarence E. Mulford. — Center Point large
print ed.
    p. cm.
  ISBN 978-1-61173-041-8 (library binding : alk. paper)
  1. Cassidy, Hopalong (Fictitious character)—Fiction. 2. Large type books. I. Title.
    II. Title: Bar-twenty days.
  PS3525.U398B43 2011
  813′.52—dc22
                                                                                    2010052180

Author's Dedication—

Affectionately dedicated to "M. D."

List of Chapters—

CHAPTER ONE

ON A STRANGE RANGE

TWO tired but happy punchers rode into the coast town and dismounted in front of the best hotel. Putting up their horses as quickly as possible, they made arrangements for sleeping-quarters and then hastened out to attend to business. Buck had been kind to delegate this mission to them and they would have it over with first of all; then they would feel free to enjoy what pleasures the town might afford. While at that time the city was not what it is now, nevertheless it was capable of satisfying what demands might be made upon it by two very active and zealous cowpunchers. Their first experience began as they left the hotel.

"Hey, you cow wrastlers!" said a not unpleasant voice, and they turned suspiciously as it continued, "You've shore got to hang up them guns with th' hotel clerk while you cavorts around on this range. This is *fence* country."

They regarded the speaker's smiling face and twinkling eyes and laughed. "Well, yo're th' foreman if you own that badge," grinned Hopalong, cheerfully. "We don't need no guns, nohow, in this town, we don't. Plumb forgot we was toting them. But mebby you can tell us where lawyer Jeremiah T. Jones grazes in daylight?"

"Right over yonder, second floor," replied the marshal. "An' come to think of it, mebby you better leave most of yore cash with th' guns—somebody'll take it away from you if you don't. It'd be an awful temptation, an' flesh is weak."

"Huh!" laughed Johnny, moving back into the hotel to leave his gun, closely followed by Hopalong. "Anybody that can turn that little trick on me an' Hoppy will shore earn every red cent; why, we've been to Kansas City!"

As they emerged again Johnny slapped his pocket, from which sounded a musical jingling. "If them weak people try anything on us, we may come between them and *their* money!" he boasted.

"From th' bottom of my heart I pity you," called the marshal, watching them depart, a broad smile illuminating his face. "In about twenty-four hours they'll put up a holler for me to go git it back for 'em," he muttered. "An' I almost believe I'll do it, too. I ain't never seen none of that breed what ever left a town without empty pockets an' aching heads—an' th' smarter they think they are th' easier they fall." A fleeting expression of discontent clouded the smile, for the lure of the open range is hard to resist when once a man has ridden free under its sky and watched its stars. "An' I wish I was one of 'em again," he muttered, sauntering on.

Jeremiah T. Jones, Esq., was busy when his door

opened, but he leaned back in his chair and smiled pleasantly at their bowlegged entry, waving them toward two chairs. Hopalong hung his sombrero on a letter press and tipped his chair back against the wall. Johnny hung grimly to his hat, sat stiffly upright until he noticed his companion's pose, and then, deciding that everything was all right, and that Hopalong was better up in etiquette than himself, pitched his sombrero dexterously over the water pitcher and also leaned against the wall. Nobody could lose him when it came to doing the right thing.

"Well, gentlemen, you look tired and thirsty. This is considered good for all human ailments of whatsoever nature, degree, or wheresoever located, in part or entirety, *ab initio*," Mr. Jones remarked, filling glasses. There was no argument and when the glasses were empty, he continued, "Now what can I do for you? From the Bar-20? Ah, yes; I was expecting you. We'll get right at it," and they did. Half an hour later they emerged on the street, free to take in the town, or to have the town take them in—which was usually the case.

"What was that he said for us to keep away from?" asked Johnny with keen interest.

"Sh! Not so loud," chuckled Hopalong, winking prodigiously.

Johnny pulled tentatively at his upper lip but before he could reply his companion had accosted a stranger.

11

"Friend, we're pilgrims in a strange land, an' we don't know th' trails. Can you tell us where th' docks are?"

"Certainly; glad to. You'll find them at the end of this street," and he smilingly waved them toward the section of the town which Jeremiah T. Jones had specifically and earnestly warned them to avoid.

"Wonder if you're as thirsty as me?" solicitously inquired Hopalong of his companion.

"I was just wondering th' same," replied Johnny. "Say," he confided in a lower voice, "blamed if I don't feel sort of lost without that Colt. Every time I lifts my right laig she goes too high—don't feel natural, nohow."

"Same here; I'm allus feeling to see if I lost it," Hopalong responded. "There ain't no rubbing, no weight, nor nothing."

"Wish I had something to put in its place, blamed if I don't."

"Why, now yo're talking—mebby we can buy something," grinned Hopalong, happily. "Here's a hardware store—come on in."

The clerk looked up and laid aside his novel. "Good morning, gentlemen; what can I do for you? We've just got in some fine new rifles," he suggested.

The customers exchanged looks and it was Hopalong who first found his voice. "Nope, don't want no rifles," he replied, glancing around. "To tell th' truth, I don't know just what we do want, but we want something, all right—got to have it. It's a funny thing, come to think of it; I can't never pass a hardware store without going in an' buying something. I've been told my father was th' same way, so I must inherit it. It's th' same with my pardner, here, only he gets his weakness from his whole family, and it's different from mine. He can't pass a saloon without going in an' buying something."

"Yo're a cheerful liar, an' you know it," retorted Johnny. "You know th' reason why I goes in saloons so much—you'd never leave 'em if I didn't drag you out. He inherits that weakness from his grandfather, twice removed," he confided to the astonished clerk, whose expression didn't know what to express.

"Let's see; a saw?" soliloquized Hopalong. "Nope; got lots of 'em, an' they're all genuine Colts," he mused thoughtfully. "Ax? Nails? Augurs? Corkscrews? Can we use a corkscrew, Johnny? Ah, thought I'd wake you up. Now, what was it cookie said for us to bring him? Bacon? Got any bacon? Too bad—oh, don't apologize; it's all right. Cold chisels—that's th' thing if you ain't got no bacon. Let me see a three-pound cold chisel about as big as that,"—extending a huge and crooked forefinger—"an' with a big bulge at one end. Straight in th' middle, circling off into a three-cornered wavy edge on the other side.

What? Look here! You can't tell us nothing about saloons that we don't know. I want a three-pound chisel, any kind, so it's cold."

Johnny nudged him. "How about them wedges?"

"Twenty-five cents a pound," explained the clerk, groping for his bearings.

"They might do," Hopalong muttered, forcing the article mentioned into his holster. "Why, they're quite hocus-pocus. You take th' brother to mine, Johnny."

"Feels good, but I dunno," his companion muttered. "Little wide at th' sharp end. Hey, got any loose shot?" he suddenly asked, whereat Hopalong beamed and the clerk gasped. It didn't seem to matter whether they bought bacon, cold chisels, wedges, or shot; yet they looked sober.

"Yes, sir; what size?"

"Three pounds of shot, I said!" Johnny rumbled in his throat. "Never mind what size."

"We never care about size when we buy shot," Hopalong smiled. "But, Johnny, wouldn't them little screws be better?" he asked, pointing eagerly.

"Mebby; reckon we better get 'em mixed—half of each," Johnny gravely replied. "Anyhow, there ain't much difference."

The clerk had been behind that counter for four years, and executing and filling orders had become a habit with him, else he would have given them six pounds of cold chisels and corkscrews, mixed. His mouth was still open when he weighed out the screws.

"Mix 'em! Mix 'em!" roared Hopalong, and the stunned clerk complied, and charged them for the whole purchase at the rate set down for screws.

Hopalong started to pour his purchase into the holster which, being open at the bottom, gayly passed the first installment through to the floor. He stopped and looked appealingly at Johnny, and Johnny, in pain from holding back screams of laughter, looked at him indignantly. Then a guileless smile crept over Hopalong's face and he stopped the opening with a wad of wrapping paper and disposed of the shot and screws, Johnny following his laudable example. After haggling a moment over the bill, they paid it and walked out, to the apparent joy of the clerk.

"Don't laugh, Kid; you'll spoil it all," warned Hopalong, as he noted signs of distress on his companion's face. "Now, then; what was it we said about thirst? Come on, I see one already."

Having entered the saloon and ordered, Hopalong beamed upon the bartender and shoved his glass back again. "One more, kind stranger; it's good stuff."

"Yes, feels like a shore-enough gun," remarked Johnny, combining two thoughts in one expression, which is brevity.

The bartender looked at him quickly and then

stood quite still and listened, a puzzled expression on his face.

Tic—tickety-tick—tic-tic, came strange sounds from the other side of the bar. Hopalong was intently studying a chromo on the wall and Johnny gazed vacantly out of the window.

"What's that? What in the deuce is that?" quickly demanded the man with the apron, swiftly reaching for his bung-starter.

Tickety-tic-tic-tic-tic-tic, the noise went on, and Hopalong, slowly rolling his eyes, looked at the floor. A screw rebounded and struck his foot, while shot were rolling recklessly.

"Them's making th' noise," Johnny explained after critical survey.

"Hang it! I knowed we ought to 'a' got them wedges!" Hopalong exclaimed, petulantly, closing the bottom of the sheath. "Why, I won't have no gun left soon 'less I holds it in." The complaint was plaintive.

"Must be filtering through th' stopper," Johnny remarked. "But don't it sound nice, especially when it hits that brass cuspidor!"

The bartender, grasping the mallet even more firmly, arose on his toes and peered over the bar, not quite sure of what he might discover. He had read of infernal machines although he had never seen one. "What th' blazes!" he ejaculated in almost a whisper; and then his face went hard. "You get out of here, quick! You've had too much already! I've seen drunks, but—G'wan! Get out!"

"But we ain't begun yet," Hopalong interposed hastily. "You see—"

"Never mind what I see! I'd hate to see what you'll be seein' before long. God help you when you finish!" rather impolitely interrupted the bartender. He waved the mallet and made for the end of the counter with no hesitancy and lots of purpose in his stride. "G'wan, now! Get out!"

"Come on, Johnny; I'd shoot him only we didn't put no powder with th' shot," Hopalong remarked sadly, leading the way out of the saloon and towards the hardware store.

"You better get out!" shouted the man with the mallet, waving the weapon defiantly. "An' don't you never come back again, neither," he warned.

"Hey, it leaked," Hopalong said pleasantly as he closed the door of the hardware store behind him, whereupon the clerk jumped and reached for the sawed-off shotgun behind the counter. Sawed-off shotguns are great institutions for arguing at short range, almost as effective as dynamite in clearing away obstacles.

"Don't you come no nearer!" he cried, white of face. "You git out, or I'll let *this* leak, an' give you *all* shot, an' more than you can carry!"

"Easy! Easy there, pardner; we want them wedges," Hopalong replied, somewhat hurriedly. "Th' others ain't no good; I choked on th' very first screw. Why, I wouldn't hurt you for th' world,"

Hopalong assured him, gazing interestedly down the twin tunnels.

Johnny leaned over a nail keg and loosed the shot and screws into it, smiling with childlike simplicity as he listened to the tintinnabulation of the metal shower among the nails. "It *does* drop when you let go of it," he observed.

"Didn't I tell you it would? I allus said so," replied Hopalong, looking back to the clerk and the shotgun. "Didn't I, stranger?"

The clerk's reply was a guttural rumbling, 90 per cent profanity, and Hopalong, nodding wisely, picked up two wedges. "Johnny, here's yore gun. If this man will stop talking to hisself and drop that lead-sprayer long enough to take our good money, we'll wear 'em."

He tossed a gold coin on the table, and the clerk, still holding tightly to the shotgun, tossed the coin into the cash box and cautiously slid the change across the counter. Hopalong picked up the money and, emptying his holster into the nail keg, followed his companion to the street, in turn followed slowly by the suspicious clerk. The door slammed shut behind them, the bolt shot home, and the clerk sat down on a box and cogitated.

Hopalong hooked his arm through Johnny's and started down the street. "I wonder what that feller thinks about us, anyhow. I'm glad Buck sent Red over to El Paso instead of us. Won't he be mad when we tell him all th' fun we've had?" he asked, grinning broadly.

They were to meet Red at Dent's store on the way back and ride home together.

They were strangely clad for their surroundings, the chaps glaringly out of place in the Seaman's Port, and winks were exchanged by the regular *habitués* when the two punchers entered the room and called for drinks. They were very tired and a little under the weather, for they had made the most of their time and spent almost all of their money; but any one counting on robbing them would have found them sober enough to look out for themselves. Night had found them ready to go to the hotel, but on the way they felt that they must have one more bracer, and finish their exploration of Jeremiah T. Jones's tabooed section. The town had begun to grow wearisome and they were vastly relieved when they realized that the rising sun would see them in the saddle and homeward bound, headed for God's country, which was the only place for cowpunchers after all.

"Long way from th' home port, ain't you, mates?" queried a tar of Hopalong. Another seaman went to the bar to hold a short, whispered consultation with the bartender, who at first frowned and then finally nodded assent.
"Too far from home, if that's what yo're driving at," Hopalong replied. "Blast these hard trails—

19

my feet are shore on th' prod. Ever meet my side pardner? Johnny, here's a friend of mine, a salt-water puncher, an' he's welcome to th' job, too."

Johnny turned his head ponderously and nodded. "Pleased to meet you, stranger. An' what'll you all have?"

"Old Holland, mate," replied the other, joining them.

"All up!" invited Hopalong, waving them forward. "Might as well do things right or not at all. Them's my sentiments, which I holds as proper. Plain rye, general, if you mean me," he replied to the bartender's look of inquiry.

He drained the glass and then made a grimace. "Tastes a little off—reckon it's my mouth; nothing tastes right in this cussed town. Now, up on our—" He stopped and caught at the bar. "Holy smoke! That's shore alcohol!"

Johnny was relaxing and vainly trying to command his will power. "Something's wrong; what's th' matter?" he muttered sleepily.

"Guess you meant beer; you ain't used to drinking whisky," grinned the bartender, derisively, and watching him closely.

"I can—drink as much whisky as—" and, muttering, Johnny slipped to the floor.

"That wasn't whisky!" cried Hopalong sleepily. "That liquor was *fixed!*" he shouted, sudden anger bracing him. "An' I'm going to fix *you,* too!" he added, reaching for his gun, and drawing forth a

20

wedge. His sailor friend leaped at him, to go down like a log, and Hopalong, seething with rage, wheeled and threw the weapon at the man behind the bar, who also went down. The wedge, glancing from his skull, swept a row of bottles and glasses from the shelf and, caroming, went through the window.

In an instant Hopalong was the vortex of a mass of struggling men and, handicapped as he was, fought valiantly, his rage for the time neutralizing the effects of the drug. But at last, too sleepy to stand or think, he, too, went down.

"By th' Lord, that man's a fighter!" enthusiastically remarked the leader, gently touching his swollen eye. "George must 'a' put an awful dose in that grog."

"Lucky for us he didn't have no gun—th' wedge was bad enough," groaned a man on the floor, slowly sitting up. "Whoever swapped him that wedge for his gun did us a good turn, all right."

A companion tentatively readjusted his lip. "I don't envy Wilkins his job breaking in that man when he gets awake."

"Don't waste no time, mates," came the order. "Up with 'em an' aboard. We've done our share; let th' mate do his, an' be hanged. Hullo, Portsmouth; coming around, eh?" he asked the man who had first felt the wedge. "I was scared you was done for that time."

"No more shanghaiing hair pants for me, no more!" thickly replied Portsmouth. "Oh, my head, it's bust open!"

"Never mind about th' bartender—let him alone; we can't waste no time with him now!" commanded the leader sharply. "Get these fellers on board before we're caught with 'em. We want our money after that."

"All clear!" came a low call from the lookout at the door, and soon a shadowy mass surged across the street and along a wharf. There was a short pause as a boat emerged out of the gloom, some whispered orders, and then the squeaking of oars grew steadily fainter in the direction of a ship which lay indistinct in the darkness.

Chapter Two

The Rebound

A MAN moaned and stirred restlessly in a bunk, muttering incoherently. A stampeded herd was thundering over him, the grinding hoofs beating him slowly to death. He saw one mad steer stop and lower its head to gore him and just as the sharp horns touched his skin, he awakened. Slowly opening his bloodshot eyes, he squinted about him, sick, weak, racking with pain where heavy shoes had struck him in the *mêlée*, his head reverberating with roars which seemed almost to split it open. Slowly he regained his full senses and began to make out his surroundings. He was in a bunk which moved up and down, from side to side, and was never still. There was a small, round window near his feet—thank heaven it was open, for he was almost suffocated by the foul air and the heat. Where was he? What had happened? Was there a salty odor in the air, or was he still dreaming? Painfully raising himself on one elbow, he looked around and caught sight of a man in a bunk across the aisle. It was Johnny Nelson! Then, bit by bit, the whole thing came to him and he cursed heartily as he reviewed it and reached the only possible conclusion. He was at sea! He, Hopalong Cassidy, the best fighting unit of a good fighting outfit, shanghaied and at sea! Drugged, beaten, and stolen to labor on a ship!

Johnny was muttering and moaning and Hopalong slowly climbed out of the narrow bunk, unsteadily crossed the moving floor, and shook him. "Reckon he's in a stampede, too!" he growled. "They shore raised hell with us. Oh, what a beating we got! But we'll pass it along with trimmings."

Johnny's eyes opened and he looked around in confusion. "Wha', Hopalong!"

"Yes, it's me, th' prize idiot of a blamed good pair of 'em. How d'you feel?"

"Sleepy an' sick. My eyes ache an' my head's splitting. Where's Buck an' the rest?"

Hopalong sat down on the edge of the bunk and swore luridly, eloquently, beautifully, with a fervor and polish which left nothing to be desired in that line, and caused his companion to gaze at him in astonishment.

"I had a mighty bad dream, but you must 'a' had one a whole lot worse, to listen to you," Johnny remarked. "Gee, you're going some! What's th' matter with you? You sick, too?"

Thereupon Hopalong unfolded the tale of woe and when Johnny had grasped its import and knew that his dream had been a stern reality he straightway loosed his vocabulary and earned a draw. "Well, I'm going back again," he finished with great decision, arising to make good his assertion.

"Swim or walk?" asked Hopalong nonchalantly.

"Huh! Oh, Lord!"

"Well, I ain't going to either swim or walk," Hopalong soliloquized. "I'm just going to stay right here in this one-by-nothing cellar an' spoil the health an' good looks of any pirate that comes down that ladder to get me out." He looked around, interested in life once more, and his trained eye grasped the strategic worth of their position. "Only one at a time, an' down that ladder," he mused, thoughtfully. "Why, Johnny, we owns this range as long as we wants to. They can't get us out. But, say, if only we had our guns!" he sighed, regretfully.

"You're right as far as you go, but you don't go to th' eating part. We'll starve an' we ain't got no water. I can drink about a bucketful right now," moodily replied his companion.

"Well, yo're right, but mebby we can find food an' water."

"Don't see no signs of none. Hey!" Johnny ejaculated, smiling faintly in his misery. "Let's get busy an' burn th' cussed thing up! Got any matches?"

"First you want to drown yoreself swimming, an' now you want to roast th' pair of us to death," Hopalong retorted, eying the rear wall of the room. "Wonder what's on th' other side of that partition?"

Johnny looked. "Why, water; an' lots of it, too."

"Naw; th' water is on th' other sides."

"Then how do I know?—sh! I hear somebody coming on th' roof."

"Tumble back in yore bunk—quick!" Hopalong hurriedly whispered. "Be asleep—if he comes down here it'll be our deal."

The steps overhead stopped at the companionway and a shadow appeared across the small patch of sunlight on the floor of the forecastle. "Tumble up here, you blasted loafers!" roared a deep voice.

No reply came from the forecastle—the silence was unbroken.

"If I have to come down there I'll—" the first mate made promises in no uncertain tones and in very impolite language. He listened for a moment, and having very good ears and hearing nothing, made more promises and came down the ladder quickly and nimbly.

"*I'll* bring you to," he muttered, reaching a brawny hand for Hopalong's nose, and missing. But he made contact with his own face, which stopped a short-arm blow from the owner of the aforesaid nose, a jolt full of enthusiasm and purpose. Beautiful and dazzling flashes of fire filled the air and just then something landed behind his ear and prolonged the pyrotechnic display. When the skyrockets went up he lost interest in the proceedings and dropped to the floor like a bag of meal.

Hopalong cut another piece from the rope in his

hand and watched his companion's busy fingers. "Tie him good, Johnny; he's th' only ace we've drawn in this game so far, an' we mustn't lose him."

Johnny tied an extra knot for luck and leaned forward, his eyes riveted on the bump under the victim's coat. His darting hand brought into sight that which pleased him greatly. "Oh, joy! Here, Hoppy, you take it."

Hopalong turned the weapon over in his hand, spun the cylinder, and gloated, the clicking sweet music to his ears. "Plumb full, too! I never reckoned I'd ever be so tickled over a snub-nosed gun like this—but I feel like singing!"

"An' I feel like dying," grunted Johnny, grabbing at his stomach. "If th' blamed shack would only stand still!" he groaned, gazing at the floor with strong disgust. "I don't reckon I've ever been so blamed sick in all my—" the sentence was unfinished, for the open porthole caught his eye and he leaped forward to use it for a collar.

Hopalong gazed at him in astonishment and sudden pity took possession of him as his pallid companion left the porthole and faced him.

"You ought to have something to eat, Kid—I'm purty hungry myself—what th' blazes!" he ejaculated, for Johnny's protesting wail was finished outside the port. Then a light broke upon him and he wondered how soon it would be his turn to pay tribute to Neptune.

"Mr. Wilkins!" shouted a voice from the deck, and Hopalong moved back a step. "Mr. Wilkins!" After a short silence the voice soliloquized, "Guess he changed his mind about it; I'll get 'em up for him," and feet came into view. When halfway down the ladder the second mate turned his head and looked blankly down a gun barrel, while a quiet but angry voice urged him further, "Keep a-coming, keep a-coming!" The second mate complained, but complied.

"Stick 'em up higher—now, Johnny, wobble around behind the nice man an' take *his* toy gun— you shut yore yap! I'm bossing this trick, not you. Got it, Kid? There's th' rope—that's right. Nobody'd think you sick to see you work. Well, that's a good draw, but it's only a pair of aces against a full, at that. Wonder who'll be th' next. Hope it's th' foreman."

Johnny, keeping up by sheer grit, pointed to the rear wall. "What about that?"

For reply his companion walked over to it, put his shoulder to it and pushed. He stepped back and hurled his weight against it, but it was firm despite its squeaking protest. Then he examined it foot by foot and found a large knot, which he drove in by a blow of the gun. Bending, he squinted through the opening for a full minute and then reported:

"Purty black in there at this end, but up at th' other there's light from a hole in th' roof, an' I could see boxes an' things like that. I reckon it's th' main cellar."

"If we could get out at th' other end with that gun you've got we could raise blazes for a while," suggested Johnny. "Anyhow, mebby they can come at us that way when they find out what we've gone an' done."

"Yo're right," Hopalong replied, looking around. Seeing an iron bar, he procured it and, pushing it through the knothole in the partition, pulled. The board, splitting and cracking under the attack, finally broke from its fastenings with a sharp report, and Hopalong, pulling it aside, stepped out of sight of his companion. Johnny was grinning at the success of his plan when he was interrupted.

"Ahoy, down there!" yelled a stentorian voice from above. "Mr. Wilkins! What th' devil are you doing so long?" and after a very short wait other feet came into sight.

Just then the second mate, having managed to slip off the gag, shouted warning, "Look out, Captain! They've got us and our guns! One of them has—" but Johnny's knee thudded into his chest and ended the sentence as a bullet sent a splinter flying from under the captain's foot.

"Hang these guns!" Johnny swore, and quickly turned to secure the gag in the mouth of the offending second mate. "You make any more yaps like that an' I'll wing you for keeps with yore own gun!" he snapped. "We're caught in yore trap an' we'll fight to a finish. You'll be th' first to go under if you gets any smart."

"Ahoy, men!" roared the captain in a towering rage, dancing frantically about on the deck and shouting for the crew to join him. He filled the air with picturesque profanity and stamped and yelled in passion at such rank mutiny.

"Hand grenades! Hand grenades!" he cried. Then he remembered that his two mates were also below and would share in the mutineers' fate, and his rage increased at his galling helplessness. When he had calmed sufficiently to think clearly he realized that it was certain death for anyone to attempt going down the ladder, and that his must be a waiting game. He glanced at his crew, 13 good men, all armed with windlass bars and belaying-pins, and gave them orders. Two were to watch the hatch and break the first head to appear, while the others returned to work. Hunger and thirst would do the rest. And what joy would be his when they were forced to surrender!

Hopalong groped his way slowly towards the patch of light, barking his shins, stumbling and falling over the barrels and crates, and finally, losing his footing at a critical moment, tumbled down upon a box marked *Cotton*. There was a splintering crash and the very faint clink of metal. Dazed and bruised, he sat up and felt of himself—and found that he had lost his gun in the fall.

"Now, where in blazes did it fly to?" he muttered angrily, peering about anxiously. His eyes suddenly opened their widest and he stared in surprise at a field gun which covered him, and then he saw parts of two more.

"Good Lord! Is this a gunboat?" he cried. "Are we up against bluejackets an' Uncle Sam?" He glanced quickly back the way he had come when he heard Johnny's shot, but he could see nothing. He figured that Johnny had sense enough to call for help if he needed it, and put that possibility out of his mind. "Naw, this ain't no gunboat—th' government don't steal men; it enlists 'em. But it's a funny pile of junk, all th' same. Where in blazes is that toy gun? *Well,* I'll be hanged!" and he plunged toward the *Cotton* box he had burst in his descent, and worked at it frantically.

"Winchesters! Winchesters!" he cried, dragging out two of them. "Whoop! Now for th' cartridges—there shore must be some to go with these guns!" He saw a keg marked *Nails,* and managed to open it after great labor—and found it full of army Colts. Forcing down the desire to turn a handspring, he slipped one of the six-shooters in his empty holster and patted it lovingly. "Old friend, I'm shore glad to see you, all right. You've been used, but that don't make no difference."

31

Searching further, he opened a full box of *machetes,* and soon after found cartridges of many kinds and calibers. It took him but a few minutes to make his selection and cram his pockets with them. Then he filled two Colts and two Winchesters—and executed a short jig to work off the dangerous pressure of his exuberance.

"But what an unholy lot of weapons," he soliloquized on his way back to Johnny. "An' they're all second-hand. Cannons, too—an' *machetes!*" he exclaimed, suddenly understanding. "Jumping Jerusalem!—a filibustering expedition bound for Cuba, or one of them wildcat republics down south! Oh, ho, my friends; I see where you have bit off more'n you can chew." In his haste to impart the joyous news to his companion, he barked his shins shamefully.

"'Way down south in the land o' cotton, cinnamon seed an'—whoa, blast you!" and Hopalong stuck his head through the opening in the partition and grinned. "Heard you shoot, Kid; I reckoned you might need me—an' these!" he finished, looking fondly upon the weapons as he shoved them into the forecastle.

Johnny groaned and held his stomach, but his eyes lighted up when he saw the guns, and he eagerly took one of each kind, a faint smile wreathing his lips. "Now we'll show these water snakes what kind of men they stole," he threatened.

Up on the deck the choleric captain still stamped and swore, and his crew, with well-concealed mirth, went about their various duties as if they were accustomed to have shanghaied men act this way. They sympathized with the unfortunate pair, realizing how they themselves would feel if shanghaied to break broncos.

Hogan, A. B., stated the feelings of his companions very well in his remarks to the men who worked alongside. "In me hear-rt I'm dommed glad av it, Yensen. I hope they bate th' old man at his own game. 'T is a shame in these days fer honest men to be took in that unlawful way. I've heard me father tell of th' press gangs on th' other side, an' 't is small business."

Yensen looked up to reply, chanced to glance aft, and dropped his calking-iron in his astonishment. "Yumping Yimminy! Luk at dat fallar!"

Hogan looked. "Th' deuce! That's a man after me own hear-rt! Kape yore pagan mouth shut! If ye take a hand agin' 'em I'll swab up th' deck wid yez. G'wan wor-rking like a sane man, ye ijit!"

"Ay ent ban fight wit dat fallar! Luk at th' gun!"

A man had climbed out of the after hatch and was walking rapidly towards them, a rifle in his hands, while at his thigh swung a Colt. He watched the two seamen closely and caught sight of Hogan's twinkling blue eyes, and a smile quivered about his mouth. Hogan shut and opened one eye and went on working.

As soon as Hopalong caught sight of the captain, the rifle went up and he announced his presence without loss of time. "Throw up yore hands, you polecat! I'm running this ranch from now on!"

The captain wheeled with a jerk and his mouth opened, and then clicked shut as he started forward, his rage acting galvanically. But he stopped quickly enough when he looked down the barrel of the Winchester and glared at the cool man behind it.

"What th' hell are you doing?" he yelled.

"Well, I ain't kidnaping cowpunchers to steal my boat," replied Hopalong. "An' you fellers stand still or I'll drop you cold!" he ordered to the assembled and restless crew. "Johnny!" he shouted, and his companion popped up through the hatch like a jack-in-the-box. "Good boy, Johnny. Tie this coyote foreman like you did th' others," he ordered. While Johnny obeyed, Hopalong looked around the circle, and his eyes rested on Hogan's face, studying it, and found something there which warmed his heart. "Friend, do you know th' back trail? Can you find that runt of a town we left?"

"Aye, aye."

"Shore, you; who'd you think I was talking to? Can you find th' way back, th' way we came?"

"Shure an' I can that, if I'm made to."

"You'll swing for mutiny if you do, you bilgewallering pirate!" roared the trussed captain. "Take that gun away from him, d'ye hear!" he yelled at the crew. "I'm captain of this ship, an' I'll hang every last one of you if you don't obey orders! This is mutiny!"

"You won't do no hanging with that load of weapons below!" retorted Hopalong. "Uncle Sam is looking for filibusters—this here gun is 'cotton,'" he said, grinning. He turned to the crew. "But you fellers are due to get shot if you sees her through," he added.

"I'm captain of this ship—" began the helpless autocrat.

"You shore look like it, all right," Hopalong replied, smiling. "If yo're th' captain you order her turned around and headed over th' back trail, or I'll drop you overboard off yore own ship!" Then fierce anger at the thought of the indignities and injuries he and his companion had suffered swept over him and prompted a one-minute speech which left no doubt as to what he would do if his demand was not complied with. Johnny, now free to watch the crew, added a word or two of endorsement, and he acted a little as if he rather hoped it would not be complied with. He itched for an excuse.

The captain did some quick thinking; the true situation could not be disguised, and with a final oath of rage he gave in. "'Bout ship, Hogan; nor' by nor'west," he growled, and the seaman started away to execute the command, but was quickly stopped by Hopalong.

"Hogan, is that right?" he demanded. "No funny business, or we'll clean up th' whole bunch, an' blamed quick, too!"

"That's th' course, sor. That's th' way back to town. I can navigate, an' me orders are plain. Ye're Irish, by th' way av ye' and 't is back to town ye go, sor." He turned to the crew, "Stand by, me boys." And in a short time the course was nor' by nor'west.

The return journey was uneventful and at nightfall the ship lay at anchor off the low Texas coast, and a boat loaded with men grounded on the sandy beach. Four of them arose and leaped out into the mild surf and dragged the boat as high up on the sand as it would go. Then the two cowpunchers followed and one of them gave a low-spoken order to the Irishman at his side.

"Yes, sor," replied Hogan, and hastened to help the captain out onto the sand and to cut the ropes which bound him. "Do ye want th' mates, too, sor?" he asked, glancing at the trussed men in the boat.

"No, th' foreman's enough," Hopalong responded, handing his weapons to Johnny and turning to face the captain, who was looking into Johnny's gun as he rubbed his arms to restore perfect circulation.

"Now, you flat-faced coyote, yo're going to get

th' beating of yore life, an' I'm going to give it to you!" Hopalong cried, warily advancing upon the man whom he held to be responsible for the miseries of the past 24 hours. "You didn't give me a square deal, but I'm man enough to give you one! When you drug an' steal any more cowpunchers—" Action stopped his words.

It was a great fight. A filibustering sea captain is no more peaceful than a wild boar and about as dangerous; and while this one was not at his best, neither was Hopalong. The latter luckily had acquired some knowledge of the rudiments of the game and had the vigor of youth to oppose to the captain's experience and his infuriated but well-timed rushes. The seamen, for the honor of their calling and perhaps with a mind to the future, cheered on the captain and danced up and down in their delight and excitement. They had a lot of respect for the prowess of their master, and for the man who could stand up against him in a fair and square fist fight. To give assistance to either in a fair fight was not to be thought of, and Johnny's gun was sufficient after-excuse for non-interference.

The *sop! sop!* of the punishing blows as they got home and the steady circling of Hopalong in avoiding the dangerous attacks, went on minute after minute. Slowly the captain's strength was giving out, and he resorted to trickery as his last chance. Retreating, he half raised his arms and lowered them as if weary, ready as a cat to strike with all his weight if the other gave an opening. It ought to have worked—it had worked before—but Hopalong was there to win, and without the momentary hesitation of the suspicious fighter he followed the retreat and his hard hand flashed in over the captain's guard a fraction of a second sooner than that surprised gentleman anticipated. The ferocious frown gave way to placid peace and the captain reclined at the feet of the battered victor, who stood waiting for him to get up and fight. The captain lay without a sign of movement and as Hopalong wondered, Hogan was the first to speak.

"Fer th' love av hiven, let him be! Ye needn't wait—he's done—I know by th' sound av it!" he exclaimed, stepping forward. "'T was a purty blow, an' 't was a gr-rand foight ye put up, sor! A gr-rand foight, but any more av that is murder. 'T is an Irishman's game, sor, an' ye did yersilf proud. But now let him be—no man, least av all a Dootchman, iver tuk more than that an' lived!"

Hopalong looked at him and slowly replied between swollen lips, "Yo're right, Hogan; we're square now, I reckon."

"That's right, sor," Hogan replied, and turned to his companions. "Put him in th' boat; an' mind ye handle him gintly—we'll be sailing under him soon. Now, sor, if it's yer pleasure, I'll be after sayin' good-by to ye, sor; an' to ye, too," he said, shaking hands with both punchers. "Fer a sick la-ad ye're a wonder, ye are that," he smiled at Johnny, "but ye want to kape away from th' water-fronts. Good-by to ye both, an' a pleasant journey home. Th' town is tin miles to me right, over beyant them hills."

"Good-by, Hogan," mumbled Hopalong gratefully. "Yo're square all th' way through; an' if you ever get out of a job or in any kind of trouble that I can help you out of, come up to th' Bar-20 an' you won't have to ask twice. Good luck!" And the two sore and aching punchers, wiser in the ways of the world, plodded doggedly toward the town, ten miles away.

The next morning found them in the saddle, bound for Dent's hotel and store near the San Miguel Canyon. When they arrived at their destination and Johnny found there was some hours to wait for Red, his restlessness sent him roaming about the country, not so much "seeking what he might devour" as hoping something might seek to devour him. He was so sore over his recent kidnaping that he longed to find a salve. He faithfully promised Hopalong that he would return at noon.

CHAPTER THREE

DICK MARTIN STARTS SOMETHING

DICK MARTIN slowly turned, leaned his back against the bar, and languidly regarded a group of Mexicans at the other end of the room. Singly, or in combinations of two or more, each was imparting all he knew, or thought he knew about the ghost of San Miguel Canyon. Their fellow-countrymen, new to the locality, seemed properly impressed. That it was the ghost of Carlos Martinez, murdered nearly 100 years before at the big bend in the canyon, was conceded by all; but there was a dispute as to why it showed itself only on Friday nights, and why it was never seen by any but a Mexican. Never had a Gringo seen it. The Mexican stranger was appealed to. Did this not prove that the murder had been committed by a Mexican? The stranger affected to consider the question.

Martin surveyed them with outward impassiveness and inward contempt. A realist, a cynic, and an absolute genius with a Colt's .45, he was well known along the border for his dare-devil exploits and reckless courage. The brainiest men in the Secret Service, Lewis, Thomas, Sayre, and even Old Jim Lane, the local chief, whose fingers at El Paso felt every vibration along the

Rio Grande, were not as well known—except to those who had seen the inside of government penitentiaries—and they were quite satisfied to be so eclipsed. But the Service knew of the ghost, as it knew everything pertaining to the border, and gave it no serious thought; if it took interest in all the ghosts and superstitions peculiar to the Mexican temperament it would have no time for serious work. Martin once, in a spirit of savage denial, had wasted the better part of several successive Friday nights in the San Miguel, but to no avail. When told that the ghost showed itself only to Mexicans he had shrugged his shoulders eloquently and laughed, also eloquently.

"A Greaser," he replied, "is one-half fear and superstition, an' th' other half imagination. There ain't no ghosts, but I know th' Greasers have seen 'em, all right. A Greaser can see anything scary if he makes up his mind to. If *I* ever see one an' he keeps on being one after I shoot, I'll either believe in ghosts or quit drinking." His eyes twinkled as he added, "An' of th' two, I think I'd *prefer* to see ghosts!"

He was flushed and restless with deviltry. His fifth glass always made him so, and tonight there was an added stimulus. He believed the strange Mexican to be Juan Alvarez, who was so clever that the government had never been able to convict him. Alvarez was fearless to recklessness and Martin, eager to test him, addressed the group with the blunt terseness for which he was famed, and hated.

"Greasers are cowards," he asserted quietly, and with a smile which invited excitement. He took a keen delight in analyzing the expressions on the faces of those hit. It was one of his favorite pastimes when feeling coltish.

The group was shocked into silence, quickly followed by great unrest and hot, muttered words. Martin did not move a muscle, the smile was set, but between the half-closed eyelids crouched combat, on its toes. The Mexicans knew it was there without looking for it—the tone of his voice, the caressing purr of his words, and his unnatural languor were signs well known to them. Not a criminal sneaking back from voluntary banishment in Mexico who had seen those signs ever forgot them, if he lived. Martin watched the group catlike, keenly scrutinizing each face, reading the changing emotions in every shifting expression. He had this art down so well that he could tell when a man was debating the pull of a gun, and beat him on the draw by a fraction of a second.

"De senor ees meestak," came the reply, as quiet and caressing as the words which provoked it. The strange Mexican was standing proudly and looking into the squinting eyes with only a grayness of face and a tigerish litheness to tell what he felt.

"None go through th' canyon after dark on Fridays," purred Martin.

"*I* go tro' de canyon nex' Friday night. Eef I do, then you mak' apology to me?"

"I'll limit my remark to all but one Greaser."

The Mexican stepped forward. "I tak' thees gloove an' leave eet at de Beeg Ben', for you to fin' in daylight," he said, tapping one of Martin's gauntlets which lay on the bar. "You geev me eet befo' I go?"

"Yes, at nine o'clock tomorrow night," Martin replied, hiding his elation. He was sure that he knew the man now.

The Mexican, cool and smiling, bowed and left the room, his companions hastening after him.

"Well, I'll bet twenty-five dollars he flunks!" breathed the bartender, straightening up.

Martin turned languidly and smiled at him. "I'll take that, Charley," he replied.

Johnny Nelson was always late, and on this occasion he was later than usual. He was to have joined Hopalong and Red, if Red had arrived, at Dent's at noon the day before, and now it was after nine o'clock at night as he rode through San Felippe without pausing and struck east for the canyon. The dropping trail down the canyon was serious enough in broad daylight, but at night to attempt its passage was foolhardy, unless one knew every turn and slant by heart, which Johnny did not. He was 33 hours late now, and he was determined to make up what he could in the next three.

When Johnny left Hopalong at Dent's he had given his word to be back on time and not to keep his companions waiting, for Red might be on time and he would chafe if he were delayed. But alas for Johnny's good intentions, his course took him through a small Mexican hamlet in which lived a senorita of remarkable beauty and rebellious eyes, and Johnny tarried in the town most of the day, riding up and down the streets, practicing the nice things he would say if he met her. She watched him from the heavily draped window, and sighed as she wondered if her dashing *Americano* would storm the house and carry her off like the knights of old. Finally he had to turn away with heavy and reluctant heart, promising himself that he would return when no petulant and sarcastic companions were waiting for him. Then—ah! what dreams youth knows.

Half an hour ahead of him on another trail rode Juan, smiling with satisfaction. He had come to San Felippe to get a look at the canyon on Friday nights, and Martin had given him an excuse entirely unexpected. For this he was truly grateful, even while he knew that the American had tried to pick a quarrel with him and thus rid the border of a man entirely too clever for the good of customs receipts; and failing in that, had hoped the treacherous canyon trail would gain that end in another manner. Old Jim Lane's fingers touched wires not one whit more sensitive than those which had sent Juan Alvarez to look over the San Miguel—and Lane's wires had been slow this time. When Juan had left the saloon the night before and had seen Manuel slip away from the group and ride off into the north, he had known that the ghost would show itself the following night.

But Juan was to be disappointed. He was still some distance from the canyon when a snarling bulk landed on the haunches of his horse. He jerked loose his gun and fired twice and then knew nothing. When he opened his eyes he lay quietly, trying to figure it out with a head throbbing with pain from his fall. The cougar must have been desperate for food to attack a man. He moved his foot and struck something soft and heavy. His shots had been lucky, but they had not saved him his horse and a sprained arm and leg. There would be no gauntlet found at the Big Bend at daylight.

When Johnny Nelson reached the twin boulders marking the beginning of the sloping run where the trail pitched down, he grinned happily at sight of the moon rising over the low hills and then grabbed at his holster, while every hair in his head stood up curiously. A wild, haunting, feminine scream arose to a quavering soprano and sobbed away into silence. No words can adequately describe the unearthly wail in that cry and it took a full half-minute for Johnny to become himself again and to understand what it was. Once more it arose, nearer, and Johnny peered into the shadows along a rough backbone of rock, his Colt balanced in his half-raised hand.

"You come 'round me an' you'll get hurt," he muttered, straining his eyes to peer into the blackness of the shadows. "Come on out, Soft-foot; th' moon's yore finish. You an' me will have it out right here an' now. I don't want no cougar trailing me through that ink-black canyon on a two-foot ledge." He thought he saw a shadow glide across a dim patch of moonlight, but when his smoke rifted he knew he had missed. "Damn it! You've got a mate 'round here somewhere," he complained. "Well, I'll have to chance it, anyhow. Come on bronc! Yo're shaking like a leaf—get out of this!"

When he began to descend into the canyon he allowed his horse to pick its own way without any guidance from him, and gave all of his attention to the trail behind him. The horse could get along better by itself in the dark, and it was more than possible that one or two lithe cougars might be slinking behind him on velvet paws. The horse scraped along gingerly, feeling its way step by step, and sending stones rattling and clattering down the precipice at his left to tinkle into the stream at the bottom.

"Gee, but I wish I'd not wasted so much time," muttered the rider uneasily. "This here canyon-cougar combination is th' worst *I* ever butted up against. I'll never be late again, not never; not for all th' girls in th' world. Easy, bronc," he cautioned, as he felt the animal slip and quiver. "Won't this trail ever start going up again?" he growled petulantly, taking his eyes off the black back trail, where no amount of scrutiny showed him anything, and turned in the saddle to peer ahead—and a yell of surprise and fear burst from him, while chills ran up and down his spine. An unearthly, piercing shriek suddenly rang out and filled the canyon with ear-splitting uproar and a glowing, sheeted half-figure of a man floated and danced 20 feet from him and over the chasm. He jerked his gun and fired, but only once, for his mount had its own ideas about some things and this particular one easily headed the list. The startled rider grabbed reins and pommel, his blood congealed with fear of the precipice less than a foot from his side, and he gave all his attention to the horse. But scared as he was he heard, or thought that he heard, a peculiar sound when he fired, and he would have sworn that he hit the mark—the striking of the bullet was not drowned in the uproar and he would never forget the sound of that impact. He rounded Big Bend as if he were coming up to the judge's stand, and when he struck the upslant of the emerging trail he had made a record. Cold sweat beaded his forehead and he was trembling from head to foot when he again rode into the moonlight on the level plain, where he tried to break another record.

Chapter Four

Johnny Arrives

MEANWHILE HOPALONG and Red quarreled petulantly and damned the erring Johnny with enthusiastic abandon, while Dent smiled at them and joked; but his efforts at levity made little impression on the irate pair. Red, true to his word, had turned up at the time set, in fact, he was half an hour ahead of time, for which miracle he endeavored to take great and disproportionate credit. Dent was secretly glad about the delay, for he found his place lonesome. He thoroughly enjoyed the company of the two gentlemen from the Bar-20, whose actions seemed to be governed by whims and who appeared to lack all regard for consequences; and they squabbled so refreshingly, and spent their money cheerfully. Now, if they would only wind up the day by fighting! Such a finish would be joy indeed. And speaking of fights, Dent was certain that Mr. Cassidy had been in one recently, for his face bore marks that could only be acquired in that way.

After supper the two guests had relapsed into a silence which endured only as long as the pleasing fullness. Then the squabbling began again, growing worse until they fell silent from lack of adequate expression. Finally Red once again spoke of their absent friend.

"We oughtn't get peevish, Hoppy—he's only thirty-six hours late," suggested Red. "An' he might be a week," he added thoughtfully, as his mind ran back over a long list of Johnny's misdeeds.

"Yes, he might. An' won't he have a fine cock-an'-bull tale to explain it," growled Hopalong reminiscently. "His excuses are th' worst part of it generally."

"Eh, does he—make excuses?" asked Dent, mildly surprised.

"He does to *us*," retorted Red savagely. "He's worse than a woman; take him all in all an' you've got th' toughest proposition that ever wore pants. But he's a good feller, at that."

"Well, you've got a lot of nerve, you have!" retorted Hopalong. "You don't want to say anything about th' Kid. If there's anybody that can beat him in being late an' acting th' fool generally, it's you. An' what's more, you know it!"

Red wheeled to reply, but was interrupted by a sudden uproar outside, fluent swearing coming toward the house. The door opened with a bang, admitting a white-faced, big-eyed man with one leg jammed through the box he had landed on in dismounting.

"Gimme a drink, quick!" he shouted wildly, dragging the box over to the bar with a cheerful disregard for chairs and other temporary obstructions. "Gimme a drink!" he reiterated.

"Give you six hops in th' neck!" yelled Red, missing and almost sitting down because of the enthusiasm he had put into his effort. Johnny side-stepped and ducked, and as he straightened up to ask for whys and wherefores, Red's eyes opened wide and he paused in his further intentions to stare at the apparition.

"Sick?" queried Hopalong, who was frightened.

"Gimme that drink!" demanded Johnny feverishly, and when he had it he leaned against the bar and mopped his face with a trembling hand.

"What's th' matter with you, anyhow?" asked Red with deep anxiety.

"Yes, for God's sake, what's happened to you?" demanded Hopalong.

Johnny breathed deeply and threw back his shoulders as if to shake off a weight. "Fellers, I had a cougar soft-footing after me in that dark canyon, my cayuse ran away on a two-foot ledge up th' wall,—*an'*—*I*—*saw*—*a*—*ghost!*"

There was a respectful silence. Johnny, waiting a reasonable length of time for replies and exclamations, flushed a bit and repeated his frank and candid statement, adding a few adjectives to it. "*A real, screeching, flying ghost!* An' I'm going *home,* an' I'm going to *stay* there. I ain't never coming back no more, not for anything. Damn this border country, *anyhow!*"

The silence continued, whereupon Johnny grew properly indignant. "You act like I told you it was going to rain! Why don't you say something? Didn't you hear what I said, you fools!" he asked pugnaciously. "Are you in th' habit of having a thing like that told you? Why don't you show some interest, you dod-blasted, thick-skulled wooden-heads?"

Red looked at Hopalong, Hopalong looked at Red, and then they both looked at Dent, whose eyes were fixed in a stare on Johnny.

"Huh!" snorted Hopalong, warily arising. "Was that all?" he asked, nodding at Red, who also arose and began to move cautiously toward their erring friend. "Didn't you see no more'n one ghost? Anybody that can see one ghost, an' no more, is wrong somewhere. Now, stop, an' think,didn't you see *two?*" He was advancing carefully while he talked, and Red was now behind the man who saw one ghost.

"Why, you—" there was a sudden flurry and Johnny's words were cut short in the *mêlée.*

"Good, Red! Ouch!" shouted Hopalong. "Look out! Got any rope, Dent? Well, hurry up: there ain't no telling what he'll do if he's loose. Th' mescal they sell down in this country ain't liquor—it's poison," he panted. "An' he can't even stand whisky!"

Finding the rope was easier than finding a place to put it, and the unequal battle raged across the room and into the next, where it sounded as if the house were falling down. Johnny's voice was shrill and full of vexation and his words were extremely impolite and lacked censoring. His feet appeared to be numerous and growing rapidly, judging from the amount of territory they covered and defended, and Red joyfully kicked Hopalong in the *mêlée*, which in this instance also stands for stomach—Red always took great pains to do more than his share in a scrimmage. Dent hovered on the flanks, his hands full of rope, and begged with great earnestness to be allowed to apply it to parts of Johnny's thrashing anatomy. But as the flanks continued to change with bewildering swiftness he begged in vain, and began to make suggestions and give advice pleasing to the three combatants. Dent knew just how it should be done, and was generous with the knowledge until Johnny zealously planted five knuckles on his one good eye, when the engagement became general.

The table skidded through the door on one leg and caromed off the bar at a graceful angle, collecting three chairs and one sand-box cuspidor on the way. The box on Johnny's leg had long since departed, as Hopalong's shin could testify. One chair dissolved unity and distributed itself lavishly over the room, while the bed shrank silently and folded itself on top of Dent, who bucked it up and down with burning zeal, and finally had sense enough to crawl from under it.

He immediately celebrated his liberation by getting a strangle hold on two legs, one of which happened to be the personal property of Hopalong Cassidy; and the battle raged on a lower plane. Red raised one hand as he carefully traced a neck to its own proper head and then his steel fingers opened and swooped down and shut off the dialect. Hopalong pushed Dent off him and managed to catch Johnny's flailing arm on the third attempt, while Dent made tentative sorties against Johnny's spurred boots.

"Phew! Can he fight like that when he's sober?" reverently asked Dent, seeing how close his fingers could come to his gaudy eye without touching it. "I won't be able to see at all in an hour," he added gloomily.

Hopalong, seated on Johnny's chest, soberly made reply as he tenderly flirted with a raw shin. "It's th' mescal. I'm going to slip some of that stuff into Pete's cayuse some of these days," he promised, happy with a new idea. Pete Wilson had no sense of humor.

"That ghost was plumb lucky," grunted Red, "an' so was th' sea captain," he finished as an afterthought, limping off toward the bar, slowly and painfully followed by his disfigured companions. "One drink; then to bed."

After Red had departed, Hopalong and Dent smoked awhile and then, knocking the ashes out of his pipe, Hopalong arose. "An' yet, Dent, there are people that believe in ghosts," he remarked, with a vast and settled contempt.

Dent gave critical scrutiny to the scratched bar for a moment. "Well, th' Greasers all say there *is* a ghost in th' San Miguel, though I never saw it. But some of them have seen it, an' no Greasers ride that trail no more."

"Huh!" snorted Hopalong. "Some Greasers must have filled th' Kid up on ghosts while he was filling hisself up on mescal. Ghosts? R-a-t-s!"

"It shows itself only to Greasers, an' then only on Friday nights," explained Dent thoughtfully. This was Friday night. Others had seen that ghost, but they were all Mexicans; now that a "white" man of Johnny's undisputed caliber had been so honored Dent's skepticism wavered and he had something to think about for days to come. True, Johnny was not a Greaser; but even ghosts might make mistakes once in a while.

Hopalong laughed, dismissing the subject from his mind as being beneath further comment. "Well, we won't argue—I'm too tired. An' I'm sorry you got that eye, Dent."

"Oh, that's all right," hastily assured the store-keeper, smiling faintly. "I was just spoiling for a fight, an' now I've had it. Feels sort of good. Yes, first thing in th' morning—breakfast'll be ready soon as you are. Good night."

But the proprietor couldn't sleep. Finally he arose and tiptoed into the room where Johnny lay wrapped in the sleep of the exhausted. After cautious and critical inspection, which was made hard because of his damaged eye, he tiptoed back to his bunk, shaking his head slowly. "He wasn't drunk," he muttered. "He saw that ghost, all right, an' I'll bet everything I've got on it!"

At daybreak three quarreling punchers rode homeward and after a monotonous journey arrived at the bunkhouse and reported. It took them two nights adequately to describe their experiences to an envious audience. The morning after the telling of the ghost story things began to happen, Red starting it by erecting a sign:

NOTISE—NO GOSTS ALOWED

An exuberant handful of the outfit watched him drive the last nail and step back to admire his work, and the running fire of comment covered all degrees of humor, and promised much hilarity in the future at the expense of the only man on the Bar-20 who had seen a ghost.

In a week Johnny and his acute vision had become a byword in that part of the country and his friends had made it a practice to stop him and gravely discuss spirit manifestations of all kinds. He had thrashed Wood Wright and been thrashed by Sandy Lucas in two beautiful and memorable fights and was only waiting to recover from the last affair before having the matter out with Rich Finn. These facts were beginning to have the effect he strove for; though Cowan still sold a new concoction of gin, brandy, and whisky which he called "Flying Ghost," and which he proudly guaranteed would show more ghosts per drink than any liquor south of the Rio Grande—and some of his patrons were eager to back up his claims with real money.

This was the condition of affairs when Hopalong Cassidy strolled into Cowan's and forgot his thirst in the story being told by a strange Mexican. It was Johnny's ghost, without a doubt, and when he had carelessly asked a few questions he was convinced that Johnny had really seen something. On the way home he cogitated upon it and two points challenged his intelligence with renewed insistence: the ghost showed itself only on Friday, and then only to "Greasers." His suspicious mind would not rest until he had reviewed the question from all sides, and his opinion was that there was something more than spiritual about the ghost of the San Miguel—and a cold, practical reason for it.

When he rode into the corral at the ranch he saw that another sign had been put on the corral wall. He had destroyed the first, speaking his mind in full at the time. He swept his gloved hand upward with a rush, tore the flimsy board from its fastenings, broke it to pieces across his saddle, and tossed the fragments from him. He was angry, for he had warned the outfit that they were carrying the joke too far, that Johnny was giving way to hysterical rage more frequently, and might easily do something that they all would regret. And he felt sorry for the Kid; he knew what Johnny's feelings were and he made up his mind to start a few fights himself if the persecution did not cease. When he stepped into the bunkhouse and faced his friends they listened to a three-minute speech that made them squirm, and as he finished talking the deep voice of the foreman endorsed the promises he had just heard made, for Buck had entered the gallery without being noticed. The joke had come to an end.

When Johnny rode in that evening he was surprised to find Hopalong waiting for him a short distance from the corral and he replied to his friend's gesture by riding over to him. "What's up now?" he asked.

"Come along with me. I want to talk to you for a few minutes," and Hopalong led the way toward the open, followed by Johnny, who was more or less suspicious. Finally Hopalong stopped, turned, and looked his companion squarely in the eyes. "Kid, I'm in dead earnest. This ain't no fool joke—now you tell me what that ghost looked like, how he acted, an' all about it. I mean what I say, because now I know that you saw *something*. If it wasn't a ghost it was made to look like one, anyhow. Now go ahead."

"I've told you a dozen times already," retorted Johnny, his face flushing. "I've begged you to believe me an' told you that I wasn't fooling. How do I know you ain't now? I'm not going to tell—"

"Hold on; yes, you are. Yo're going to tell it slow, an' just like you saw it," Hopalong interrupted hastily. "I know I've doubted it, but who wouldn't! Wait a minute—I've done a heap of thinking in th' last few days an' I know that you saw a ghost. Now, everybody knows that there ain't no such thing as ghosts; then what was it you saw? There's a game on, Kid, an' it's a dandy; an' you an' me are going to bust it up an' get th' laugh on th' whole blasted crowd, from Buck to Cowan."

Johnny's suspicions left him with a rush, for his old Hoppy was one man in a thousand, and when he spoke like that, with such sharp decision, Johnny knew what it meant. Hopalong listened intently and when the short account was finished he put out his hand and smiled.

"We're th' fools, Kid, not you. There's something crooked going on in that canyon, an' I know it! But keep mum about what we think."

Johnny lost his grouch so suddenly and beamed upon his friends with such a superior air that they began to worry about what was in the wind. The suspense wore on them, for with Hopalong's assistance, Johnny might spring some game on them all that would more than pay up for the fun they had enjoyed at his expense; and the longer the suspense lasted the worse it became. They never lost sight of him while he was around and Hopalong had to endure the same surveillance, and it was no uncommon thing to see small groups of the anxious men engaged in deep discussion. When they found that Buck must have been told and noticed his smile was as fixed as Hopalong's or Johnny's, they were certain that trouble of some nature was in store for them.

Several weeks later Buck Peters drew rein and waited for a stranger to join him.

"Howdy. Is yore name Peters?" asked the newcomer, sizing him up in one trained glance.

"Well, who are you, an' what do you want?"

"I want to see Peters, Buck Peters. That yore name?"

"Yes; what of it?"

"My name's Fox. Old Jim Lane gave me a message for you," and the stranger spoke earnestly to some length. "There, that's th' situation. We've got to have shrewd men that they don't know an' won't suspect. Lane wants to pay a couple of yore men their wages for a month or two. He said he was shore he could count on you to help him out."

"He's right; he can. I don't forget favors. I've got a couple of men that—there's one of 'em now. Hey, Hoppy! Whoop-e, Hoppy!"

Mr. Cassidy arrived quickly, listened eagerly, named Red and Johnny to accompany him, overruled his companions by insisting that if

Johnny didn't go the whole thing was off, carried his point, and galloped off to find the lucky two, his eyes gleaming with anticipation and joy. Fox laughed, thanked the foreman, and rode on his way north, and that night three cowpunchers rode south, all strangely elated. And the friends who watched them go heaved sighs of relief, for the reprisals evidently were to be postponed for a while.

Chapter Five

The Ghost of the San Miguel

JUAN ALVAREZ had not been in San Felippe since Dick Martin left, which meant for over a month. Martin was down the river looking for a man who did not wish to be found; and some said that Martin cared nothing about international boundaries when he wanted any one real bad. And there was that geologist who wore blue glasses and was always puttering around in the canyon and hammering chips of rock off the steep walls; he must have slipped one noon, because his body was found on a flat boulder at the edge of the stream. Manuel had found it and wanted to be paid for his trouble in bringing it to town— but Manuel was a fool. Who, indeed, would pay good money for a dead Gringo, especially after he was dead? And there were three cowpunchers holding a herd of 6-X cattle up north, an hour or so from the town. They wanted to buy steers from Senor Rodriguez, but said that he was a robber and threatened to cut his ears off. Cannot a man name his own price? These cowpunchers liked to get drunk and gallop through San Felippe, shooting like crazy men. They got drunk one Friday night and went shouting and singing to the Big Bend in the canyon to see the flying ghost, and they called it names and fired off their pistols and sang loudly, and for a week they insulted all the Mexicans in town by calling them liars and cowards. Was it the fault of any one that the ghost would show itself only to Mexicans? Oh, these Gringos—might the good God punish them for their sins!

Thus the peons complained to the padre while they kept one eye open for the advent of the rowdy cowpunchers, who always wanted to drink, and then to fight with someone, either with fists or pistols. Why should anyone fight with them, especially with such things as fists?

"Let them fight among themselves. What have you to do with heretics?" reproved the good padre, who ostracized himself from the pleasant parts of the wide world that he might make easier the life and struggles of his ignorant flock. "God is not hasty—He will punish in His own way when it best suits Him. And perhaps you will profit much if you are more regular to mass instead of wasting the cool hours of the morning in bed. Think well of what I have said, my children."

But the cowpunchers were not punished and they swore they would not leave the vicinity until they had all the steers they wanted, and at their own price. And one night their herd stampeded and was checked only in time to save it from going over the canyon's edge. And for some reason Sanchez kept out of the padre's way and did not go to confess when he should, for the padre spoke plainly and set hard obligations for penance.

The cowpunchers swore that it had been done by some Mexican and said that they would come to town some day soon and kill three Mexicans unless the guilty one was found and brought to them. Then the padre mounted his donkey and went out to them to argue and they finally told him they would wait for two weeks. But the padre was too smart for them—he sent a messenger to find Senor Martin, and in one week Senor Martin came to town. There was no fight. The Gringo rowdies were cowards at heart and Martin could not shoot them down in cold blood, and he could not arrest them, because he was not a policeman or even a sheriff, but only a revenue officer, which was a most foolish law. But he watched them all the time and wanted them to fight—there was no more shooting or drunkenness in town. Nobody wanted to fight Senor Martin, for he was a great man. He even went so far as to talk with them about it and wave his arms, but they were as frightened at him as little children might be.

So the Mexicans gossiped and exulted, some of the bolder of them even swaggering out to the Gringo camp, but Martin drove them back again, saying he would not allow them to bully men who could not retaliate, which was right and fair. Then, afraid to go away and leave the mad cowpunchers so close to town, he ordered them to drive their herd farther east, nearer to Dent's store, and never to return to San Felippe unless they needed the padre, and they obeyed him after a long talk. After seeing them settled in their new camp, which was on Monday morning, Martin returned to San Felippe and told the padre where he could be found and then rode away again. San Felippe celebrated for a whole day and two Mexican babies were christened after Senor Dick Martin, which was honor all around.

Friday, when Manuel went over to spy upon the cowpunchers in their new camp, he found them so drunk that they could not stand, and before he crept away at dusk two of them were sleeping like gorged snakes and the third was firing off his revolver at random, which diversion had not a little to do with Manuel's departure.

When Manuel crept away he headed straight for a crevice near the wall of the canyon at the Big Bend and, reaching it, looked all around and then dropped into it. Not long thereafter another Mexican appeared, this one from San Felippe, and also disappeared into the crevice. As darkness fell Manuel reappeared with something under his jacket and a moment later a light gleamed at the base of a slender sapling which grew on the edge of the canyon wall and leaned out over the abyss. It was cleverly placed, for only at one spot on the Mexican side of the distant Rio Grande could it be seen—the high canyon walls farther down screened it from anyone who might be riding on the north bank of the river. In a moment there came an answering twinkle and Manuel, covering the lantern with a blanket, was swallowed up in the darkness of the crevice.

Without a trace of emotion, Dick Martin, from his place of concealment, caught the answering gleam, and he watched Manuel disappear. "Cassidy was right in every point; Lewis or Sayre couldn't 'a' done this better. I hope he won't be late," he muttered, and settled himself more comfortably to wait for the cue for action, smiling as the moon poked its rim over the low hills to his right. "This means promotion for me, or I've very much mistaken," he chuckled.

Hopalong was not late and as soon as it was dark he and his companions stole into the canyon on foot. They felt their way down the east end of the trail, not far from Dent's, toward the Big Bend, which they gained without a mishap. Johnny was sent up to a place they had noticed and marked in their memories at the time they had rioted down to defy the ghost. He was to stop anyone trying to escape up the San Felippe end of the canyon trail, and his confidence in his ability to do this was exuberant. Hopalong and Red slowly and laboriously worked their way down the perilous path leading to the bottom, forded the stream, and crept up the other side, where they found cover not far from a wide crack in the canyon wall. Upon the occasion of their hilarious visit to the Big Bend they had observed that a faint trail led to the crack and had cogitated deeply upon this fact.

Three hours passed before the watchers in and above the canyon were rewarded by anything further; and then a light flickered far down the canyon and close to the edge of the stream. Immediately strange noises were heard and suddenly the ghost swung out of the opening in the rock wall near Hopalong and Red and danced above their heads, while the shrieking which had so frightened Johnny and his horse filled the canyon with uproar and sent Martin wriggling nearer to the crevice which he had watched so closely. The noise soon ceased, but the ghost danced on, and the sound of men stumbling along the rocky ledge bordering the stream became more and more audible. Four were in the party and they all carried bulky loads on their backs and grunted with pleasure and relief as they entered the entrance in the wall. When the last man had disappeared and the noise of their passing had died out, Johnny's rope sailed up and out, and the ghost swayed violently and then began to sag in an unaccountable manner towards the trail as the owner of the rope hitched its free end around a spur of rock and made it fast. Then he feverishly scrambled down the steep path to join his friends.

Hopalong and Red, wriggling on their stomachs

toward the crack in the wall, paused in amazement and stared across the canyon; and then the former chuckled and whispered something in his companion's ear. "That was why he lugged his rope along! He's just idiot enough to want a souveneer an' plaything at th' risk of losing th' game. Come on!—they'll tumble to what's up an' get away if we don't hustle."

When the two punchers cautiously and noiselessly entered the crack and felt their way along its rock walls they heard fluent swearing in Spanish by the man who worked the ghost, and who could not understand its sudden ambition to take root. It was made painfully clear to him a moment later when a pair of brawny hands reached out of the darkness behind him and encircled his throat a hand's width below his gleaming cigarette. Another pair used cords with deftness and despatch and he was left by himself to browse upon the gag when all his senses returned.

Hopalong, with Red inconsiderately stepping on his heels, felt his way along the wall of the crevice, alert and silent, his Colt nestling comfortably in his right hand, while the left was pushed out ahead feeling for trouble. As they worked farther away from the canyon distant voices could be heard and they forthwith proceeded even more cautiously. When Hopalong came to the second bend in the narrow passage he peered around it and stopped so abruptly that

Red's nose almost spread itself over the back of his head. Red's indignation was all the harder to bear because it must bloom unheard.

In a huge, irregular room, whose roof could not be discerned in the dim light of the few candles, five men were resting in various attitudes of ease as they discussed the events of the night and tried to compute their profits. They were secure, for Manuel, having by this time put away the ghost and megaphone, was on duty at the mouth of the crevice, and he was as sensitive to danger as a hound.

"The risk is not much and the profits are large," remarked Pedro, in Spanish. "We must burn a candle for the repose of the soul of Carlos Martinez. It is he that made our plans safe. And a candle is not much when we—"

"Hands up!" said a quiet voice, followed by grim commands.

The Mexicans jumped as if stung by a scorpion, and could just discern two of the rowdy Gringo cowpunchers in the heavy shadows of the opposite wall, but the candle light glinted in rings on the muzzles of their six-shooters. Had Manuel betrayed them? But they had little time or inclination for cogitation regarding Manuel.

"Easy there!" shouted Red, and Pedro's hand stopped when halfway to his chest. Pedro was a gambler by nature, but the odds were too heavy and he sullenly obeyed the command.

"Stick 'em up! Stick 'em up! Higher yet, an' hold 'em there," purred a soft voice from the other end of the room, where Dick Martin smiled pleasantly upon them and wondered if there was anything on earth harder to pound good common sense into than a Greaser's head. His gun was blue, but it was, nevertheless, the most prominent part of his make-up, even if the light was poor.

One of the Mexicans reached involuntarily for his gun, for he was a gunman by training, while his companions felt for their knives, deadly weapons in a *mêlée*.

Martin, crying, "Watch 'em, Cassidy!" side-stepped and lunged forward with the speed and skill of a boxer, and his hard left hand landed on the point of Juan Alvarez's jaw with a force and precision not to be withstood. But to make more certain that the Mexican would not take part in any possible demonstration of resistance, Martin's right circled up in a short half-hook and stopped against Juan's short ribs. Martin weighed 180 pounds and packed no fat on his well-knit frame.

At this moment a two-legged cyclone burst upon the scene in the person of Johnny Nelson, whose rage had been worked up almost to the weeping point because he had lost so much time hunting for the crevice where it was not. Seeing Juan fall, and the glint of knives, he started in to clean things up, yelling, "I'm a ghost! I'm a ghost! Take 'em alive! Take 'em alive!"

Hopalong and Red felt that they were in his way, and taking care of one Mexican between them, while Martin knocked out another, they watched the exits—for anything was possible in such a chaotic mix-up—and gave Johnny plenty of room. The latter paused, triumphant, looked around to see if he had missed any, and then advanced upon his friends and shoved his jaw up close to Hopalong's face.

"Tried to lose me, didn't you! Wouldn't wait for me, eh! For seven cents an' a toothbrush I'd give you what's left!"

Red grabbed him by trousers and collar and heaved him into the passageway. "Go out an' play with yore souveneer or we'll step on you!"

Johnny sat up, rubbed certain portions of his anatomy, and grinned. "Oh, I've got it, all right! I'm shore going to take that ghost home an' make some of them fools *eat* it!"

Martin smiled as he finished tying the last prisoner. "That's right, Nelson, you've got it on 'em this time. Make 'em chew it."

Chapter Six

Hopalong Loses a Horse

FOR a month after their return from the San Miguel, Hopalong and his companions worked with renewed zest, and told and retold the other members of the outfit of their unusual experiences near the Mexican border. Word had come up to them that Martin had secured the conviction of the smugglers and was in line for immediate advancement. No one on the range had the heart to meet Johnny Nelson, for Johnny carried with him a piece of the ghost, and became pugnacious if his once-jeering friends and acquaintances refused to nibble on it. Cowan still sold his remarkable drink, but he had yielded to Johnny's persuasive methods and now called it "Nelson's Pet."

One bright day the outfit started rounding up a small herd of three-year-olds, which Buck had sold, and by the end of the week the herd was complete and ready for the drive. This took two weeks and when Hopalong led his drive outfit through Hoyt's Corners on its homeward journey he felt the pull of the town of Grant, some miles distant, and it was too strong to be resisted. Flinging a word of explanation to the nearest puncher, he turned to lope away, when Red's voice checked him. Red wanted to delay his home-going for a day or two and attend to a purely personal matter at a ranch lying to the west. Hopalong, knowing the reason for Red's wish, grinned and told him to go, and not to propose until he had thought the matter over very carefully. Red's reply was characteristic, and after arranging a rendezvous and naming the time, the two separated and rode toward their destinations, while the rest of the outfit kept on toward their ranch.

"A man owes something to *all* his friends," Hopalong mused. In this case he owed a return game of draw poker to certain of Grant's leading citizens, and he liked to pay his obligations when opportunity offered.

It was mid-forenoon when he topped a rise and saw below him the handful of shacks making up the town. A look of pleased interest flickered across his face as he noticed a patched and dirty tent pitched close up to the nearest shack. "Show!" he ejaculated. "Now, ain't that luck! I'll shore take it in. If it's a circus, mebby it has a trick mule to ride—I'll never forget that one up in Kansas City," he grinned. But almost instantly a doubt arose and tempered the grin. "Huh! Mebby it's th' branding-chute of some gospel sharp." As he drew near he focussed his eyes on the canvas and found that his fears were justified.

"All Are Welcome," he spelled out slowly. "Shore they are!" he muttered. "I never nowhere

saw such hard-working, all-embracing rustlers as them fellers. They'll stick their iron on anything from a wobbly calf or dying dogie to a staggering-with-age mosshead, an' shout 'tally one' with th' same joy. Well, not for mine, *this* trip. I'm going to graze loose an' buck-jump all I want. Anyhow, if I did let him brand me I'd only backslide in a week," and Hopalong pressed his pony to a more rapid gait as two men emerged from the tent. "There's th' sky pilot now," he muttered—"an' there's Dave!" he shouted, waving his arm. "Oh, Dave! Dave!"

Dave Wilkes looked up, and his grin of delight threatened to engulf his ears. "Hullo, Cassidy! Glad to see you! Keep right on for th' store—I'll be with you in a minute." When Dave told his companion the visitor's name the evangelist held up his hand eloquently and spoke.

"I know all about him!" he ejaculated sorrowfully. "If I can lead him out of his wickedness I will rest content though I save no more souls this fortnight. Is it all true?"

"Huh! What true?"

"All that I have heard about him."

"Well, I dunno what you've heard," replied Dave with grave caution, "but I reckon it might be if it didn't cover lying, stealing, cowardice, an' such coyote traits. He's shore a holy terror with a short gun, all right, but lemme tell you something mebby you *ain't* heard; there ain't a square man in this part of th' country that won't feel some honored an' proud to be called a friend of Hopalong Cassidy. Them's th' sentiments rampaging hereabouts. I ain't denying that he's gone an' killed off a lot of men first an' last—but th' only trouble there is that he didn't get 'em soon enough. They all had lived too blamed long when they went an' stacked up agin him an' that lightning short gun of his'n. But, say, if yo're calculating to tackle him at yore game, lead him gentle—don't push none. He comes to life real sudden when he's shoved. So long; see you later, mebby."

The revivalist looked after him and mused, "I hope I was informed wrong, but this much I have to be thankful for: the wickedness of most of these men, these over-grown children, is manly, stalwart, and open; few of them are vicious or contemptible. Their one great curse is drink."

When Hopalong entered the store he was vociferously welcomed by two men, and the proprietor joining them, the circle was complete. When the conversation threatened to repeat itself cards were brought and the next two hours passed very rapidly. They were expensive hours to the Bar-20 puncher, who finally arose with an apologetic grin and slapped his thigh significantly.

"Well, you've got it all; I'm busted wide open, except for a measly dollar, an' I shore hope you don't want that," he laughed. "You play a whole lot better than you did th' last time I was here. I've got to move along. I'm going east an' see Wallace an' from there I've got to meet Red an' ride home with him. But you come down an' see us when you can—it's *me* that wants revenge this time."

"Huh, you'll be wanting it worse than ever if we do," smiled Dave.

"Say, Hoppy," advised Tom Lawrence, "better drop in an' hear th' sky pilot's palaver before you go. It'll do you a whole lot of good, an' it can't do you no harm, anyhow."

"You going?" asked Hopalong suspiciously.

"Can't—got too much work to do," quickly responded Tom, his brother Art nodding happy confirmation.

"Huh, I reckoned so!" snorted Hopalong sarcastically as he shook hands all around. "You all know where to find us—drop in an' see us when you get down our way," he invited.

"Sorry you can't stay longer, Cassidy," remarked Dave, as his friend mounted. "But come up again soon—an' be shore to tell all the boys we was asking for 'em," he called.

Considering the speed with which Hopalong started for Wallace's, he might have been expecting a relay of quarter horses to keep it going, but he pulled up short at the tent. Such inconsistency is trying to the temper of the best-mannered horse, and this particular animal was not in the least good-mannered, wherefore its rider was obliged to soothe its resentment in his own peculiar way, listening meanwhile to the loud and impassioned voice of the evangelist haranguing his small audience.

"I wonder," said Hopalong, glancing through the door, "if them friends of mine reckon I'm any ascared to go in that tent? Huh, I'll just show 'em anyhow!" whereupon he dismounted, flung the reins over his horse's head, and strode through the doorway.

The nearest seat, a bench made by placing a bottom board of the evangelist's wagon across two up-ended boxes, was close enough to the exhorter and he dropped into it and glanced carelessly at his nearest neighbor. The carelessness went out of his bearing as his eyes fastened themselves in a stare on the man's neckerchief. Hopalong was hardened to awful sights and at his best was not an artistic soul, but the villainous riot of fiery crimson, gaudy yellow, and pugnacious and domineering green which flaunted defiance and insolence from the stranger's neck caused his breath to hang over one count and then come doubly strong at the next exhalation. "Gee whiz!" he whispered.

The stranger slowly turned his head and looked coldly upon the impudent disturber of his reverent reflections. "Meaning?" he questioned, with an upward slant in his voice. The neckerchief seemed to grow suddenly malignant and about to spring. "Meaning?" repeated the other with great insolence, while his eyes looked a challenge.

While Hopalong's eyes left the scrambled color-insult and tried to banish the horrible after-image, his mind groped for the rules of etiquette governing free fist fights in gospel tents, and while he hesitated as to whether he should dent the classic profile of the color-bearer or just twist his nose as a sign of displeasure, the voice of the evangelist arose to a roar and thundered out. Hopalong ducked instinctively.

"—Stop! Stop before it is too late, before death takes you in the wallow of your sins! Repent and gain salvation—"

Hopalong felt relieved, but his face retained its expression of childlike innocence even after he realized that he was not being personally addressed; and he glanced around. It took him 97 seconds to see everything there was to be seen, and his eyes were drawn irresistibly back to the stranger's kerchief. "Awful! Awful thing for a drinking man to wear, or run up against unexpectedly!" he muttered, blinking. "Worse than snakes," he added thoughtfully.

"Look ahere, you—" began the owner of the offensive decoration, if it might be called such, but the evangelist drowned his voice in another flight of eloquence.

"—*Peace! Peace* is the message of the Lord to

His children," roared the voice from the upturned soap box, and when the speaker turned and looked in the direction of the two men-with-a-difference he found them sitting up very straight and apparently drinking in his words with great relish whereupon he felt that he was making gratifying progress toward the salvation of their spotted souls. He was very glad, indeed, that he had been so grievously misinformed about the personal attributes of one Hopalong Cassidy—glad and thankful.

"Death cometh as a thief in the night," the voice went on. "Think of the friends who have gone before; who were well one minute and gone the next! And it must come to all of us, to all of us, to me and to you—"

The man with the afflicted neck started rocking the bench.

"Something is coming to somebody purty soon," murmured Hopalong. He began to sidle over towards his neighbor, his near hand doubled up into a huge knot of protuberant knuckles and white-streaked fingers, but as he was about to deliver his hint that he was greatly displeased at the antics of the bench a sob came to his ears. Turning his head swiftly, he caught sight of the stranger's face, and sorrow was marked so strongly upon it that the sight made Hopalong gape. His hand opened slowly and he cautiously sidled back again, disgruntled, puzzled, and vexed at himself for having strayed into a game where he was so hopelessly at sea. He thought it all over carefully and then gave it up as being too deep for him to solve. But he determined one thing: he was not going to leave before the other man did, anyhow.

"An' if I catch that howling kerchief outside—" he muttered, smacking his lips with satisfaction at what was in store for it. His visit to Wallace was not very important, anyway, and it could wait on more important events.

"There sits a sinner!" thundered out the exhorter, and Hopalong looked stealthily around for a sight of a villain. "God only has the right to punish. 'Vengeance is mine,' saith the Lord, and whosoever takes the law into his own hands, whosoever takes human life, defies the Creator. There sits a man who has killed his fellow men, his brothers! Are you not a sinner, *Cassidy?*"

Cassidy jumped clear of the bench as he jerked his head around and stared over the suddenly outstretched arm and pointing finger of the speaker and into his accusing eyes.

"Answer me! Are you not a sinner?"

Hopalong stood up, confused, bewildered, and then his suspended thoughts stirred and formed. "Guilty, I reckon, an' in th' first degree. But they didn't get no more'n what was coming to 'em, no more'n they earned. An' that's straight!"

"How do you know they didn't? How do you

know they earned it? How do you *know?*" demanded the evangelist, who was delighted with the chance to argue with a sinner. He had great faith in "personal contact," and his was the assurance of training, of the man well rehearsed and fully prepared. And he knew that if he should be pinned into a corner by logic and asked for *his* proofs, that he could squirm out easily and take the offensive again by appealing to faith, the last word in sophistry, and a greater and more powerful weapon than intelligence. *This* was his game, and it was fixed; he could not lose if he could arouse enough interest in a man to hold him to the end of the argument. He continued to drive, to crowd. "What right have you to think so? What right have you to judge them? Have you divine insight? Are you inspired? 'Judge not lest ye be judged,' saith the Lord, and you *dare* to fly in the face of that great command!"

"You've got me picking the pea in *this* game, all right," responded Hopalong, dropping back on the bench. "But lemme tell you one thing: command or no command, devine or not devine, I know when a man has lived too long, an' when he's going to try to get me. An' all th' gospel sharps south of heaven can't stop me from handing a thief what he's earned. Go on with th' show, but count me out."

While the evangelist warmed to the attack, vaguely realizing that he had made a mistake in not heeding Dave Wilkes's tip, Hopalong became conscious of a sense of relief stealing over him and he looked around wonderingly for the cause. The man with the kerchief had "folded his tents" and departed, and Hopalong, heaving a sigh of satisfaction, settled himself more comfortably and gave real attention to the discourse, although he did not reply to the warm and eloquent man on the soap box. Suddenly he sat up with a start as he remembered that he had a long and hard ride before him if he wished to see Wallace, and arising, strode towards the exit, his chest up and his chin thrust out. The only reply he made to the excited and personal remarks of the revivalist was to stop at the door and drop his last dollar into the yeast box before passing out.

For a moment he stood still and pondered, his head too full of what he had heard to notice that anything out of the ordinary had happened. Although the evangelist had adopted the wrong method he had gained more than he knew and Hopalong had something to take home with him and wrestle out for himself in spare moments— that is, he would have had but for one thing: As he slowly looked around for his horse he came to himself with a sharp jerk, and hot profanity routed the germ of religion incubating in his soul. His horse was missing! Here was a pretty mess, he thought savagely, and then his expression of anger and perplexity gave way to a flickering grin as the probable solution came to his mind.

"By th' Lord, I never saw such a bunch to play jokes," he laughed. "Won't they never grow up? They was watching me when I went inside an' sneaked up and rustled my cayuse. Well, I'll get it back again without much trouble, all right. They ought to know me better by this time."

"Hey, stranger!" he called to a man who was riding past, "have you seen anything of a skinny roan cayuse fifteen han's high, white stocking on th' near foreleg, an' a bandage on th' off fetlock, Bar-20 being th' brand?"

The stranger, knowing the grinning inquisitor by sight, suspected that a joke was being played; he also knew Dave Wilkes and that gentleman's friends. He chuckled and determined to help it along a little. "Shore did, pardner; saw a man leading him real cautious. Was he yourn?"

"Oh, no, not at all. He belonged to my great-great-grandfather, who left him to my second cousin. You see, I borrowed it," he grinned, making his way leisurely toward the general store, kept by his friend Dave, the joker. "Funny how everybody likes a joke," he muttered, opening the door of the store. "Hey, Dave," he called.

Mr. Wilkes wheeled suddenly and stared. "Why, I thought you was halfway to Wallace's by now!" he exclaimed. "Did you come back to lose that lone dollar?"

"Oh, I lost that too. But yo're a real smart cuss, now ain't you?" queried Hopalong, his eyes twinkling and his face wreathed with good humor. "An' how innocent you act, too. Thought you could scare me, didn't you? Thought I'd go tearing 'round this fool town like a house afire, hey? Well, I reckon you can guess again. Now, I'm owning up that th' joke's on me, so you hand over my cayuse, an' I'll make up for lost time."

Dave Wilkes's face expressed several things, but surprise was dominant. "Why, I ain't even seen yore ol' cayuse, you chump! Last time I saw it you was on him, goin' like th' devil. Did somebody pull you off it an' take it away from you?" he demanded with great sarcasm. "Is somebody abusing you?"

Hopalong bit into a generous handful of dried apricots, chewed complacently for a moment, and replied, "'At's aw right, I wan' my c'use." Swallowing hastily, he continued: "I want it, an' I've come to th' right place for it, too. Hand it over, David."

"Dod blast it, I tell you I ain't got it!" retorted Dave, beginning to suspect that something was radically wrong. "I ain't seen it, an' I don't know nothing about it."

Hopalong wiped his mouth with his sleeve. "Well, then, Tom or Art does, all right."

"No, they don't, neither; I watched 'em leave an' they rode straight out of town, an' went th' other way, same as they allus do." Dave was getting irritated. "Look here, you; are you joking or drunk, or both, or is that animule of yourn really missing?"

"Huh!" snorted Hopalong, trying some new prunes. " 'Ese prunes er purty good," he mumbled in grave congratulation. "I don' get prunes like 'ese very of'n."

"I reckon you don't! They ought to be good. Cost me thirty cents a half-pound," Dave retorted with asperity, anxiously shifting his feet. It didn't take much of a loss to wipe out a day's profits with him.

"An' I don't reckon you paid none too much for 'em, at that," Mr. Cassidy responded, nodding his head in comprehension. "Ain't no worms in 'em, is there?"

"Shore there is!" exploded Dave. "Plumb full of 'em!"

"You don't say! Hardly know whether to take a chance with th' worms or try th' apricots. Ain't no worms in them, anyhow. But when am I going to get my cayuse? I've got a long way to go, an' delay is costly—how much did you say these yaller fellers cost?" he asked significantly, trying another handful of apricots.

"On th' dead level, cross my heart an' hope to die, but I ain't seen yore cayuse since you left here," earnestly replied Dave. "If you don't know where it is, then somebody went an' lifted it. It looks like it's up to you to do some hunting, 'stead of cultivating a belly ache at *my* expense. *I* ain't trying to keep you, God knows!"

Hopalong glanced out of the window as he considered, and saw, entering the saloon, the same puncher who had confessed to seeing his horse. "Hey, Dave; wait a minute!" and he dashed out of the store and made good time towards the liquid-refreshment parlor. Dave promptly nailed the covers on the boxes of prunes and apricots and leaned innocently against the cracker box to await results, thinking hard all the while. It looked like a plain case of horse stealing to him.

"Stranger," cried Hopalong, bouncing into the bar-room, "where did you see that cayuse of mine?"

"Th' ancient relic of yore fambly was aheading toward Hoyt's Corners," the stranger replied, grinning broadly. "It's a long walk. Have something before you start?"

"Damn th' walk! Who was riding him?"

"Nobody at all."

"What do you mean?"

"He wasn't being rid when I saw him."

"Hang it, man, that cayuse was stole from me!"

"Somewhat in th' nature of a calamity, now ain't it?" smiled the stranger, enjoying his contribution to the success of the joke.

"You bet yore life it is!" shouted Hopalong, growing red and then pale. "You tell me who was leading him, understand?"

"Well, I couldn't see his face, honest I couldn't," replied the stranger. "Every time I tried it I was shore blinded by th' most awful an' horrible neckerchief I've ever had th' hard luck to lay my eyes on. Of all th' drunks I ever met, them there colors was—Hey! Wait a minute!" he shouted at Hopalong's back.

"Dave, gimme yore cayuse an' a rifle—quick!" cried Hopalong from the middle of the street as he ran toward the store. "Hypocrite son-of-a-hoss-thief went an' run mine off. Might 'a' knowed nobody but a thief would wear such a kerchief!"

"I'm with you!" shouted Dave, leading the way on a run toward the corral in the rear of his store.

"No, you ain't with me, neither!" replied Hopalong, deftly saddling. "This ain't no plain hoss-thief case—it's a private grudge. See you later, mebby," and he was pacing a cloud of dust toward the outskirts of the town.

Dave looked after him. "Well, that feller has shore got a big start on you, but he can't keep ahead of that Doll of mine for very long. She can out-run anything in these parts. 'Sides, Cassidy's cayuse looked sort of done up, while mine's as fresh as a bird. That thief will get what's coming to him, all right."

CHAPTER SEVEN

MR. CASSIDY COGITATES

WHILE Hopalong tried to find his horse, Ben Ferris pushed forward, circling steadily to the east and away from the direction of Hoyt's Corners, which was as much a menace to his health and happiness as the town of Grant, 20 miles to his rear. If he could have been certain that no danger was nearer to him than these two towns, he would have felt vastly relieved, even if his horse were not fresh. During the last hour he had not urged it as hard as he had in the beginning of his flight and it had dropped to a walk for minutes at a stretch. This was not because he felt that he had plenty of time, but for the reason that he understood horses and could not afford to exhaust his mount so early in the chase. He glanced back from time to time as if fearing what might be on his trail, and well he might fear. According to all the traditions and customs of the range, both of which he knew well, somewhere between him and Grant was a posse of hard-riding cowpunchers, all anxious and eager for a glance at him over their sights. In his mind's eye he could see them, silent, grim, tenacious, reeling off the miles on that distance-eating lope. He had stolen a horse, and that meant death if they caught him. He loosened his gaudy kerchief and gulped in fear, not of what pursued, but of what was miles before him. His own saddle, strapped behind the one he sat in, bumped against him with each reach of the horse and had already made his back sore—but he must endure it for a time. Never in all his life had minutes been so precious.

Another hour passed and the horse seemed to be doing well, much better than he had hoped—he would rest it for a few minutes at the next water while he drank his fill and changed the bumping saddle. As he rounded a turn and entered a heavily grassed valley he saw a stream close at hand and, leaping off, fixed the saddle first. As he knelt to drink he caught a movement and jumped up to catch his mount. Time after time he almost touched it, but it evaded him and kept up the game, cropping a mouthful of grass during each respite.

"All right!" he muttered as he let it eat. "I'll get my drink while you eat an' then I'll get you!"

He knelt by the stream again and drank long and deep. As he paused for breath something made him leap up and to one side, reaching for his Colt at the same instant. His fingers found only leather and he swore fiercely as he remembered—he had sold the Colt for food and kept the rifle for defence. As he faced the rear, a horseman rounded the turn and the fugitive, wheeling, dashed for the stolen horse 40 yards away, where his rifle lay in its saddle sheath. But an angry command and the sharp hum of a bullet fired in front of him checked his flight and he stopped short and swore.

"I reckon th' jig's up," remarked Mr. Cassidy, balancing the upraised Colt with nicety and indifference.

"Yes, I reckon so," sullenly replied the other, tears running into his eyes.

"Well, I'm damned!" snorted Hopalong with cutting contempt. "Cryin' like a li'l baby! Got nerve enough to steal my cayuse, an' then go an' beller like a lost calf when I catch you. Yo're a fine specimen of a hoss thief, I don't think!"

"Yo're a liar!" retorted the other, clenching his fists and growing red.

Mr. Cassidy's mouth opened and then clicked shut as his Colt swung down. But he did not shoot; something inside of him held his trigger finger and he swore instead. The idea of a man stealing his horse, being caught red-handed and unarmed, and still possessed of sufficient courage to call his captor a name never tolerated or overlooked in that country! And the idea that he, Hopalong Cassidy, of the Bar-20, could not shoot such a thief! "Damn that sky pilot! He's shore gone an' made me loco," he muttered, savagely, and then addressed his prisoner. "Oh, you ain't crying? Wind got in yore eyes, I reckon, an' sort of made 'em leak a little—that it? Or mebby them unholy green roses an' yaller grass on that blasted fool neckerchief of yourn are too much for *your* eyes, too!"

"Look ahere!" snapped the man on the ground, stepping forward, one fist upraised. "I came nigh onto licking you this noon in that gospel sharp's tent for making fun of that scarf, an' I'll do it yet if you get any smart about it! You mind yore own business an' close yore fool eyes if you don't like my clothes!"

"Say! You ain't no cry-baby after all. Hanged if I even think yo're a real genuine hoss thief!" enthused Mr. Cassidy. "You act like a twin brother, but what th' devil ever made you steal that cayuse, anyhow?"

"An' that's none of yore business, neither, but I'll tell you, just th' same," replied the thief. "I had to have it; that's why. I'll fight you rough-an'-tumble to see if I keep it, or if you take th' cayuse an' shoot me besides. Is it a go?"

Hopalong stared at him and then a grin struggled for life, got it, and spread slowly over his tanned countenance. "Yore gall is refreshing! Damned if it ain't worse than th' scarf. Here, you tell me what made you take a chance like stealing a cayuse this noon—I'm getting to like you, bad as you are, hanged if I ain't!"

"Oh, what's th' use?" demanded the other, tears again coming into his eyes. "You'll think I'm lying an' trying to crawl out—an' I won't do neither."

"*I* didn't say *you* was a liar," replied Hopalong. "It was th' other way about. Reckon you can try me, anyhow, can't you?"

"Yes, I s'pose so," responded the other slowly and in a milder tone of voice. "An' when I called you that I was mad an' desperate. I was hasty— you see, my wife's dying, or dead, over in Winchester. I was riding hard to get to her before it was too late when my cayuse stepped into a hole just th' other side of Grant—you know what happened. I shot th' animal, stripped off my saddle an' hoofed it to town, an' dropped into that gospel dealer's layout to see if he could make me feel any better—which he could not. I just couldn't stand his palaver about death an' slipped out. I was going to lay for you an' lick you for th' way you acted about this scarf—had to do something or go loco. But when I got outside there was yore cayuse, all saddled an' ready to go. I just up an' threw my saddle on it, followed suit with myself an' was ten miles out of town before I realized just what I'd done. But th' realizing part of it didn't make no difference to me—I'd 'a' done it just th' same if I had stopped to think it over. That's flat, an' straight. I've got to get to that li'l woman as quick as I can, an' I'd steal all th' cayuses in th' whole damned country if they'd do me any good. That's all of it—take it or leave it. I put it up to you. That's yore cayuse, but you ain't going to get it without fighting me for it! If you shoot me down without giving me a chance, all right! I'll cut a throat for that wore-out bronc!"

Hopalong was buried in thought and came to himself just in time to cover the other and stop him not six feet away. "Just a minute, before you make me shoot you! I want to think about it."

"Damn that gun!" swore the fugitive, nervously shifting his feet and preparing to spring. "We'd 'a' been fighting by this time if it wasn't for that!"

"You stand still or I'll blow you apart," retorted Hopalong, grimly. "A man's got a right to think, ain't he? An' if I had somebody here to mind these guns so you couldn't sneak 'em on me I'd fight you so blamed quick that you'd be licked before you knew you was at it. But we ain't going to fight—*stand still!* You ain't got no show at all when yo're dead!"

"Then you gimme that cayuse—my God, man! Do you know th' hell I've been through for th' last two days? Got th' word up at Daly's Crossing an' ain't slept since. I'll go loco if th' strain lasts much longer! She asking for me, begging to see me—an' me, like a damned idiot, wasting time out here talking to another. Ride with me, behind me—it's only forty miles more—tie me to th' saddle an' blow me to pieces if you find I'm lying—do anything you want, but let me get to Winchester before dark!"

Hopalong was watching him closely and at the end of the other's outburst threw back his head. "I reckon I'm a plain fool, a jackass, but I don't care. I'll rope that cayuse for you. You come along to save time," Hopalong ordered, spurring forward. His borrowed rope sailed out, tightened, and in a moment he was working at the saddle. "Here, you; I'm going to swamp mounts with you—this one is fresher an' faster." He had his own saddle off and the other on in record time, and stepped back. "There; don't stand there like a fool—wake up an' hustle! I might change my mind—that's th' way to move! Gimme that neckerchief for a souveneer, an' get out. Send that cayuse back to Dave Wilkes, at Grant—it's his'n. Don't thank me; just gimme that scarf an' ride like th' devil."

The other, already mounted, tore the kerchief from his throat and handed it quickly to his benefactor. "If you ever want a man to take you out of hell, send to Winchester for Ben Ferris—that's me. So long!"

Mr. Cassidy sat on his saddle where he had dropped it after making the exchange and looked after the galloping horseman, and when a distant rise had shut him from sight, turned his eyes on the scarf in his hand and cogitated. Finally, with a long-drawn sigh he arose, and, placing the scarf on the ground, caught and saddled his horse. Riding gloomily back to where the riot of color fluttered on the grass he drew his Colt and sent six bullets through it with a great amount of satisfaction. Not content with the damage he had inflicted, he leaned over and swooped it up. Riding further he also swooped up a stone and tied the kerchief around it, and then stood up in his stirrups and drew back his arm with critical judgment. He sat quietly for a time after the gaudy missile had disappeared into the stream and then, wheeling, cantered away. But he did not return to the town of Grant—he lacked the nerve to face Dave Wilkes and tell his childish and improbable story. He would ride on and meet Red as they had agreed; a letter would do for Mr. Wilkes, and after he had broken the shock in that manner he could pay him a personal visit sometime soon. Dave would never believe the story and when it was told Hopalong wanted to have the value of the horse in his trousers pocket. Of course, Ben Ferris *might* have told the truth and he might return the horse according to directions. Hopalong emerged from his reverie long enough to appeal to his mount, "Bronc, I've been thinking. Am I or am I not a jackass?"

Chapter Eight

Red Brings Trouble

AFTER a night spent on the plain and a cigarette for his breakfast, Hopalong, grouchy and hungry, rode slowly to the place appointed for his meeting with Red, but Mr. Connors was over two hours late. It was now mid-forenoon and Hopalong occupied his time for a while by riding out fancy designs on the sand, but he soon tired of this makeshift diversion and grew petulant. Red's tardiness was all the worse because the erring party to the agreement had turned in his saddle at Hoyt's Corners and loosed a flippant and entirely uncalled-for remark about his friend's ideas regarding appointments.

"Well, that redheaded Romeo is shore late this time," Hopalong muttered. "Why don't he find a girl closer to home, anyhow? Thank th' Lord I ain't got no use for shell games of any kind. Here I am, without anything to eat an' no prospects of anything, sitting up on this locoed layout like a sore thumb, an' can't move without hitting myself! An' it'll be late today before I can get any grub, too. Oh, well," he sighed, "I ain't in love, so things might be a whole lot worse with me. An' he ain't in love, neither, only he won't listen to reason. He gets mad an' calls me a sage hen an' says I'm stuck on myself because some fool told me I had brains."

He laughed as he pictured the object of his friend's affections. "Huh, anybody that got one good, square look at her wouldn't ever accuse him of having brains. But he'll forget her in a month. That was th' life of his last hobbling fit an' it was th' worst he ever had."

Grinning at his friend's peculiarly human characteristics, he leaned back in the saddle and felt for tobacco and papers. As he finished pouring the chopped alfalfa into the paper he glanced up and saw a mounted man top the sky line of the distant hills and shoot down the slope at full speed.

"I knowed it: started three hours late an' now he's trying to make it up in th' last mile," Hopalong muttered, dexterously spreading the tobacco along the groove and quickly rolling the cigarette. Lighting it, he looked up again and saw that the horseman was wildly waving a sombrero.

"Huh! Wigwagging for forgiveness," laughed the man who waited. "Old son-of-a-gun, I'd wait a week if I had some grub, an' he knows it. Couldn't get mad at him if I tried."

Mr. Connors's antics now became frantic and he shouted something at the top of his voice. His friend spurred his mount. "Come on, bronc; wake up. His girl said 'yes' an' now he wants me to get him out of his trouble." Whereupon he jogged forward. "What's that?" he shouted, sitting up very straight. "What's that?"

Red energetically swept the sombrero behind him and pointed to the rear. "War whoops! W-a-r w-h-o-o-p-s! Injuns, you chump!" Mr. Connors appeared to be mildly exasperated.

"Yes?" sarcastically rejoined Mr. Cassidy in his throat, and then shouted in reply: "Love an' liquor don't mix very well in you. Wake up! Come out of it!"

"That's straight—I mean it!" cried Mr. Connors, close enough now to save the remainder of his lungs. "It's a bunch of young bucks on their first war trail, I reckon. 'T ain't Geronimo, all right; I wouldn't be here now if it was. Three of 'em chased me an' th' two that are left are coming hot-foot somewhere th' other side of them hills. They act sort of mad, too."

"Mebby they ain't acting at all," cheerily replied his companion. "An' then that's th' way you got that graze, eh?"—pointing to a bloody furrow on Mr. Connors's cheek. "But just th' same it looks like th' trail left by a woman's fingernail."

"Fingernail nothing," retorted Mr. Connors, flushing a little. "But, for God's sake, are you going to sit here like a wart on a dead dog an' wait for 'em?" he demanded with a rising inflection. "Do you reckon yo're running a dance, or a party, or something like that?"

"How many?" placidly inquired Mr. Cassidy,

gazing intently towards the high sky line of the distant hills.

"Two—an' I won't tell you again, neither!" snapped the owner of the furrowed cheek. "Th' others are 'way behind now—but we're standing *still!*"

"Why didn't you say there was others?" reproved Hopalong. "Naturally I didn't see no use of getting all het up just because two sprouted papooses feel like crowding us a bit; it wouldn't be none of *our* funeral, would it?" and the indignant Mr. Cassidy hurriedly dismounted and hid his horse in a near-by chaparral and returned to his companion at a run.

"Red, gimme yore Winchester an' then hustle on for a ways, have an accident, fall off yore cayuse, an' act scared to death, if you know how. It's that little trick Buck told us about, an' it shore ought to work fine here. We'll see if two infant feather-dusters can lick th' Bar-20. Get a-going!"

They traded rifles, Hopalong taking the repeater in place of the single-shot gun he carried, and Red departed as bidden, his face gradually breaking into an enthusiastic grin as he ruminated upon the plan. "Level-headed old cuss; he's a wonder when it comes to planning or fighting. An' lucky—well, I reckon!"

Hopalong ran forward for a short distance and slid down the steep bank of a narrow arroyo and waited, the repeater thrust out through the dense fringe of grass and shrubs which bordered the edge. When settled to his complete satisfaction and certain that he was effectually screened from the sight of anyone in front of him, he arose on his toes and looked around for his companion, and laughed. Mr. Connors was bending very dejectedly apparently over his prostrate horse, but in reality was swearing heartily at the ignorant quadruped because it strove with might and main to get its master's foot off its head so it could arise. The man in the arroyo turned again and watched the hills and it was not long before he saw two Indians burst into view over the crest and gallop toward his friend. They were not to be blamed because they did not know the pursued had joined a friend, for the second trail was yet some distance in front of them.

"Pair of budding warriors, all right, an' awful important. Somebody must 'a' told *them* they had brains," Mr. Cassidy muttered. "They're just at th' age when they know it all an' have to go 'round raising hell all th' time. Wonder when they jumped th' reservation."

The Indians, seeing Mr. Connors arguing with his prostrate horse, and taking it for granted that he was not stopping for pleasure or to view the scenery, let out a yell and dashed ahead at greater speed, at the same time separating so as to encircle him and attack him front and rear at the same time. They had a great amount of respect for cowboys.

This maneuver was entirely unexpected and clashed violently with Mr. Cassidy's plan of procedure, so two irate punchers swore heartily at their rank stupidity in not counting on it. Of course everybody that knew anything at all about such warfare knew that they would do just such a thing, which made it all the more bitter. But Red had cultivated the habit of thinking quickly and he saw at once that the remedy lay with him; he astonished the exultant savages by straddling his disgruntled horse as it scrambled to its feet and galloping away from them, bearing slightly to the south, because he wished to lure his pursuers to ride closer to his anxious and eager friend.

This action was a success, for the yelling warriors, slowing perceptibly because of their natural astonishment at the resurrection and speed of an animal regarded as dead or useless, spurred on again, drawing closer together, and along the chord of the arc made by Mr. Connors's trail. Evidently the fool white man was either crazy or had original and startling ideas about the way to rest a horse when hard pressed, which pleased them much, since he had lost so much time. The pleasures of the war trail would be vastly greater if all white men had similar ideas.

Hopalong, the light of fighting burning strong in his eyes, watched them sweep nearer and nearer, splendid examples of their type and seeming to be a part of their mounts. Then two shots rang out in quick succession and a cloud of pungent smoke arose lazily from the edge of the arroyo as the warriors fell from their mounts not 60 yards from the hidden marksman.

Mr. Connors's rifle spat fire once to make assurance doubly sure and he hastily rejoined his friend as that person climbed out of the arroyo.

"Huh! They must have been half-breeds!" snorted Red in great disgust, watching his friend shed sand from his clothes. "I allus opined that 'Paches was too blamed slick to bite on a game like that."

"Well, they are purty 'lusive animals, 'Paches, but there are exceptions," replied Hopalong, smiling at the success of their scheme. "Them two ain't 'Paches—they're th' exceptions. But let me tell you that's a good game, just the same. It is as long as they don't see th' second trail in time. Didn't Buck and Skinny get two that way?"

"Yes, I reckon so. But what'll we do now? What's th' next play?" asked Red, hurriedly, his eyes searching the sky line of the hills. "Th' rest of th' coyotes will be here purty soon, an' they'll be madder than ever now. An' you better gimme back that gun, too."

"Take yore old gun—who wants th' blamed thing, anyhow?" Hopalong demanded, throwing the weapon at his friend as he ran to bring up the hidden horse. When he returned he grinned pleasantly. "Why, we'll go on like we was greased for calamity, that's what we'll do. Did you reckon we was going to play leapfrog around here an' wait for th' rest of them paint shops, like a blamed-fool pair of idiots?"

"I didn't know what *you* might do, remembering how you acted when I met you," retorted Red, shifting his cartridge belt so the empty loops were behind and out of the way. "But I shore knowed what we ought to do, all right."

"Well, mebby you also know how many's headed this way; do you?"

"You've got me stumped there; but there's a round dozen, anyway," Red replied. "You see, th' three that chased me were out scouting ahead of th' main bunch; an' I didn't have no time to take no blasted census."

"Then we've got to hit th' home trail, an' hit it hard. Wind up that four-laigged excuse of yourn, an' take my dust," Hopalong responded, leading the way. "If we can get home there'll be a lot of disgusted braves hitting th' high spots on th' back trail trying to find a way out. Buck an' th' rest of th' boys will be a whole lot pleased, too. We can muster thirty men in two hours if we get to Buckskin, an' that's twenty more than we'll need."

"Tell you one thing, Hoppy, we can get as far as Powers's old ranch house, an' that's shore," replied Red, thoughtfully.

"Yas!" exploded his companion in scorn and

pity. "That old sieve of a shack ain't good enough for *me* to die in, no matter what you think about it. Why, it's as full of holes as a stiff hat in a *mêlée*. Yo're on th' wrong trail. Think again."

Mr. Cassidy objected not because he believed that Powers's old ranch house was unworthy of serious consideration as a place of refuge and defense, but for the reason that he wished to reach Buckskin so his friends might all get in on the treat. Times were very dull on the ranch, and this was an occasion far too precious to let slip by. Besides, he then would have the pleasure of leading his friends against the enemy and battling on even terms. If he sought shelter he and Red would have to fight on the defensive, which was a game he hated cordially because it put him in a relatively subordinate position and thereby hurt his pride.

"Let me tell you that it's a whole lot better than thin air with a hard-working circle around us—an' you know what that means," retorted Mr. Connors. "But if you don't want to take a chance in th' shack, why mebby we can make Wallace's, or th' Cross-O-Cross. That is, if we don't get turned out of our way."

"We don't head for no Cross-O-Cross or Wallace's," rejoined his friend with emphasis, "an' we won't waste no time in Powers's shack, neither; we'll push right through as hard as we can go for Buckskin. Let them fellers find their own hunting—our outfit comes first. An' besides that'll mean a detour in a country fine for ambushes. We'd never get through."

"Well, have it yore own way, then!" snapped Red. "You allus was a hard-headed old mule, anyhow." In his heart Red knew that Hopalong was right about Wallace's and the Cross-O-Cross.

Some time after the two punchers had quitted the scene of their trap, several Apaches loped up, read the story of the tragedy at a glance, and galloped on in pursuit. They had left the reservation a fortnight before under the able leadership of that veteran of many war trails—Black Bear. Their leader, chafing at inaction and sick of the monotony of reservation life, had yielded to the entreaties of a score of restless young men and slipped away at their head, eager for the joys of raiding and plundering. But instead of stealing horses and murdering isolated whites as they had expected, they met with heavy repulses and were now without the mind of their leader. They had fled from one defeat to another and twice had barely eluded the cavalry which pursued them. Now two more of their dwindling force were dead and another had been found but an hour before. Rage and ferocity seethed in each savage heart and they determined to get the puncher they had chased, and that other whose trail they now saw for the first time. They would place at least one victory against the string of their defeats, and at any cost. Whips rose and fell and the war party shot forward in a compact group, two scouts thrown ahead to feel the way.

Red and Hopalong rode on rejoicing, for there were three less Apaches loose in the Southwest for the inhabitants to swear about and fear, and there was an excellent chance of more to follow. The Southwest had no toleration for the Government's policy of dealing with Indians and derived a great amount of satisfaction every time an Apache was killed. It still clung to the time-honored belief that the only good Indian was a dead one. Mr. Cassidy voiced his elation and then rubbed an empty stomach in vain regret—when a bullet shrilled past his head, so unexpectedly as to cause him to duck instinctively and then glance apologetically at his red-haired friend; and both spurred their mounts to greater speed. Next Mr. Connors grabbed frantically at his perforated sombrero and grew petulant and loquacious.

"Both them shots was lucky, Hoppy; th' feller that fired at me did it on th' dead run, but that won't help us none if one of 'em connects with us. You gimme that Sharps—got to show 'em that they're taking big chances crowding us this way." He took the heavy rifle and turned in the saddle. "It's an even thousand, if it's a yard. He don't look very big, can't hardly tell him from his cayuse; an' th' wind's puffy. Why don't you dirty or rust this gun? Th' sun glitters all along th' barrel. Well, here goes."

"Missed by a mile," reproved Hopalong, who would have been stunned by such a thing as a hit under the circumstances, even if his good-shooting friend had made it.

"Yes! Missed th' coyote I aimed for, but I got th' cayuse of his off pardner; see it?"

"Talk about luck!"

"That's all right: it takes blamed good shooting to miss that close in this case. Look! It's slowed 'em up a bit, an' that's about all I hoped to do. Bet they think I'm a real, shore-'nuff medicine man. Now gimme another cartridge."

"I will not; no use wasting lead at this range. We'll need all th' cartridges we got before we get out of this hole. You can't do nothing without stopping—an' that takes time."

"Then I'll stop! Th' blazes with th' time! Gimme another, d'ye hear?"

Mr. Cassidy heard, complied, and stopped beside his companion, who was very intent upon the matter at hand. It took some figuring to make a hit when the range was so great and the sun so blinding and the wind so capricious. He lowered the rifle and peered through the smoke at the confusion he had caused by dropping the nearest warrior. He was said to be the best rifle shot in the Southwest, which means a great deal, and his enemies did not deny it. But since the Sharps shot a special cartridge and was reliable up to the limit of its sight gauge, a matter of 1800 yards, he did not regard the hit as anything worthy of especial mention. Not so his friend, who grinned joyously and loosed his admiration.

"Yo're a shore wonder with that gun, Red! Why don't you lose that repeater an' get a gun like mine? Lord, if I could use a rifle like you, I wouldn't have that gun of yourn for a gift. Just look at what you did with it!"

"I'm plumb satisfied with th' repeater," replied Red. "I don't miss very often at eight hundred with it, an' that's long enough range for most anybody. An' if I do miss, I can send another that won't, an' right on th' tail of th' first, too."

"Ah, th' devil! You make me disgusted with yore fool talk about that carbine!" snapped his companion, and the subject was dropped.

The merits of their respective rifles had always been a bone of contention between them and one well chewed, at that. Red was very well satisfied with his Winchester, and he was a good judge.

"You did stop 'em a little," asserted Mr. Cassidy some time later when he looked back. "You stopped 'em coming straight, but they're spreading out to work up around us. Now, if we had good cayuses instead of these wooden wonders, we could run away from 'em dead easy, draw their best mounted warriors to th' front, an' then close with 'em. Good thing their cayuses are well tired out, for as it is we've got to make a stand purty soon. Gee! They don't like you, Red; they're calling you names in th' sign language. Just look at 'em cuss you!"

"How much water have you got?" inquired his friend with anxiety.

"Canteen plumb full. How're you fixed?"

"I got th' same, less one drink. That gives us enough for a couple of days with some to spare, if we're careful," Mr. Connors replied. New Mexican canteens are built on generous lines and are known as life preservers.

"Look at that glory hunter go!" exclaimed Red, watching a brave who was riding half a mile to their right and rapidly coming abreast of them. "Wonder how he got over there without us seeing him."

"Here, stop him!" suggested Hopalong, holding out his Sharps. "We can't let him get ahead of us and lay in ambush—that's what he's playing to do."

"My gun's good, and better, for me, at this range, but you know I can't hit a jack rabbit going over rough country as fast as that feller is," replied his companion, standing up in his stirrups and firing.

"Huh! Never touched him! But he's edging off a-plenty. See him cuss you. What's he calling you, anyhow?"

"Aw, shut up! How th' devil do *I* know? I don't talk with my arms."

"Are you superstitious, Red?"

"No! Shut up!"

"Well, I am. See that feller over there? If he gets in front of us it's a shore sign that somebody's going to get hurt. He'll have plenty of time to get cover an' pick us off as we come up."

"Don't you worry—his cayuse is deader'n ours. They must 'a' been pushing on purty hard th' last few days. See it stumble?—what'd I tell you!"

"Yes; but they're gaining on us slow but shore. We've got to make a stand purty soon—how much further do you reckon that infernal shack is, anyhow?" Hopalong asked sharply.

" 'T ain't fur off—see it any minute now."

"Here," remarked Hopalong, holding out his rifle, "stencil yore mark on his hide; catch him just as he strikes th' top of that little rise."

"Ain't got time—that shack can't be much further."

And it wasn't, for as they galloped over a rise they saw, half a mile ahead of them, an adobe building in poor state of preservation. It was Powers's old ranch house, and as they neared it, they saw that there was no doubt about the holes.

"Told you it was a sieve," grunted Hopalong, swinging in on the trail of his companion. "Not worth a hang for anything," he added bitterly.

"It'll answer, all right," retorted Red grimly.

Chapter Nine

Mr. Holden Drops In

MR. CASSIDY dismounted and viewed the building with open disgust, walking around it to see what held it up, and when he finally realized that it was self-supporting his astonishment was profound. Undoubtedly there were shacks in the United States in worse condition, but he hoped their number was small. Of course he knew that the building would make a very good place of defense, but for the sake of argument he called to his companion and urged that they be satisfied with what defense they could extemporize in the open. Mr. Connors hotly and hastily dissented as he led the horses into the building, and straightway the subject was arbitrated with much feeling and snappy eloquence. Finally Hopalong thought that Red was a chump, and said so out loud, whereat Red said unpleasant things about his good friend's pedigree, attributes, intelligence, *et al.*, even going so far as to prognosticate his friend's place of eternal abode.

The remarks were fast getting to be somewhat personal in tenor when a whine in the air swept up the scale to a vicious shriek as it passed between them, dropped rapidly to a whine again and quickly died out in the distance, a flat report coming to their ears a few seconds later. Invisible bees seemed to be winging through the air, the angry and venomous droning becoming more pronounced each passing moment, and the irregular cracking of rifles grew louder rapidly. An angry *s-p-a-t!* told of where a stone behind them had launched the ricochet which hurtled skyward with a wheezing scream. A handful of 'dobe dust sprang from the corner of the building and sifted down upon them, causing Red to cough.

"That ricochet was a Sharps!" exclaimed Hopalong, and they lost no time in getting into the building, where the discussion was renewed as they prepared for the final struggle. Red grunted his cheerful approval, for now he was out of the blazing sun and where he could better appreciate the musical tones of the flying bullets, but his companion, slamming shut the door and propping it with a fallen roof beam, grumbled and finally gave rein to his rancor by sneering at the Winchester.

"It shore gets me that after all I have said about that gun you will tote it around with you and force yoreself into a suicide's grave," quoth Mr. Cassidy with exuberant pugnacity. "I ain't in no way objecting to th' suicide part of it, but I can't see that it's at all fair to drag *me* onto th' edge of everlasting eternity with you. If you ain't got no regard for yore own life you shore ought to think a little about yore friend's. Now you'll waste all yore ca'tridges an' then come snooping around me to borrow my gun. Why don't you lose th' damned thing?"

"What I pack ain't none of yore business, which same I'll uphold," retorted Mr. Connors, at last able to make himself heard. "You get over on yore own side an' use yore Colt; I've wondered a whole lot where you ever got th' sense to use a Colt—*I* wouldn't be a heap surprised to see you toting a pearl-handled .22, like th' kids use. Now you 'tend to yore graveyard aspirants, an' lemme do th' same with mine."

"Th' Lord knows I've stood a whole lot from you because you just can't help being foolish, but I've got plumb weary and sick of it. It stops right here or you won't get no 'Paches," snorted Hopalong, peering intently through a hole in the shack. The more they squabbled the better they liked it—controversies had become so common that they were merely a habit, and they served to take the grimness out of desperate situations.

"Aw, you can't lick one side of me," averred Red loftily. "You never did stop anybody that was anything," he jeered as he fired from his window. "Why, you couldn't even hit th' bottom of th' Grand Canyon if you leaned over th' edge."

"You could, if you leaned too far, you red-headed wart of a half-breed," snapped Hopalong. "But how about th' Joneses, Tarantula Charley,

Slim Travennes, an' all th' rest? How about them, hey?"

"Huh! You couldn't 'a' got any of 'em if they had been sober," and Mr. Connors shook so with mirth that the Indian at whom he had fired got away with a whole skin and cheerfully derided the marksman. "That 'Pache shore reckons it was you shooting at him, I missed him so far. Now, you shut up—I want to get some so we can go home. I don't want to stay out here all night an' th' next day as well," Red grumbled, his words dying slowly in his throat as he voiced other thoughts.

Hopalong caught sight of an Apache who moved cautiously through a chaparral lying about 900 yards away. As long as the distant enemy lay quietly he could not be discerned, but he was not content with assured safety and took a chance. Hopalong raised his rifle to his shoulder as the Indian fired and the latter's bullet, striking the edge of the hole through which Mr. Cassidy peered, kicked up a generous handful of dust, some of which found lodgment in that individual's eyes.

"Oh! Oh! Oh! Wow!" yelled the unfortunate, dancing blindly around the room in rage and pain, and dropping his rifle to grab at his eyes. "Oh! Oh! Oh!"

His companion wheeled like a flash and grabbed him as he stumbled past. "Are you plugged bad,

Hoppy? Where did they get you? Are you hit bad?" and Red's heart was in his voice.

"No, I ain't plugged bad!" mimicked Hopalong. "I ain't plugged at all!" he blazed, kicking enthusiastically at his solicitous friend. "Get me some water, you jackass! Don't stand there like a fool! I ain't going to fall down. Don't you know my eyes are full of 'dobe?"

Red, avoiding another kick, hastily complied, and as hastily left Mr. Cassidy to wash out the dirt while he returned to his post by the window. "Anybody'd think you was full of redeye, th' way you act," muttered Red peevishly.

Hopalong, rubbing his eyes of the dirt, went back to the hole in the wall and looked out. "Hey, Red! Come over here an' spill that brave's conceit. I can't keep my eyes open long enough to aim, an' it's a nice shot, too. It'd serve him right if you got him!"

Mr. Connors obeyed the summons and peered out cautiously. "I can't see him, nohow; where is th' coyote?"

"Over there in that little chaparral—see him now? *There!* See him moving. Do you mean to tell me—"

"Yep, I see him, all right. You watch," was the reply. "He's just over nine hundred—where's yore Sharps?" He took the weapon, glanced at the Buffington sight, which he found to be set right, and aimed carefully.

Hopalong blinked through another hole as his friend fired and saw the Indian flop down and crawl aimlessly about on hands and knees. "What's he doing now, Red?"

"Playing marbles, you chump, an' here goes for his agate," replied the man with the Sharps, firing again. "There! Gee!" he exclaimed, as a bullet hummed in through the window he had quitted for the moment, and thudded into the wall, making the dry adobe fly. It had missed him by only a few inches and he now crept along the floor to the rear of the room and shoved his rifle out among the branches of a stunted mesquite which grew before a fissure in the wall. "You keep away from that windy for a minute, Hoppy," he warned as he waited.

A terror-stricken lizard flashed out of the fissure and along the wall where the roof had fallen in and flitted into a hole, while a fly buzzed loudly and hovered persistently around Red's head, to the rage of that individual. "Ah, ha!" he grunted, lowering the rifle and peering through the smoke. A yell reached his ears and he forthwith returned to his window, whistling softly.

Evidently Mr. Cassidy's eyes were better and his temper sweeter, for he hummed *Dixie* and then jumped to *Yankee Doodle*, mixing the two airs with careless impartiality, which was a sign that he was thinking deeply. "Wonder whatever became of Powers, Red. Peculiar feller, he was."

"In jail, I reckon, if drink hasn't killed him."

"Yes, I reckon so," and Mr. Cassidy continued his medley, which prompted his friend quickly to announce his unqualified disapproval.

"You can make more of a mess of them two songs than anybody I ever heard murder 'em! *Shut up!*"—and the concert stopped, the vocalist venting his feelings at an Indian, and killing the horse instead.

"Did you get him?" queried Red.

"Nope, but I got his cayuse," Hopalong replied, shoving a fresh cartridge into the foul, greasy breech of the Sharps. "An' here's where I get him—got to square up for my eyes some way," he muttered, firing. "Missed! Now, what do you think of that!" he ejaculated.

"Better take my Winchester," suggested Red, in a matter-of-fact way, but he chuckled softly and listened for the reply.

"Aw, you go to th' devil!" snapped Mr. Cassidy, firing again. "Whoop! Got him that time!"

"Where?" asked his companion, with strong suspicion.

"None of yore business!"

"Aw, darn it! Who spilled th' water?" yelled Red, staring blankly at the overturned canteen.

"Pshaw! Reckon I did, Red," apologized his friend ruefully. "Now of all th' cussed luck!"

"Oh, well, we've got another, an' you had to wash out yore eyes. Lucky we each had one—

holy smoke! It's most all gone! Th' top is loose!"

Heartfelt profanity filled the room and the two disgusted punchers went sullenly back to their posts. It was a calamity of no small magnitude, for while food could be dispensed with for a long time if necessary, going without water was another question. It was as necessary as cartridges.

Then Hopalong laughed at the ludicrous side of the whole affair, thereby revealing one of the characteristics which endeared him to his friends. No matter how desperate a situation might be, he could always find in it something at which to laugh. He laughed going into danger and coming out of it, with a joke or a pleasantry always trembling on the end of his tongue.

"Red, did it ever strike you how cussed thirsty a feller gets just as soon as he knows he can't have no drink? But it don't make much difference, nohow. We'll get out of this little scrape just as we've allus got out of trouble. There's some mad war whoops outside that are worse off than we are, because they are at th' wrong end of yore gun. I feel sort of sorry for 'em."

"Yo're shore a happy idiot," grinned Red. "Hey! Listen!"

Galloping was heard and Hopalong, running to the door, looked out through a crack as sudden firing broke out around the rear of the shack, and fell to pulling away the props, crying, "It's a puncher, Red—he's riding this way! Come on an' help him in!"

"He's a blamed fool to ride this way! I'm with you!" replied Red, running to his side.

Half a mile from the house, coming across the open space as fast as he could urge his horse, rode a cowboy, and not far behind him raced about a dozen Apaches, yelling and firing.

Red picked up his companion's rifle, and steadying it against the jamb of the door, fired, dropping one of the foremost of the pursuers. Quickly reloading again, he fired and missed. The third shot struck another horse, and then taking up his own gun he began to fire rapidly, as rapidly as he could work the lever and yet make his shots tell. Hopalong drew his Colt and ran back to watch the rear of the house, and it was well that he did so, for an Apache in that direction, believing that the trapped punchers were so busily engaged with the new developments as to forget for the moment, sprinted towards the back window; and he had gotten within 20 paces of the goal when Hopalong's Colt cracked a protest. Seeing that the warrior was no longer a combatant, Mr. Cassidy ran back to the door just as the stranger fell from his horse and crawled past Red. The door slammed shut, the props fell against it, and the two friends turned to the work of driving back the second band, which, however, had given up all hope of rushing the house in the face of Red's telling fire, and had sought cover instead.

The stranger dragged himself to the canteens and drank what little water remained, and then turned to watch the two men moving from place to place, firing coolly and methodically. He thought he recognized one of them from the descriptions he had heard, but he was not sure.

"My name's Holden," he whispered hoarsely, but the cracking of the rifles drowned his voice. During a lull he tried again: "My name's Holden," he repeated weakly. "I'm from th' Cross-O-Cross, an' can't get back there again."

"Mine's Cassidy, an' that's Connors, of th' Bar-20. Are you hurt very bad?"

"No, not very bad," lied Holden, trying to smile. "Gee, but I'm glad I fell in with you two fellers," he exclaimed. He was but little more than a boy, and to him Hopalong Cassidy and Red Connors were names with which to conjure. "But I'm plumb sorry I went an' brought you more trouble," he added regretfully.

"Oh, pshaw! We had it before you came—you needn't do no worrying about that, Holden; besides, I reckon you couldn't help it," Hopalong grinned facetiously. "But tell us how you came to mix up with that bunch," he continued.

Holden shuddered and hesitated a moment, his companions alertly shifting from crack to crack, window to window, their rifles cracking at intervals. They appeared to him to act as if they had done nothing else all their lives but fight Indians from that shack, and he braced up a little at their example of coolness.

"It's an awful story, awful!" he began. "I was riding toward Hoyt's Corners an' when I got about halfway there I topped a rise an' saw a nester's house about half a mile away. It wasn't there th' last time I rode that way, an' it looked so peaceful an' homelike that I stopped an' looked at it a few minutes. I was just going to start again when that war party rode out of a barranca close to th' house an' went straight for it at top speed. It seemed like a dream, 'cause I thought Apaches never got so far east. They don't, do they? I thought not—these must 'a' got turned out of their way an' had to hustle for safety. Well, it was all over purty quick. I saw 'em drag out two women an'—an'—purty soon a man. He was fighting like fury, but he didn't last long. Then they set fire to th' house an' threw th' man's body up on th' roof. I couldn't seem to move till th' flames shot up, but then I must 'a' went sort of loco, because I emptied my gun at 'em, which was plumb foolish at that distance, for me. Th' next thing I knowed was that half of 'em was coming my way as hard as they could ride, an' I lit out instanter; an' here I am. I can't get that sight outen my head nohow—it'll drive me loco!" he screamed, sobbing like a child from the horror of it all.

125

His auditors still moved around the room, growing more and more vindictive all the while and more zealously endeavoring to create a still greater deficit in one Apache war party. They knew what he had looked upon, for they themselves had become familiar with the work of Apaches in Arizona. They could picture it vividly in all its devilish horror. Neither of them paid any apparent attention to their companion, for they could not spare the time, and, also, they believed it best to let him fight out his own battles unassisted.

Holden sobbed and muttered as the minutes dragged along, at times acting so strangely as to draw a covert side glance from one or both of the Bar-20 punchers. Then Mr. Connors saw his boon companion suddenly lean out of a window and immediately become the target for the hard-working enemy. He swore angrily at the criminal recklessness of it. "Hey, you! Come in out of that! Ain't you got no brains at all, you blasted idiot! Don't you know that we need every gun?"

"Yes, that's right. I sort of forgot," grinned the reckless one, obeying with alacrity and looking sheepish. "But you know there's two thundering big tarantulas out there fighting like blazes. You ought to see 'em jump! It's a sort of a leapfrog fight, Red."

"Fool!" snorted Mr. Connors belligerently. "*You'd* 'a' jumped if one of them slugs had 'a' got you! Yo're th' damnedest fool that ever walked on two laigs, you blasted sage hen!" Mr. Connors was beginning to lose his temper and talk in his throat.

"Well, they didn't get me, did they? What you yelling about, anyhow?" growled Hopalong, trying to brazen it out.

"An' *you* talking about suicide to me!" snapped Mr. Connors, determined to rub it in and have the last word.

Mr. Holden stared, open-mouthed, at the man who could enjoy a miserable spider fight under such circumstances, and his shaken nerves became steadier as he gave thought to the fact that he was a companion of the two men about whose exploits he had heard so much. Evidently the stories had not been exaggerated. What must they think of him for giving away as he had? He arose to his feet in time to see a horse blunder into the open on Red's side of the house, and after it blundered its owner, who immediately lost all need of earthly conveyances. Holden laughed from the joy of being with a man who could shoot like that, and he took up his rifle and turned to a crack in the wall, filled with the determination to let his companions know that he was built of the right kind of timber after all, wounded as he was.

Red's only comment, as he pumped a fresh cartridge into the barrel, was, "He must 'a' thought he saw a spider fight, too."

"Hey, Red," called Hopalong. "Th' big one is dead."

"What big one?"

"Why, don't you remember? That big tarantula I was watching. One was bigger than th' other, but th' little feller shore waded into him an'—"

"Go to th' devil!" shouted Red, who had to grin despite his anger.

"Presently, presently," replied Hopalong, laughing.

So the day passed, and when darkness came upon them all of the defenders were wounded, Holden desperately so.

"Red, one of us has got to try to make th' ranch," Hopalong suddenly announced, and his friend knew he was right. Since Holden had appeared upon the scene they had known that they could not try a dash; one of them had to stay.

"We'll toss for it—heads, I go," Red suggested, flipping a coin.

"Tails!" cried Hopalong. "It's only thirty miles to Buckskin, an' if I can get away from here I'm good to make it by eleven tonight. I'll stop at Cowan's an' have him send word to Lucas an' Bartlett, so there'll be enough in case any of our boys are out on th' range in some line house. We can pick 'em up on th' way back, so there won't be no time lost. If I get through you can expect excitement on th' outside of this sieve by daylight. You an' Holden can hold her till then, because they never attack at night. It's th' only way out of this for us—we ain't got cartridges or water enough to last another day."

Red, knowing that Hopalong was taking a desperate chance in working through the cordon of Indians which surrounded them, and that the house was safe when compared to running such a gantlet, offered to go through the danger line with him. For several minutes a wordy war raged and finally Red accepted a compromise: he was to help, but not to work through the line.

"But what's th' use of all this argument?" feebly demanded Holden. "Why don't you both go? I ain't a-going to live, nohow, so there ain't no use of anybody staying here with me, to die with me. Put a bullet through me so them devils can't play with me like they do with others, an' then get away while you've got a chance. Two men can get through as easy as one." He sank back, exhausted by the effort.

"No more of that!" cried Red, trying to be stern. "I'm going to stay with you an' see things through. I'd be a fine sort of a coyote to sneak off an' leave you for them fiends. An' besides, I can't get away; my cayuse is hit too hard an' yourn is dead," he lied cheerfully. "An' yo're going to get well, all right. I've seen fellers hit harder than you are pull through."

Hopalong walked over to the prostrate man and shook hands with him. "I'm awful glad I met you, Holden. Yo're pure grit all th' way through, an' I like to tie to that kind of a man. Don't you worry about nothing; Red can handle this proposition, and we'll have you in Buckskin by tomorrow night. You'll be riding again in two weeks. So long."

He turned to Red and shook hands silently, led his horse out of the building and mounted, glad that the moon had not yet come up, for in the darkness he had a chance.

"Good luck, Hoppy!" cried Red, running to the door. "Good luck!"

"You bet—an' lots of it, too," groaned Holden, but he was gone.

Then Red wheeled. "Holden, keep yore eyes an' ears open. I'm going out to see that he gets off. He may run into a—" and he too was gone.

Holden watched the doors and windows, striving to resist the weak, giddy feeling in his head, and ten minutes later he heard a shot and then several more in quick succession. Shortly afterward Red called out, and almost immediately the Bar-20 puncher crawled in through a window.

"Well?" anxiously cried the man on the floor. "Did he make it?"

"I reckon so. He got away from th' first crowd, anyhow. I wasn't very far behind him, an' by th' time they woke up to what was going on he was through an' riding like blazes. I heard him call 'em half-breeds a minute later an' it sounded far off.

They hit me—fired at my flash, like I drilled one of them. But it ain't much, anyhow. How are you feeling now?"

"Fine!" lied the other. "That Cassidy is shore a wonder—he's all right, an' so are you. I'll never see him again, but I shore hope he gets through!"

"Don't be foolish. Here, you finish th' water in yore canteen—I picked it up outside by yore cayuse. Then go to sleep," ordered Red. "I'll do all th' watching that's necessary."

"I will if you'll call me when you get sleepy."

"Why, shore I will. But don't you want th' rest of th' water? I ain't a bit thirsty—I had all I could hold just before you came," Red remarked as his companion pushed the canteen against him in the dark. He was choking with thirst. "Well, then, all right," and Red pretended to drink. "Now, then, you go to sleep—a good snooze will do you a world of good—it's just what you need."

CHAPTER TEN

BUCK TAKES A HAND

COWAN'S saloon, club, and place of general assembly for the town of Buckskin and the near-by ranches, held a merry crowd, for it was payday on the range, and laughter and liquor ran a close race. Buck Peters, his hands full of cigars, passed through the happy-go-lucky, do-as-you-please crowd and invited everybody to smoke, which nobody refused to do. Wood Wright, of the C-80, tuned his fiddle anew and swung into a rousing quick-step. Partners were chosen, the "women" wearing handkerchiefs on their arms to indicate the fact, and the room shook and quivered as the scraping of heavy boots filled the air with a cloud of dust. *"Allemande left!"* cried the prompter, and then the dance stopped as if by magic. The door had crashed open and a blood-stained man staggered in and toward the bar, crying, "Buck! Red's hemmed in by 'Paches!"

"Good God!" roared the foreman of the Bar-20, leaping forward, the cigars falling to the floor to be crushed and ground into powder by careless feet. He grasped his puncher and steadied him while Cowan slid an extra-generous glassful of brandy across the bar for the wounded man. The room was in an uproar, men grabbing rifles and running out to get their horses, for it was plain to be seen that there was hard work to be done, and quickly. Questions, threats, curses filled the air, those who remained inside to get the story listening intently to the jerky narrative; those outside, caring less for the facts of an action past than for the action to come, shouted impatiently for a start to be made, even threatening to go on and tackle the proposition by themselves if there were not more haste. Hopalong told in a graphic, terse manner all that was necessary, while Buck and Cowan hurriedly bandaged his wounds.

"Come on! Come on!" shouted the mounted crowd outside, angry, and impatient for a start, the prancing of horses and the clinking of metal adding to the noise. "Get a move on! *Will* you hurry up!"

"Listen, Hoppy!" pleaded Buck, in a furore. "Shut up, you outside!" he yelled. "You say they know that you got away, Hoppy?" he asked. "All right—*Lanky!*" he shouted. *"Lanky!"*

"All right, Buck!" and Lanky Smith roughly pushed his way through the crowd to his foreman's side. "Here I am."

"Take Skinny and Pete with you, an' a lead horse apiece. Strike straight for Powers's old ranch house. Them Injuns'll have pickets out looking for Hoppy's friends. You three get th' pickets nearest th' old trail through that arroyo to th' southeast, an' then wait for us. We'll come along th' high bank on th' left. Don't make no noise doing it, neither, if you can help it. Understand? Good! Now ride like th' devil!"

Lanky grabbed Pete and Skinny on his way out and disappeared into the corral; and very soon thereafter hoofbeats thudded softly in the sandy street and pounded into the darkness of the north, soon lost to the ear. An uproar of advice and good wishes crashed after them, for the game had begun.

"It's Powers's old shack, boys!" shouted a man in the door to the restless force outside, which immediately became more restless. "Hey! Don't go yet!" he begged. "Wait for me an' th' rest. Don't be a lot of idiots!"

Excited and impatient voices replied from the darkness, vexed, grouchy, and querulous. "Then get a move on—*whoa!*—it'll be light before we get there if you don't hustle!" roared one voice above the confusion. "You know what *that* means!"

"Come on! Come on! For God's sake, are you tied to th' bar?"

"Yo're a lot of old grandmothers! Come on!"

Hopalong appeared in the door. "I'll show you th' way, boys!" he shouted. "Cowan, put my saddle on yore cayuse—*pronto!*"

"Good for you, Hoppy!" came from the street. "We'll wait!"

"You stay here; yo're hurt too much!" cried

135

Buck to his puncher, as he grabbed up a box of cartridges from a shelf behind the bar. "Ain't you got no sense? There's enough of us to take care of this without you!"

Hopalong wheeled and looked his foreman squarely in the eyes. "Red's out there, waiting for me—I'm going! I'd be a fine sort of a coyote to leave him in that hell-hole an' not go back, wouldn't I!" he said, with quiet determination.

"Good for you, Cassidy!" cried a man who hastened out to mount.

"Well, then, come on," replied Buck. "There's blamed few like you," he muttered, following Hopalong outside.

"Here's th' cayuse, Cassidy," cried Cowan, turning the animal over to him. "*Wait,* Buck!" and he leaped into the building and ran out again, shoving a bottle of brandy and a package of food into the impatient foreman's hand. "Mebby Red or Hoppy'll need it—so long, an' good luck!" and he was alone in a choking cloud of dust, peering through the darkness along the river trail after a black mass that was swallowed up almost instantly. Then, as he watched, the moon pushed its rim up over the hills and he laughed joyously as he realized what its light would mean to the crowd. "There'll be great doings when *that* gang cuts loose," he muttered with savage elation. "Wish I was with 'em. Damn Injuns, anyhow!"

Far ahead of the main fighting force rode the

three special-duty men, reeling off the miles at top speed and constantly distancing their friends, for they changed mounts at need, thanks to the lead horses provided by Mr. Peters's cool-headed foresight. It was a race against dawn, and every effort was made to win—the life of Red Connors hung in the balance and a minute might turn the scale.

In Powers's old ranch house the night dragged along slowly to the grim watcher, and the man huddled in the corner stirred uneasily and babbled, ofttimes crying out in horror at the vivid dreams of his disordered mind. Pacing ceaselessly from window to window, crack to crack, when the moon came up, Mr. Connors scanned the bare, level plain with anxious eyes, searching out the few covers and looking for dark spots on the dull gray sand. They never attacked at night, but still — Through the void came the quavering call of a coyote, and he listened for the reply, which soon came from the black chaparral across the clearing. He knew where two of them were hiding, anyhow. Holden was muttering and tried to answer the calls, and Red looked at him for the hundredth time that night. He glanced out of the window again and noticed that there was a glow in the eastern sky, and shortly afterwards dawn swiftly developed.

Pouring the last few drops of the precious water

between the wounded man's parched and swollen lips, he tossed the empty canteen from him and stood erect.

"Pore devil," he muttered, shaking his head sorrowfully as he realized that Holden's delirium was getting worse all the time. "If you was all right we could give them wolves hell to dance to. Well, you won't know nothing about it if we go under, an' that's some consolation." He examined his rifle and saw that the Colt at his thigh was fully loaded and in good working order. "An' they'll pay us for their victory, by God! They'll pay for it!" He stepped closer to the window, throwing the rifle into the hollow of his arm. "It's about time for th' rush; about time for th' game—"

There was movement by that small chaparral to the south! To the east something stirred into bounding life and action; a coyote called twice— and then they came, on foot and silently as fleeting shadows, leaning forward to bring into play every ounce of energy in the slim, red legs. Smoke filled the room with its acrid sting. The crashing of the Winchester, worked with wonderful speed and deadly accuracy by the best rifle shot in the Southwest, brought the prostrate man to his feet in an instinctive response to the call to action, the necessity of defense. He grasped his Colt and stumbled blindly to a window to help the man who had stayed with him.

On Red's side of the house one warrior threw up his arms and fell forward, sprawling with arms and legs extended; another pitched to one side and rolled over twice before he lay still; the legs of the third collapsed and threw him headlong, bunched up in a grotesque pile of lifeless flesh; the fourth leaped high into the air and turned a somersault before he struck the sand, badly wounded, and out of the fight. Holden, steadying himself against the wall, leaned in a window on the other side of the shack and emptied his Colt in a dazed manner—doing his very best. Then the man with the rifle staggered back with a muttered curse, his right arm useless, and dropped the weapon to draw his Colt with the other hand.

Holden shrieked once and sank down, wagging his head slowly from side to side, blood oozing from his mouth and nostrils; and his companion, goaded into a frenzy of blood lust and insane rage at the sight, threw himself against the door and out into the open, to die under the clear sky, to go like the man he was if he must die. "Damn you! It'll cost you more yet!" he screamed, wheeling to place his back against the wall.

The triumphant yells of the exultant savages were cut short and turned to howls of dismay by a fusillade which thundered from the south, where a crowd of hard-riding, hard-shooting cow-punchers tore out of the thicket like an avalanche and swept over the open sand, yelling and cursing, and then separated to go in hot pursuit of the sprinting Apaches. Some stood up in their stirrups and fired down at a slant, making short, chopping motions with their heavy Colts; others leaned forward, far over the necks of their horses, and shot with stationary guns; while yet others, with reins dangling free, worked the levers of blue Winchesters so rapidly that the flashes seemed to merge into a continuous flame.

"Thank God! Thank God—an' Hoppy!" groaned the man at the door of the shack, staggering forward to meet the two men who had lost no time in pursuit of the enemy, but had ridden straight to him.

"I was scared stiff you was done fer!" cried Hopalong, leaping off his horse and shaking hands with his friend, whose handclasp was not as strong as usual. "How's Holden?" he demanded, anxiously.

"He passed. It was a close—" began Red, weakly, but his foreman interposed.

"Shut up, an' drink this!" ordered Buck, kindly but sternly. "We'll do th' talking for a while; you can tell us all about it later on. Why, *hullo!*" he cried as Lanky Smith and his two happy companions rode up. "Reckon you must 'a' got them pickets."

"Shore we did! Stalked 'em on our bellies, didn't we, Skinny?" modestly replied Mr. Smith, the roping expert of the Bar-20. "Ropes an'

140

clubbed guns did th' rest. Anyhow, there was only two anywhere near th' trail."

"We didn't see you," responded the foreman, tying the knot of a bandage on Mr. Connors's arm. "An' we looked sharp, too."

"Reckon we was hunting for more—we sort of forgot what you said about waiting for you," Mr. Smith replied, grinning broadly.

"An' you've got a good memory now," smiled Mr. Peters.

"We didn't find no more, though," offered Mr. Pete Wilson, with grave regret. "An' we looked good, too. But we got Red, an' that's th' whole game. Red, you old son-of-a-gun, you can lick yore weight in powder!"

"It's too bad about Holden," muttered Red sullenly.

CHAPTER ELEVEN

HOPALONG NURSES A GROUCH

AFTER the excitement incident to the affair at Powers's shack had died down and the Bar-20 outfit worked over its range in the old, placid way, there began to be heard low mutterings, and an air of peevish discontent began to be manifested in various childish ways. And it was all caused by the fact that Hopalong Cassidy had a grouch, and a big one. It was two months old and growing worse daily, and the signs threatened contagion. His foreman, tired and sick of the snarling, fidgety, petulant atmosphere that Hopalong had created on the ranch, and driven to desperation, eagerly sought some chance to get rid of the "sore-thumb" temporarily and give him an opportunity to shed his generous mantle of the blues. And at last it came.

No one knew the cause for Hoppy's unusual state of mind, although there were many conjectures, and they covered the field rather thoroughly, but they did not strike on the cause. Even Red Connors, now well over all ill effects of the wounds acquired in the old ranch house, was forced to guess, and when Red had to do that about anything concerning Hopalong he was well warranted in believing the matter to be very serious.

Johnny Nelson made no secret of his opinion and derived from it a great amount of satisfaction, which he admitted with a grin to his foreman.

"Buck," he said, "Hoppy told me he went broke playing poker over in Grant with Dave Wilkes and them two Lawrence boys, an' that shore explains it all. He's got pack sores from carrying his unholy licking. It was due to come to him, an' Dave Wilkes is just th' boy to deliver it. That's th' whole trouble, an' I know it, an' I'm damned glad they trimmed him. But he ain't got no right of making *us* miserable because he lost a few measly dollars."

"Yo're wrong, son—dead, dead wrong," Buck replied. "He takes his beatings with a grin, an' money never did bother him. No poker game that ever was played could leave a welt on him like th' one we all mourn an' cuss. He's been doing something that he don't want us to know—made a fool of hisself some way, most likely, an' feels so ashamed that he's sore. I've knowed him too long an' well to believe that gambling had anything to do with it. But this little trip he's taking will fix him up all right, an' I couldn't 'a' picked a better man—or one that I'd ruther get rid of just now."

"Well, lemme tell you it's blamed lucky for him that you picked him to go," rejoined Johnny, who thought more of the woeful absentee than he did of his own skin. "I was going to lick him, shore, if it went on much longer. Me an' Red an' Billy was going to beat him up good till he forgot his dead injuries an' took more interest in his friends."

Buck laughed heartily. "Well, th' three of you might 'a' done it if you worked hard an' didn't get careless, but I have my doubts. Now look here—you've been hanging around th' bunkhouse too blamed much lately. Henceforth an' hereafter you've got to earn yore grub. Get out on that west line an' hustle."

"You know I've had a toothache!" snorted Johnny with a show of indignation, his face as sober as that of a judge.

"An' you'll have a bellyache from lack of grub if you don't earn yore right to eat purty soon," retorted Buck. "You ain't had a toothache in yore whole life, an' you don't know what one is. G'wan, now, or I'll give you a backache that'll ache!"

"Huh! Devil of a way to treat a sick man!" Johnny retorted, but he departed exultantly, whistling with much noise and no music. But he was sorry for one thing: he sincerely regretted that he had not been present when Hopalong met his Waterloo. It would have been pleasing to look upon.

While the outfit blessed the proposed lease of range that took him out of their small circle for a time, Hopalong rode farther and farther into the northwest, frequently lost in abstraction which, judging by its effect upon him, must have been caused by something serious. He had not heard from Dave Wilkes about that individual's good horse which had been loaned to Ben Ferris, of Winchester. Did Dave think he had been killed or was still pursuing the man whose neckerchief had aroused such animosity in Hopalong's heart? Or had the horse actually been returned? The animal was a good one, a successful contender in all distances from one to five miles, and had earned its owner and backers much money—and Hopalong had parted with it as easily as he would have borrowed five dollars from Red. The story, as he had often reflected since, was as old as lying—a broken-legged horse, a wife dying 40 miles away, and a horse all saddled which needed only to be mounted and ridden.

These thoughts kept him company for a day and when he dismounted before Stevenson's "Hotel" in Hoyt's Corners he summed up his feelings for the enlightenment of his horse.

"Damn it, bronc! I'd give ten dollars right now to know if I was a jackass or not," he growled. "But he was an awful slick talker if he lied. An' I've got to go up an' face Dave Wilkes to find out about it!"

Mr. Cassidy was not known by sight to the citizens of Hoyt's Corners, however well versed they might be in his numerous exploits of wisdom and folly. Therefore the *habitués* of Stevenson's Hotel did not recognize him in the gloomy and morose individual who dropped his saddle on the floor with a crash and stamped over to the three-legged table at dusk and surlily demanded shelter for the night.

"Gimme a bed an' something to eat," he demanded, eying the three men seated with their chairs tilted against the wall. "Do I get 'em?" he asked impatiently.

"You do," replied a one-eyed man, lazily arising and approaching him. "One dollar, now."

"An' take th' rocks outen that bed—I want to sleep."

"A dollar per for every rock you find," grinned Stevenson pleasantly. "There ain't no rocks in *my* beds," he added.

"Some folks likes to be rocked to sleep," facetiously remarked one of the pair by the wall, laughing contentedly at his own pun. He bore all the earmarks of being regarded as the wit of the locality—every hamlet has one; I have seen some myself.

"Hee, hee, hee! Yo're a droll feller, Charley," chuckled Old John Ferris, rubbing his ear with unconcealed delight. "That's a good un."

"One drink, now," growled Hopalong, mimicking the proprietor, and glaring savagely at the "droll feller" and his companion. "An' mind that it's a good one," he admonished the host.

"It's better," smiled Stevenson, whereat Old

John crossed his legs and chuckled again. Stevenson winked.

"Riding long?" he asked.

"Since I started."

"Going fur?"

"Till I stop."

"Where do you belong?" Stevenson's pique was urging him against the ethics of the range, which forbade personal questions.

Hopalong looked at him with a light in his eye that told the host he had gone too far. "Under my sombrero!" he snapped.

"Hee, hee, hee!" chortled Old John, rubbing his ear again and nudging Charley. "He ain't no fool, eh?"

"Why, I don't know, John; he won't tell," replied Charley.

Hopalong wheeled and glared at him, and Charley, smiling uneasily, made an appeal: "Ain't mad, are you?"

"Not yet," and Hopalong turned to the bar again, took up his liquor, and tossed it off. Considering a moment, he shoved the glass back again, while Old John tongued his lips in anticipation of a treat. "It is good—fill it again."

The third was even better and by the time the fourth and fifth had joined their predecessors Hopalong began to feel a little more cheerful. But even the liquor and an exceptionally well-cooked supper could not separate him from his persistent and set grouch. And of liquor he had already taken more than his limit. He had always boasted, with truth, that he had never been drunk, although there had been two occasions when he was not far from it. That was one doubtful luxury which he could not afford for the reason that there were men who would have been glad to see him, if only for a few seconds, when liquor had dulled his brain and slowed his speed of hand. He could never tell when and where he might meet one of these.

He dropped into a chair by a card table and, baffling all attempts to engage him in conversation, reviewed his troubles in a mumbled soliloquy, the liquor gradually making him careless. But of all the jumbled words his companions' diligent ears heard they recognized and retained only the bare term "Winchester," and their conjectures were limited only by their imaginations.

Hopalong stirred and looked up, shaking off the hand which had aroused him. "Better go to bed, stranger," the proprietor was saying. "You an' me are th' last two up. It's after twelve, an' you look tired and sleepy."

"Said his wife was sick," muttered the puncher. "Oh, what you saying?"

"You'll find a bed better'n this table, stranger—it's after twelve an' I want to close up an' get some sleep. I'm tired myself."

"Oh, that all? Shore I'll go to bed—like to see anybody stop me! Ain't no rocks in it, hey?"

"Nary a rock," laughingly reassured the host, picking up Hopalong's saddle and leading the way to a small room off the "office," his guest stumbling after him and growling about the rocks that lived in Winchester. When Stevenson had dropped the saddle by the window and departed, Hopalong sat on the edge of the bed to close his eyes for just a moment before tackling the labor of removing his clothes. A crash and a jar awakened him and he found himself on the floor with his back to the bed. He was hot and his head ached, and his back was skinned a little—and how hot and stuffy and choking the room had become! He thought he had blown out the light, but it still burned, and three-quarters of the chimney was thickly covered with soot. He was stifling and could not endure it any longer. After three attempts he put out the light, stumbled against his saddle and, opening the window, leaned out to breathe the pure air. As his lungs filled he chuckled wisely and, picking up the saddle, managed to get it and himself through the window and on the ground without serious mishap. He would ride for an hour, give the room time to freshen and cool off, and come back feeling much better. Not a star could be seen as he groped his way unsteadily toward the rear of the building, where he vaguely remembered having seen the corral as he rode up.

"Huh! Said he lived in Winchester an' 's name

was Bill—no, Ben Ferris," he muttered, stumbling towards a noise he knew was made by a horse rubbing against the corral fence. Then his feet got tangled up in the cinch of his saddle, which he had kicked before him, and after great labor he arose, muttering savagely, and continued on his wobbly way. "Goo' Lord, it's darker'n cats in—*oof!*" he grunted, recoiling from forcible contact with the fence he sought. Growling words unholy, he felt his way along it and finally his arm slipped through an opening and he bumped his head solidly against the top bar of the gate. As he righted himself his hand struck the nose of a horse and closed mechanically over it. Cow ponies look alike in the dark and he grinned jubilantly as he complimented himself upon finding his own so unerringly.

"Anything is easy, when you know how. Can't fool me, ol' cayuse," he beamed, fumbling at the bars with his free hand and getting them down with a fool's luck. "You can't do it—I got you firs', las', an' always, an' I got you good. Yessir, I got you good. Quit that rearing, you ol' fool! Stan' still, can't you?"

The pony sidled as the saddle hit its back and evoked profane abuse from the indignant puncher as he risked his balance in picking it up to try again, this time successfully. He began to fasten the girth, and then paused in wonder and thought deeply, for the pin in the buckle would slide to no hole but the first. "Huh! Gettin' fat, ain't you, piebald?" he demanded with withering sarcasm. "You blow yoreself up any more'n I'll bust you wide open!"—heaving with all his might on the free end of the strap, one knee pushing against the animal's side. The "fat" disappeared and Hopalong laughed. "Been learnin' new tricks, ain't you? Got smart since you been travelin', hey?" He fumbled with the bars again and got two of them back in place and then, throwing himself across the saddle as the horse started forward as hard as it could go, slipped off, but managed to save himself by hopping along the ground. As soon as he had secured the grip he wished he mounted with the ease of habit and felt for the reins. "G'wan, now, an' easy—it's plumb dark an' my head's bustin'."

When he saddled his mount at the corral he was not aware that two of the three remaining horses had taken advantage of their opportunity and had walked out and made off in the darkness before he replaced the bars, and he was too drunk to care if he had known it.

The night air felt so good that it moved him to song, but it was not long before the words faltered more and more and soon ceased altogether and a subdued snore rasped from him. He awakened from time to time, but only for a moment, for he was tired and sleepy.

His mount very quickly learned that something

was wrong and that it was being given its head. As long as it could go where it pleased it could do nothing better than head for home, and it quickened its pace toward Winchester. Some time after daylight it pricked up its ears and broke into a canter, which soon developed signs of irritation in its rider. Finally Hopalong opened his heavy eyes and looked around for his bearings. Not knowing where he was and too tired and miserable to give much thought to a matter of such slight importance, he glanced around for a place to finish his sleep. A tree some distance ahead of him looked inviting and toward it he rode. Habit made him picket the horse before he lay down and as he fell asleep he had vague recollections of handling a strange picket rope some time recently. The horse slowly turned and stared at the already snoring figure, glanced over the landscape, back to the queerest man it had ever met, and then fell to grazing in quiet content. A slinking coyote topped a rise a short distance away and stopped instantly, regarding the sleeping man with grave curiosity and strong suspicion. Deciding that there was nothing good to eat in that vicinity and that the man was carrying out a fell plot for the death of coyotes, it backed away out of sight and loped on to other hunting-grounds.

CHAPTER TWELVE

A FRIEND IN NEED

STEVENSON, having started the fire for breakfast, took a pail and departed toward the spring, but he got no farther than the corral gate, where he dropped the pail and stared. There was only one horse in the enclosure where the night before there had been four. He wasted no time in surmises, but wheeled and dashed back toward the hotel, and his vigorous shouts brought Old John to the door, sleepy and peevish. Old John's mouth dropped open as he beheld his habitually indolent host marking off long distances on the sand with each falling foot.

"What's got inter you?" demanded Old John.

"Our broncs are gone! Our broncs are gone!" yelled Stevenson, shoving Old John roughly to one side as he dashed through the doorway and on into the room he had assigned to the sullen and bibulous stranger. "I knowed it! I knowed it!" he wailed, popping out again as if on springs. "He's gone, an' he's took our broncs with him, th' measly, low-down dog! I knowed he wasn't no good! I could see it in his eye, an' he wasn't drunk, not by a darn sight. Go out an' see for yoreself if they ain't gone!" he snapped in reply to Old John's look. "Go on out, while I throw some cold grub on th' table—won't have no time this morning to do no cooking. He's got five hours' start on us, an' it'll take some right smart riding to get him before dark, but we'll do it, an' hang him, too!"

"What's all this here rumpus?" demanded a sleepy voice from upstairs. "Who's hanged?" and Charley entered the room, very much interested. His interest increased remarkably when the calamity was made known and he lost no time in joining Old John in the corral to verify the news.

Old John waved his hands over the scene and carefully explained what he had read in the tracks, to his companion's great irritation, for Charley's keen eyes and good training had already told him all there was to learn, and his reading did not exactly agree with that of his companion.

"Charley, he's gone and took our cayuses, an' that's th' very way he came—'round th' corner of th' hotel. He got all tangled up an' fell over there, an' here he bumped inter th' palisade, an' dropped his saddle. When he opened th' bars he took my roan gelding because it was th' best an' fastest, an' then he let out th' others to mix us up on th' tracks. See how he went? Had to hop four times on one foot afore he could get inter th' saddle. An' that proves he was sober, for no drunk could hop four times like that without falling down an' being drug to death. An' he left his own critter behind because he knowed it wasn't no good. It's all as plain as th' nose on your face, Charley," and Old John proudly rubbed his ear. "Hee, hee, hee! You can't fool Old John, even if he is gettin' old. No, sir, b'gum."

Charley had just returned from inside the corral, where he had looked at the brand on the far side of the one horse left, and he waited impatiently for his companion to cease talking. He took quick advantage of the first pause Old John made and spoke crisply.

"I don't care what corner he came 'round or what he bumped inter, an' any fool can see that. An' if he left that cayuse behind because he thought it wasn't no good, he *was* drunk. That's a Bar-20 cayuse, an' no hoss thief ever worked for that ranch. He left it behind because he stole it, that's why. An' he didn't let them others out because he wanted to mix us up, neither. How'd he know if we couldn't tell th' tracks of our own animals? He did that to make us lose time, that's what he did it for. An' he couldn't tell what bronc he took last night—it was too dark. He must 'a' struck a match an' seen where that Bar-20 cayuse was an' then took th' first one nearest that wasn't it. An' now you tell me how th' devil he knowed yourn was th' fastest, which it ain't," he finished sarcastically, gloating over a chance to rub it into the man he had always regarded as a windy old nuisance.

"Well, mebby what you said is—"

"Mebby nothin'!" snapped Charley. "If he wanted to mix th' tracks would he 'a' hopped like that so we couldn't help tellin' what cayuse he rode? He knowed we'd pick his trail quick an' he knowed that every minute counted, that's why he hopped—why, yore roan was goin' like the wind afore he got in th' saddle. If you don't believe it, look at them toe prints!"

"H'm, reckon yo're right, Charley. My eyes ain't nigh as good as they once was. But I heard him say something 'bout Winchester," replied Old John, glad to change the subject. "Bet he's goin' over there, too. He won't get through that town on no critter wearin' my brand. Everybody knows that roan, an'—"

"Quit guessin'!" snapped Charley, beginning to lose some of the tattered remnant of his respect for old age. "He's a whole lot likely to head for a town on a stolen cayuse, now ain't he! But we don't care where he's heading; we'll foller th' trail."

"Grub pile!" shouted Stevenson, and the two made haste to obey.

"Charley, gimme a chaw of yore tobacker," and Old John, biting off a generous chunk, quietly slipped it into his pocket, there to lay until after he had eaten his breakfast.

All talk was tabled while the three men gulped down a cold and uninviting meal. Ten minutes later they had finished and separated to find horses and spread the news; in 15 more they had them and were riding along the plain trail at top speed, with three other men close at their heels. Three hundred yards from the corral they pounded out of an arroyo, and Charley, who was leading, stood up in his stirrups and looked keenly ahead. Another trail joined the one they were following and ran with and on top of it. This, he reasoned, had been made by one of the strays and would turn away soon. He kept his eyes looking well ahead and soon saw that he was right in his surmise, and without checking the speed of his horse in the slightest degree he went ahead on the trail of the smaller hoofprints. In a moment Old John spurred forward and gained his side and began to argue hotheadedly.

"Hey! Charley!" he cried. "Why are you follerin' this track?" he demanded.

"Because it's his, that's why."

"Well, here, wait a minute!" and Old John was getting red from excitement. "How do you know it is? Mebby he took th' other!"

"He started out on th' cayuse that made these little tracks," retorted Charley, "an' I don't see no reason to think he swapped animules. Don't you know th' prints of yore own cayuse?"

"Lawd, no!" answered Old John. "Why, I don't hardly ride th' same cayuse th' second day, straight hand-runnin'. I tell you we ought to foller that other trail. He's just cute enough to play some trick on us."

"Well, you better do that for us," Charley replied, hoping against hope that the old man would chase off on the other and give his companions a rest.

"He ain't got sand enough to tackle a thing like that singlehanded," laughed Jed White, winking to the others.

Old John wheeled. "Ain't, hey! I am going to do that same thing an' prove that you are a pack of fools. I'm too old to be fooled by a common trick like that. An' I don't need no help—I'll ketch him all by myself, an' hang him, too!" And he wheeled to follow the other trail, angry and outraged: "Young fools," he muttered. "Why, I was fightin' all around these parts afore any of 'em knowed th' difference between day an' night!"

"Hard-headed old fool," remarked Charley, frowning, as he led the way again.

"He's gittin' old an' childish," excused Stevenson. "They say warn't nobody in these parts could hold a candle to him in his prime."

Hopalong muttered and stirred and opened his eyes to gaze blankly into those of one of the men who was tugging at his hands, and as he stared he started his stupefied brain sluggishly to work in an endeavor to explain the unusual experience. There were five men around him and the two who hauled at his hands stepped back and kicked him. A look of pained indignation slowly spread

160

over his countenance as he realized beyond doubt that they were really kicking him, and with sturdy vigor. He considered a moment and then decided that such treatment was most unwarranted and outrageous and, furthermore, that he must defend himself and chastise the perpetrators.

"Hey!" he snorted, "what do you reckon yo're doing, anyhow? If you want to do any kickin', why, kick each other an' I'll help you! But I'll lick th' whole blasted bunch of you if you don't quit maulin' me. Ain't you got no manners? Don't you know anything? Come 'round wakin' a feller up an' manhandling—"

"Get up!" snapped Stevenson angrily.

"Why, ain't I seen you before? Somewhere? Sometime?" queried Hopalong, his brow wrinkling from intense concentration of thought. "I ain't dreamin'; I've seen a one-eyed coyote som'ers lately, ain't I?" he appealed anxiously to the others.

"Get up!" ordered Charley shortly.

"An' I've seen you, too. Funny, all right."

"You've seen me, all right," retorted Stevenson. "Get up, damn you! Get up!"

"Why, I can't—my han's are tied!" exclaimed Hopalong in great wonder, pausing in his exertions to cogitate deeply upon this most remarkable phenomenon. "Tied up! Now what th' devil do you think—"

"Use yore feet, you thief!" rejoined Stevenson

roughly, stepping forward and delivering another kick. "Use yore feet!" he reiterated.

"Thief! Me a thief! Shore I'll use my feet, you yaller dog!" yelled the prostrate man, and his boot heel sank into the stomach of the offending Mr. Stevenson with sickening force and laudable precision. He drew it back slowly, as if debating shoving it farther. "Call me a thief, hey! Come pokin' 'round kickin' hones' punchers an' callin' 'em names! Anybody want th' other boot?" he inquired with grave solicitation.

Stevenson sat down forcibly and rocked to and fro, doubled up and gasping for breath, and Hopalong squinted at him and grinned with happiness. "Hear him sing! Reg'lar ol' brass band. Sounds like a cow pullin' its hoofs outen th' mud. Called me a thief, he did, jus' now. An' I won't let nobody kick me an' call me names; he's a liar, jus' a plain, squaw's dog liar, he—"

Two men grabbed him and raised him up, holding him tightly, and they were not over-careful to handle him gently, which he naturally resented. Charley stepped in front of him to go to the aid of Stevenson and caught the other boot in his groin, dropping as if he had been shot. The man on the prisoner's left emitted a yell and loosed his hold to sympathize with a bruised shinbone, and his companion promptly knocked the bound and still intoxicated man down. Bill Thomas swore and eyed the prostrate figure with

162

resentment and regret. "Hate to hit a man who can fight like that when he's loaded an' tied. I'm glad, all th' same, that he ain't sober an' loose."

"An' you ain't going to hit him no more!" snapped Jed White, reddening with anger. "I'm ready to hang him, 'cause that's what he deserves, an' what we're here for, but I'm damned if I'll stand for any more mauling. I don't blame him for fightin', an' they didn't have no right to kick him in th' beginning."

"Didn't kick him in th' beginning," grinned Bill. "Kicked him in th' ending. Anyhow," he continued seriously, "I didn't hit him hard—didn't have to. Just let him go an' shoved him quick."

"I'm just naturally goin' to clean house," muttered the prisoner, sitting up and glaring around. "Untie my han's an' gimme a gun or a club or anythin', an' watch yoreselves get licked. Called me a thief! What are you fellers, then?— stickin' me up an' 'busing me for a few measly dollars. Why didn't you take my money an' lemme sleep, 'stead of wakin' me up an' kickin' me? I wouldn't 'a' cared then."

"Come on, now, get up. We ain't through with you yet, not by a whole lot," growled Bill, helping him to his feet and steadying him. "I'm plumb glad you kicked 'em; it was comin' to 'em."

"No, you ain't; you can't fool me," gravely assured Hopalong. "Yo're lyin', an' you know it. What you goin' to do now? Ain't I got money enough? Wish I had an even break with you fellers! Wish my outfit was here!"

Stevenson, on his feet again, walked painfully up and shook his fist at the captive, from the side. "You'll find out what we want of you, you damned hoss thief!" he cried. "We're goin' to tie you to that there limb so yore feet'll swing above th' grass, that's what we're goin' to do."

Bill and Jed had their hands full for a moment and as they finally mastered the puncher, Charley came up with a rope. "Hurry up—no use draggin' it out this way. I want to get back to th' ranch some time before next week."

"W'y, *I* ain't no hoss thief, you liar!" Hopalong yelled. "My name's Hopalong Cassidy of th' Bar-20, an' w'en I tell my friends about what you've gone an' done they'll make you hard to find! You gimme any kind of a chance an' I'll do it all by myself, sick as I am, you yaller dogs!"

"Is that yore cayuse?" demanded Charley, pointing.

Hopalong squinted towards the animal indicated. "W'ich one?"

"There's only one there, you fool!"

"Tha' so?" replied Hopalong, surprised. "Well, I never seen it afore. My cayuse is—is—where th' devil *is* it?" he asked, looking around anxiously.

"How'd you get that one, then, if it ain't yours?"

"Never had it—'tain't mine, nohow," replied

Hopalong with strong conviction. "Mine was a *hoss*."

"You stole that cayuse las' night outen Stevenson's corral," continued Charley, merely as a matter of form. Charley believed that a man had the right to be heard before he died—it wouldn't change the result and so could not do any harm.

"Did I? W'y—" his forehead became furrowed again, but the events of the night before were vague in his memory and he only stumbled in his soliloquy. "But *I* wouldn't swap my cayuse for that spavined, saddle-galled, ring-boned bone-yard! Why, it interferes, an' it's got th' heaves somethin' awful!" he finished triumphantly, as if an appeal to common sense would clinch things. But he made no headway against them, for the rope went around his neck almost before he had finished talking and a flurry of excitement ensued. When the dust settled he was on his back again and the rope was being tossed over the limb.

The crowd had been too busily occupied to notice anything away from the scene of their strife and were greatly surprised when they heard a hail and saw a stranger sliding to a stand not 20 feet from them. "What's this?" demanded the newcomer angrily.

Charley's gun glinted as it swung up and the stranger swore again. "What you doin'?" he shouted. "Take that gun off'n me or I'll blow you apart!"

"Mind yore business an' sit still!" Charley snapped. "You ain't in no position to blow anything apart. We've got a hoss thief an' we're shore goin' to hang him regardless."

"An' if there's any trouble about it we can hang two as well as we can one," suggested Stevenson placidly. "You sit tight an' mind yore own affairs, stranger," he warned.

Hopalong turned his head slowly. "He's a liar, stranger—just a plain, squaw's dog of a liar. An' I'll be much obliged if you'll lick hell out'n 'em an' let—*why, hullo, hoss thief!*" he shouted, at once recognizing the other. It was the man he had met in the gospel tent, the man he had chased for a horse thief and then swapped mounts with. "Stole any more cayuses?" he asked, grinning, believing that everything was all right now. "Did you take that cayuse back to Grant's?" he finished.

"Han's up!" roared Stevenson, also covering the stranger. "So yo're another one of 'em, hey? We're in luck today. Watch him, boys, till I get his gun. If he moves, drop him quick."

"You damned fool!" cried Ferris, white with rage. "He ain't no thief, an' neither am I! My name's Ben Ferris an' I live in Winchester. Why, that man you've got is Hopalong Cassidy—Cassidy, of th' Bar-20!"

"Sit still—you can talk later, mebby," replied Stevenson, warily approaching him. "Watch him, boys!"

"Hold on!" shouted Ferris, murder in his eyes. "Don't you try that on me! I'll get one of you before I go; I'll shore get one! You can listen a minute, an' I can't get away."

"All right, talk quick."

Ferris pleaded as hard as he knew how and called attention to the condition of the prisoner. "If he did take th' wrong cayuse he was too blind drunk to know it! Can't you *see* he was?" he cried.

"Yep—through yet?" asked Stevenson quietly.

"No! I ain't started yet!" Ferris yelled. "He did me a good turn once, one that I can't never repay, an' I'm going to stop this murder or go with him. If I go I'll take one of you with me, an' my friends an' outfit'll get th' rest."

"Wait till Old John gets here," suggested Jed to Charley. "He ought to know this feller."

"For th' Lord's sake!" snorted Charley. "He won't show up for a week. Did you hear that, fellers?" he laughed, turning to the others.

"Stranger," began Stevenson, moving slowly ahead again. "You give us yore guns an' sit quiet till we gets this feller out of th' way. We'll wait till Old John Ferris comes before doing anything with you. He ought to know you."

"He knows me all right, an' he'd like to see me hung," replied the stranger. "I won't give up my guns, an' you won't lynch Hopalong Cassidy while I can pull a trigger. That's flat!" He began to talk feverishly to gain time and his eyes lighted suddenly. Seeing that Jed White was wavering, Stevenson ordered them to go on with the work they had come to perform, and he watched Ferris as a cat watches a mouse, knowing that he would be the first man hit if the stranger got a chance to shoot. But Ferris stood up very slowly in his stirrups so as not to alarm the five with any quick movement, and shouted at the top of his voice, grabbing off his sombrero and waving it frantically. A faint cheer reached his ears and made the lynchers turn quickly and look behind them. Nine men were tearing towards them at a dead gallop and had already begun to forsake their bunched-up formation in favor of an extended line. They were due to arrive in a very few minutes and caused Mr. Ferris's heart to overflow with joy.

"Me an' my outfit," he said, laughing softly and waving his hand toward the newcomers, "started out this morning to round up a bunch of cows, an' we got jackasses instead. Now lynch him, damn you!"

The nine swept up in skirmish order, guns out and ready for anything in the nature of trouble that might zephyr up. "What's th' matter, Ben?" asked Tom Murphy ominously. As underforeman of the ranch he regarded himself as spokesman. And at that instant catching sight of the rope, he swore savagely under his breath.

"Nothing, Tom, nothing now," responded Mr.

Ferris. "They was going to hang my friend there, Mr. Hopalong Cassidy, of th' Bar-20. He's th' feller that lent me his cayuse to get home on when Molly was sick. I'm going to take him back to th' ranch when he gets sober an' introduce him to some very good friends of his'n that he ain't never seen. Ain't I, Cassidy?" he demanded with a laugh.

But Mr. Cassidy made no reply. He was sound asleep, as he had been since the advent of his very good and capable friend, Mr. Ben Ferris, of Winchester.

CHAPTER THIRTEEN

MR. TOWNSEND, MARSHAL

MR. CASSIDY went to the ranch and lived like a lord until shame drove him away. He had no business to live on cake and pie and wonderful dishes that Mrs. Ferris and her sister literally forced on him, and let Buck's mission wait on his convenience. So he tore himself away and made up for lost time as he continued his journey on his own horse, for which Tom Murphy and three men had faced down the scowling population of Hoyt's Corners. The rest of his journey was without incident until, on his return home along another route, he rode into Rawhide and heard about the marshal, Mr. Townsend.

This individual was unanimously regarded as an affliction upon society and there had been objections to his continued existence, which had been overruled by the object himself. Then word had gone forth that a substantial reward and the undying gratitude of a considerable number of people awaited the man who would rid the community of the pest who seemed to be ubiquitous. Several had come in response to the call, one had returned in a wagon, and the others were now looked upon as martyrs and as examples of asinine foolhardiness. Then it had been decided to elect a marshal, or perhaps two or three, to preserve the peace of the town; but this was a flat failure. In the first place, Mr. Townsend had dispersed the meeting with no date set for a new one; in the second, no man wanted the office; and as a finish to the comedy, Mr. Townsend cheerfully announced that hereafter and henceforth he was the marshal, self-appointed and self-sustained. Those who did not like it could easily move to other localities.

With this touch of officeholding came ambition, and of stern stuff. The marshal asked himself why he could not be more officers than one and found no reason. Thereupon he announced that he was marshal, town council, mayor, justice, and poundkeeper. He did not go to the trouble of incorporating himself as the Town of Rawhide, because he knew nothing of such immaterial things; but he was the town, and that sufficed.

He had been grievously troubled about finances in the past, and he firmly believed that genius such as his should be above such petty annoyances as being broke. That was why he constituted himself the keeper of the public pound, which contented him for a short time, but later, feeling that he needed more money than the pound was giving him, he decided that the spirit of the times demanded public improvements, and therefore, as the executive head of the town, he levied taxes and improved the town by improving his wardrobe and the manner of his living. Each saloon must pay into the town treasury the sum of $100 per year, which entitled it to police protection and assured it that no new competitors would be allowed to do business in Rawhide.

Needless to say he was not furiously popular, and the crowds congregated where he was not. His tyranny was based upon his uncanny faculty of anticipating the other man's draw. The citizens were not unaccustomed to seeing swift death result to the slower man from misplaced confidence in his speed of hand—that was in the game—an even break, but to oppose an individual who *always* knew what you were going to do before you knew it yourself—this was very discouraging. Therefore, he flourished and waxed fat.

Of late, however, he had been very low in finances and could expect no taxes to be paid for three months. Even the pound had yielded him nothing for over a week, the old patrons of Rawhide's stores and saloons preferring to ride 20 miles farther in another direction than to redeem impounded horses. Perhaps his prices had been too high, he thought, so he assembled the town council, the mayor, the marshal, and the keeper of the public pound to consult upon the matter. He decided that the prices were too high and at once posted a new notice announcing the cut. It was hard to fall from a dollar to two bits, but the treasury was low—the times were panicky.

As soon as he had changed the notice he strolled up to the Paradise to inform the bartender that impounding fines had been cut to bargain prices and to ask him to make the fact generally known through his patrons. As he came within sight of the building he jumped with pleasure, for a horse was standing dejectedly before the door. Joy of joys, trade was picking up—a stranger had come to town! Hastening back to the corral, he added a cipher to the posted figure, added a decimal point, and changed the cents sign to that of a dollar. Two dollars and fifty cents was now the price prescribed by law. Returning hastily to the Paradise, he led the animal away, impounded it, and then sat down in front of the corral gate with his Winchester across his knees. Two dollars and fifty cents! Prosperity had indeed returned!

"Where th' CG ranch is I dunno, but I do know where one of their cayuses is," he mused, glancing between two of the corral posts at the sleepy animal. "If I has to auction it off to pay for its keep and th' fine, th' saddle will bring a good, round sum. I allus knowed that a dollar wasn't enough, nohow."

Nat Fisher, punching cows for the CG and tired of his job, leaned comfortably back in his chair in the Paradise and swapped lies with the all-wise bartender. After a while he realized that he was hopelessly outclassed at this diversion and he dug down into his pocket and brought to light some loose silver and regarded it thoughtfully. It was all the money he had and was beginning to grow interesting.

"Say, was you ever broke?" he asked suddenly, a trace of sadness in his voice.

The bartender glanced at him quickly, but remained judiciously silent, smelling the preamble of a touch.

"Well, I have been, am now, an' allus will be, more or less," continued Fisher in soliloquy, not waiting for an answer to his question. "Money an' me don't ride th' same range, not any. Here I am fifty miles away from my ranch, with four dollars and ninety-five cents between me an' starvation an' thirst, an' me not going home for three days yet. I was going to quit th' CG this month, but now I gotta go on workin' for it till another pay-day. I don't even own a cayuse. Now, just to show you what kind of a prickly pear I am, I'll cut th' cards with you to see who owns this," he suggested, smiling brightly at his companion.

The bartender laughed, treated on the house, and shuffled out from behind the bar with a pack of greasy playing-cards. "All at once, or a dollar a shot?" he asked, shuffling deftly.

"Any way it suits you," responded Fisher nonchalantly. He knew how a sport should talk;

once he had cut the cards to see who should own his full month's pay. He hoped he would be more successful this time.

"Don't make no difference to me," rejoined the bartender.

"All right, all at once, an' have it over with. It's a kid's game, at that."

"High wins, of course?"

"High wins."

The bartender pushed the cards across the table for his companion to cut. Nat did so, and turned up a deuce. "Oh, don't bother," he said, sliding the four dollars and ninety-five cents across the table.

"Wait," grinned the bartender, who was a stickler for rules. He reached over and turned up a card, and then laughed. "Matched, by George!"

"Try again," grinned Fisher, his face clearing with hope.

The bartender shuffled, and Fisher turned a five, which proved to be just one point shy when his companion had shown his card.

"Now," remarked Fisher, watching his money disappear into the bartender's pocket, "I'll put up my gun agin ten of yore dollars if yo're game. How about it?"

"Done—that's a good weapon."

"None better. Ah, a jack!"

"I say queen—nope, *king!*" exulted the dispenser of liquids. "Say, mebby you can get a job around here when you quit th' CG," he suggested.

"That's a good idea," replied Fisher. "But let's finish this while we're at it. I got a good saddle outside on my cayuse—go look it over an' tell me how much you'll put up agin it. If you win it an' can't use it, you can sell it. It's first-class."

The bartender walked to the door, looked carefully around for a moment, his eyes fastening upon a trail in the sandy street. Then he laughed. "There ain't no saddle out here," he reported, well knowing where it could be found.

"What! Has that ornery piebald—well, what do you think of that!" exclaimed Fisher, looking up and down the street. "This is th' first time that ever happened to me. Why, some coyote stole it! Look at th'e tracks!"

"No, it ain't stolen," the bartender responded. He considered a moment and then made a suggestion. "Mebby th' marshal can tell you where it is—he knows everything like that. Nobody can take a cayuse out of this town while th' marshal is up an' well."

"Lucky town, all right," chirped Fisher. "An' where is th' marshal?"

"You'll find him down th' back way a couple of hundred yards—can't miss him. He allus hangs out there when there are cayuses in town."

"Good for him! I'll chase right down an' see him; an' when I get that piebald—!"

The bartender watched him go around the corner and shook his head sadly. "Yes, hell of a lucky town," he snorted bitterly, listening for the riot to begin.

The marshal still sat against the corral gate and stroked the Winchester in beatific contemplation. He had a fine job and he was happy. Suddenly leaning forward to look up the road, he smiled derisively and shifted the gun. A cowpuncher was coming his way rapidly, and on foot.

"Are you th' marshal of this flea of a town?" politely inquired the newcomer.

"I am th' same," replied the man with the rifle. "Anything I kin do for you?"

"Yes; have you seen a piebald cayuse straying around loose-like, or anybody leadin' one—CG being th' brand?"

"I did; it was straying."

"An' which way did it go?"

"Into th' town pound."

"What! Pond! What'n blazes is it doin' with a pond? Couldn't it drink without getting in? Where's th' pond?"

"Right here. It's eating its fool head off. I said pound, not pond. P-o-u-n-d—which means that it's pawned, in hock, for destroyin' th' vegetation of Rawhide an' disturbin' th' public peace."

"Good joke on th' piebald, all right; it was never locked up before," laughed Fisher, trying to read a sign that faced away from him at a slight angle. "Get it out for me an' I'll disturb *its* peace. Sorry it put you to all that trouble," he sympathized.

"Two dollars an' four bits, an' a dollar initiation fee—it wasn't never in th' pound before. That makes three an' a half. Got th' money with you?"

"What!" yelled Fisher, emerging from his trance. "What!" he yelled again.

"I ain't none deaf," placidly replied the marshal. "Got th' money, th' three an' a half?"

"If you think yo're going to skin me outen three-fifty, one-fifty, or one measly cent, you need some medicine, an' I'll give it to you in pill form! You'd make a bum-lookin' angel, so get up an' hand over that cayuse, *an' do it damned quick!*"

"Three-fifty, an' two bits extry for feed. It'll cost you 'bout a dollar a day for feed. At th' end of the week I'll sell that cayuse at auction to pay its bills if you don't cough up. Got th' money?"

"I've got a lead slug for you if I can borrow my gun for five minutes!" retorted Fisher, seeing double from anger.

"Five dollars more for contempt of court," pleasantly responded Mr. Townsend. "As Justice of th' Peace of this community I must allow no disrespect, no contempt of th' sovereign law of this town to go unpunished. That makes it eight-seventy-five."

"An' to think I lost my gun!" shouted Fisher, dancing with rage. "I'll get that cayuse out an' I won't pay a cent, not a damned cent! An' I'll get you at th' same time!"

"Now you dust around for fifteen dollars even

179

an' stop yore contempt of court an' threats or I'll drill you just for luck!" rejoined Mr. Townsend angrily. "If you keep on workin' yore mouth like that there won't be nothin' comin' to you when I sell that cayuse of yourn. Turn around an' strike out or I'll put you with yore ancestors!"

CHAPTER FOURTEEN

THE STRANGER'S PLAN

FISHER, wild with rage, returned to the Paradise and profanely unfolded the tale of his burning wrongs to the bartender and demanded the loan of his gun, which the bartender promptly refused. The present owner of the gun liked Fisher very much for being such a sport and sympathized with him deeply, but he did not want to have such a pleasing acquaintance killed.

"Now, see here, you cool down an' I'll lend you fifteen dollars on that saddle of yourn. You go up an' get that cayuse out before th' price goes up any higher—you don't know that man like I do," remarked the man behind the bar earnestly. "That feller Townsend can shoot th' eyes out of a small dog at ten miles, purty nigh. Do you savvy my drift?"

"I won't pay him a cussed cent, an' when he goes to sell that piebald at auction, I'll be on hand with a gun—I'll get one somewhere, all right, even if I have to steal it. Then I'll shoot out *his* eyes at ten paces. Why, he's a two-legged holdup! That man would—" he stopped as a stranger entered the room. "Hey, stranger! Don't you leave that cayuse of yourn outside all alone or that coyote of a marshal will steal it, shore. He's th' biggest thief I ever knowed. He'll lift yore animal quick as a wink!" Fisher warned excitedly.

The stranger looked at him in surprise and then smiled. "Is it usual for a marshal to steal cayuses? Somewhat out of line, ain't it?" he asked Fisher, glancing at the bartender for light.

"I don't care what's th' rule—that marshal just stole my cayuse, an' he'll take yourn, too, if you ain't careful," Fisher replied.

"Well," drawled the stranger, smiling still more, "I reckon I ain't goin' to stay out there an' watch it, an' I can't bring it in here. But I reckon it'll be all right. You see, I carry 'big medicine' agin hoss thieves," he replied, tapping his holster and smiling as he remembered the time, not long past, when he himself had been accused of being one. "I'll take a chance if he will—what'll you all have?"

"Little whisky," replied Fisher uneasily, worrying because he could not stand for a return treat. "But, say, you keep yore eye on that animal, just th' same," he added, and then hurriedly gave his reasons. "An' th' worst part of th' whole thing is that I ain't got no gun, an' can't seem to borrow none, either," he added, wistfully eying the stranger's Colt. "I gambled mine away to th' bartender here, an' he won't lemme borrow it for five minutes!"

"Why, I never heard tell of such a thing before!" exclaimed the stranger, hardly believing his ears, and aghast at the thought that such conditions could exist. "Friend," he said, addressing the bartender, "how is it that this sort of thing can go on in this town?" When the bartender had explained at some length, his interested listener smote the bar with a heavy fist and voiced his outraged feelings. "I'll shore be plumb happy to spread that coyote marshal all over his cussed pound! Say, come with me; I'm going down there right now an' get that cayuse, an' if th' marshal opens his mouth to peep I'll get him, too. I'm itching for a chance to tunnel a man like him. Come on an' see th' show!"

"Not much!" retorted Fisher. "While I am some pleased to meet a white man, an' have a deep an' abiding gratitude for yore noble offer, I can't let you do it. He put it over on me, an' I'm th' one that's got to shoot him up. He's mine, my pudding, an' I'm hogging him all to myself. That is one luxury I can indulge in even if I am broke, an' I'm sorry, but I can't give you cards. Seein', however, as you are so friendly to th' cause of liberty an' justice, suppose you lend me yore gun for about three minutes by th' watch. From what I've been told about this town such an act will win for you th' eternal love an' gratitude of a down-trodden people; yore gun will blaze th' way to liberty an' light, freedom an' th' right to own yore own property, an' keep it. All I ask is that I be th' undeservin' medium."

"A-men," sighed the bartender. "Deacon Jones will now pass down th' aisle an' collect th' buttons an' tin money."

"Stranger," continued Fisher, warming up, when he saw that his words had not produced the desired result, "King James th' Twelfth, on th' memorable an' blood-soaked field of Trafalgar, gave men their rights. On that great day he signed th' Magnet Charter, and proved himself as great a liberator as th' sainted Lincoln. You, on this most auspicious occasion, hold in yore strong right hand th' destiny of this town—th' women an' children in this cursed community will rise up an' bless you forever an' pass yore name down to their ancestors as a man of deeds an' honor! Let us pause to consider this—"

"Hold that pause!" interrupted the astounded bartender hurriedly and with shaking voice. "String it out till I get untangled! I ain't up much on history, so I won't take no chance with that, but I want to tell our eloquent guest that there ain't no women *or* children in this town. An' if there was, I sort of reckon their ancestors would be born first. What do you think about it—"

"Let us pause to consider th' shameful an' burnin' in*dig*nity perpetrated upon us today!" continued Fisher, unheeding the bartender's words. "I, a peaceful, law-abidin' *cit*izen of this *glor*ious Commonwealth, a free an' *e*qual member of a liberty-lovin' nation, a nation whose standard

184

is, *now* and forever, 'Gimme liberty or gimme det', a *nat*ion that stands for all th' conceivable benefits that mankind may enjoy, a *nat*ion that scintillates pyrotechnically over the prostitution of power—"

Bang! went the bartender's fist on the counter. "Hey! Pause again! Wait a minute! Go back to 'shameful an' burnin',' and gimme a chance!"

"—that stands for an even break, I, Nathaniel G. Fisher, have been deprived of one of my inalienable rights, th' right of locomotion to distant an' other parts. *An'* I say, right here an' now, that I won't allow no spavined individual with thieving prehensils to—"

"Has that poundkeeper got a rifle?" calmly interrupted the stranger, without a pang of remorse.

"He has. Thus has it allus been with tyrants—well armed, fortified by habit an' tradition—"

"Then you won't get my gun, savvy? We'll find another way to get that cayuse as long as you feel that th' marshal is yore hunting. Besides, this man's gall deserves some respect; it is genius, an' to pump genius full of cold lead is to act rash. Now, suppose you tell me when this auction is due to come off."

"Oh, not for a week; he wants to run up th' board-an'-keep expenses. Tyrants, such as him—"

"Shore," interposed the bartender, "he'll make th' expenses equal what he gets for th' cayuse, no matter what it comes to. An' he's th' whole town, an' th' justice of th' peace, besides. What he says goes."

"Well, I'm th' Governor of th' State an' I've got th' Supreme Court right here in my holster, so I reckon I can reverse his official acts an' fill his legal opinions full of holes," the stranger replied, laughing heartily. "Bartender, will you help me play a little joke on His Honor, th' Town—just a little harmless joke?"

"Well, that all depends whether th' joke is harmless on *me*. You see, he can shoot like th'devil—he allus knows when a man is going to draw, an' gets his gun out first. I ain't got no respect for him, but I take off my hat to his gunplay, all right."

The stranger smiled. "Well, I can shoot a bit myself. But I shore wish he'd hold that auction quick—I've got to go on home without losing any more time. Fisher, suppose you go down to th' pound and dare that tumble-bug to hold th' auction this afternoon. Tell him that you'll shoot him full of holes if he goes pulling off any auction today, an' dare him to try it. I want it to come off before night, an' I reckon that'll hustle it along."

"I'll do anything to get th' edge on that thief," replied Fisher quickly, "but don't you reckon I'd better tote a gun, goin' down an' beardin' such a thief in his own den? You know I allus like to shoot when I'm bein' shot at."

"Well, I don't blame you, it's only a petty weakness," grinned the stranger, hanging onto his Colt as if fearing that the other would snatch it and run. "But you'll do better without any gun—me an' th' bartender don't want to have to go down there an' bring you back on a plank."

"All right, then," sighed Fisher reluctantly, "but he'll jump th' price again. He'll fine me for contempt of court an' make me pay money I ain't got for disturbin' him. But I'm game—so long."

When he had gained the street, the stranger turned to the bartender. "Now, friend, you tell me if this man of gall, this Mr. Townsend, has got many friends in town—anybody that'll be likely to pot-shoot from th' back when things get warm. I can't watch both ends unless I know what I'm up against."

"*No!* Every man in town hates him," answered the bartender hastily and with emphasis.

"Ah, that's good. Now, I wonder if you could see 'most everybody that's in town now an' get 'em to promise to help me by lettin' me run this all by myself. All I want them to do is not to say a word. It ain't hard to keep still when you want to."

"Why, I reckon I might see 'em—there ain't many here this time of day," responded the bartender. "But what's yore game, anyhow?" he asked, suddenly growing suspicious.

"It's just a little scheme I figgered out," the stranger replied, and then he confided in the bartender, who jigged a few fancy steps to show his appreciation of the other's genius. His suspicions left him at once, and he hastened out to tell the inhabitants of the town to follow his instructions to the letter, and he knew they would obey and be glad, hilariously glad, to do so. While he was hurrying around giving his instructions, the CG puncher returned to the hotel and reported.

"Well, it worked, all right," Fisher growled. "I told him what I'd do to him if he tried to auction that cayuse off an' he retorted that if I didn't shut up an' mind my own business, that he'd sell th' horse this noon, at twelve o'clock, in th' public square, wherever that is. I told him he was a coyote and dared him to do it. Told him I'd pump him full of air ducts if he didn't wait till next week. Said I had th' promise of a gun an' that it'd give me great pleasure to use it on him if he tried any auctioneering at my expense this noon. Then he fined me five dollars more, swore that he'd show me what it meant to dare the marshal of Rawhide an' insult th' dignity of th' court an' town council, an' also that he'd shoot my liver all through my system if I didn't leave him to his reflections. Now look here, stranger, noon is only two hours away an' I'm due to lose my outfit: what are *you* going to do to get me out of this mess?" he finished anxiously, hands on hips.

"You did real well, very fine, indeed," replied the stranger, smiling with content. "An' don't you worry about that outfit—I'm going to get it back for you an' a little bit more. So, as long as you don't lose nothin', you ain't got no kick coming, have you? An' you ain't got no interest in what I'm going to do. Just sit tight an' keep yore eyes an' ears open at noon. Meantime, if you want something to do to keep you busy, practice makin' speeches—you ought to be ashamed to be punchin' cows an' workin' for a living when you could use yore talents an' get a lot of graft besides. Any man who can say as much on nothing as you can ought to be in th' Senate representing some railroad company or waterpower steal—you don't have to work there, just loaf an' take easy money for cheating th' people what put you there. Now, don't get mad—I'm only stringing you: I wouldn't be mean enough to call you a senator. To tell th' truth, I think yo're too honest to even think of such a thing. But go ahead an' practice—*I* don't mind it a bit."

"Huh! I couldn't go to Congress," laughed Fisher. "I'd have to practice by gettin' elected mayor of some town an' then go to th' Legislature for th' finishing touches."

"Mr. Townsend would beat you out," murmured the stranger, looking out of the window and wishing for noon. He sauntered over to a chair, placed it where he could see his horse, and took things easy. The bartender returned with several men at his heels, and all were grinning and joking.

They took up their places against the bar and indulged in frequent fits of chuckling, not letting their eyes stray from the man in the chair and the open street through the door, where the auction was to be held. They regarded the stranger in the light of a would-be public benefactor, a martyr, who was to provide the town with a little excitement before he followed his predecessors into the grave. Perhaps he would *not* be killed, perhaps he would shoot the poundkeeper and general public nuisance—but ah, this was the stuff of which dreams were made: the marshal would never be killed, he would thrive and outlive his fellow townsmen, and die in bed at a ripe old age.

One of the citizens, dangling his legs from the card table, again looked closely at the man with the plan, and then turned to a companion beside him. "I've seen that there feller som'ers, sometime," he whispered. "I *know* I have. But I'll be teetotally dod-blasted if I can place him."

"Well, Jim, I never saw him afore, an' I don't know who he is," replied the other, refilling his pipe with elaborate care, "but if he can kill Townsend today, I'll be so plumb joyous I won't know what to do with m'self."

"I'm afraid he won't, though," remarked another, lolling back against the bar. "Th' marshal was born to hang—nobody can beat him on th' draw. But, anyhow, we're going to see some fun."

The first speaker, still straining his memory for

a clue to the stranger's identity, pulled out a handful of silver and placed it on the table. "I'll bet that he makes good," he offered, but there were no takers.

The stranger now lazily arose and stepped into the doorway, leaning against the jamb and shaking his holster sharply to loosen the gun for action. He glanced quickly behind him and spoke curtly: "Remember, now—*I* am to do all th' talking at this auction; you fellers just look on."

A mumble of assent replied to him, and the townsmen craned their necks to look out. A procession slowly wended its way up the street, led by the marshal, astride a piebald horse bearing the crude brand of the CG. Three men followed him and numerous dogs of several colors, sizes, and ages roamed at will, in a listless, bored way, between the horse and the men. The dust arose sluggishly and slowly dissipated in the hot, shimmering air, and a fly buzzed with wearying persistence against the dirty glass in the front window.

The marshal, peering out from under the pulled-down brim of his Stetson, looked critically at the sleepy horse standing near the open door of the Paradise and sought its brand, but in vain, for it was standing with the wrong side toward him. Then he glanced at the man in the door, a puzzled expression stealing over his face. He had known that man once, but time and events had wiped him nearly out of his memory and he could not place him. He decided that the other horse could wait until he had sold the one he was on, and, stopping before the door of the Paradise, he raised his left arm, his right arm lying close to his side, not far from the holster on his thigh.

"Gentlemen an' feller citizens," he began, "as marshal of this bloomin' city, I am about to offer for sale to th' highest bidder this A Number 1 piebald, pursooant to th' decree of th' local court an' with th' sanction of th' town council an' th' mayor. This same sale is for to pay th' town for th' board an' keep of this animal, an' to square th' fine in such cases made an' provided. It's sound in wind an' limb, fourteen han's high, an' in all ways a beauti-ful piece of hoss flesh. Now, gentlemen, how much am I bid for this cayuse? Remember, before you make me any offer, that this animal is broke to punching cows an' is a first-class cayuse."

The crowd in the Paradise had flocked out into the street and oozed along the front of the building, while the stranger now leaned carelessly against his own horse, critically looking over the one on sale. Fisher, uneasy and worried, squirmed close at hand and glanced covertly from his horse and saddle to the guns in the belts on the members of the crowd.

It was the stranger who broke the silence: "Two bits I bid—two bits," he said very quietly, whereat the crowd indulged in a faint snicker and a few nudges.

The marshal looked at him and then ignored him. "How much, gentlemen?" he asked, facing the crowd again.

"Two bits," repeated the stranger, as the crowd remained silent.

"Two bits!" yelled the marshal, glaring at him angrily. "*Two bits! Why, th' look* in this cayuse's eyes is worth four! Look at th' spirit in them eyes, look at th' intelligence! Th' saddle alone is worth a clean forty dollars of any man's money. I am out here to sell this animal to th' highest bidder th' sale's begun, an' I want bids, not jokes. Now, who'll start it off?" he demanded, glancing around, but no one had anything to say except the terse stranger, who appeared to be getting irritated.

"You've got a starter—I've given you a bid. I bid two bits—t-w-o b-i-t-s, twenty-five cents. Now go ahead with yore auction."

The marshal thought he saw an attempt at humor, and since he was feeling quite happy, and since he knew that good humor is conducive to good bidding, he smiled, all the time, however, racking his memory for the name of the humorist. So he accepted the bid: "All right, this gentleman bids two bits. Two bits I am bid—two bits. Twenty-five cents. Who'll make it twenty-five dollars? Two bits—who says twenty-five dollars?

Ah, did *you* say twenty-five dollars?" he snapped, leveling an accusing and threatening forefinger at the man nearest him, who squirmed restlessly and glanced at the stranger. *"Did you say twenty-five dollars?"* he shouted.

The stranger came to the rescue. "He did not. He hasn't opened his mouth. But *I* said twenty-five *cents*," quietly observed the humorist.

"Who'll gimme thirty? Who'll gimme thirty dollars? Did I hear thirty dollars? Did I hear twenty-five dollars bid? Who said thirty dollars? Did *you* say twenty-five dollars?"

"How could he when he was talkin' politics to th' man behind him?" asked the stranger. "I said two bits," he added complacently, as he watched the auctioneer closely.

"I want twenty-five dollars—an' you shut yore blasted mouth!" snapped the marshal at the persistent twenty-five-cent man. He did not see the fire smouldering in the squinting eyes so alertly watching him. "Twenty-five dollars—not a cent less takes the cayuse. Why, gentlemen, he's worth twenty in *cans!* Gimme twenty-five dollars, somebody. *I* bid twenty-five. I want thirty. I want thirty, gentlemen; you must gimme thirty. *I* bid twenty-five dollars—who's going to make it thirty?"

"Show us yore twenty-five an' she's yourn," remarked the stranger, with exasperating assurance, while Fisher grew pale with excitement.

The stranger was standing clear of his horse now, and alert readiness was stamped all over him. "You accepted my bid—show yore twenty-five dollars or take my two bits."

"You close that face of yourn!" exploded the marshal angrily. "I don't mind a little fun, but you've got altogether too damned much to say. You've queered th' biddin', an' now you shut up!"

"I said two bits an' I mean just that. You show yore twenty-five or gimme that cayuse on my bid," retorted the stranger.

"By th' pants of Julius Caesar!" shouted the marshal. "I'll put you to sleep so you'll never wake up if I hear any more about you an' yore two bits!"

"Show me, Rednose," snapped the other, his gun out in a flash. "I want that cayuse, an' I want it quick. You show me twenty-five dollars or I'll take it out from under you on my bid, you yaller dog! *Stop it!* Shut up! That's suicide, that is. Others have tried it an' failed, an' yo're no sleight-of-hand gunman. This is th' first time I ever paid a hoss thief in *silver,* or bought stolen goods, but everything has to have a beginnin'. You get nervous with that hand of yourn an' I'll cure you of it! Git off that piebald, an' quick!"

The marshal felt stunned and groped for a way out, but the gun under his nose was as steady as a rock. He sat there stupidly, not knowing enough to obey orders.

"Come, get off that cayuse," sharply commanded the stranger. "An' I'll take yore Winchester as a fine for this high-handed business you've been carryin' on. You may be th' local court an' all th' town officials, but I'm th' Governor, an' here's my Supreme Court, as I was saying to th' boys a little while ago. Yo're overruled. Get off that cayuse, an' don't waste no more time about it, neither!"

The marshal glared into the muzzle of the weapon and felt a sinking in the pit of his stomach. Never before had he failed to anticipate the pull of a gun. As the stranger said, there must always be a beginning, a first time. He was thinking quickly now; he was master of himself again, but he realized that he was in a tight place unless he obeyed the man with the drop. Not a man in town would help him; on the other hand, they were all against him, and hugely enjoying his discomfiture. With some men he could afford to take chances and jerk at his gun even when at such a disadvantage, but—

"Stranger," he said slowly, "what's yore name?"

The crowd listened eagerly.

"My *friends* call me Hopalong Cassidy—other people, other things—you gimme that cayuse an' that Winchester. Here! Hand th' gun to Fisher, so there won't be no lamentable accidents: I don't want to shoot you, 'less I have to."

"They're both yourn," sighed Mr. Townsend,

remembering a certain day over near Alameda, when he had seen Mr. Cassidy at gunplay. He dismounted slowly and sorrowfully. "Do I—do I get my two bits?" he asked.

"You shore do—yore gall is worth it," said Mr. Cassidy, turning the piebald over to its overjoyed owner, who was already arranging further gambling with his friend, the bartender.

Mr. Townsend pocketed the one bid, surveyed glumly the hilarious crowd flocking in to the bar to drink to their joy in his defeat, and wandered disconsolately back to the pound. He was never again seen in that locality, or by any of the citizens of Rawhide, for between dark and dawn he resumed his travels, bound for some locality far removed from limping, redheaded drawbacks.

CHAPTER FIFTEEN

JOHNNY LEARNS SOMETHING

FOR several weeks after Hopalong got back to the ranch, full of interesting stories and minus the grouch, things went on in a way placid enough for the most peacefully inclined individual that ever sat a saddle. And then trouble drifted down from the north and caused a look of anxiety to spoil Buck Peters's pleasant expression, and began to show on the faces of his men. When one finds the carcasses of two cows on the same day, and both are skinned, there can be only one conclusion. The killing and skinning of two cows out of herds that are numbered by thousands need not, in themselves, bring lines of worry to any foreman's brow; but there is the sting of being cheated, the possibility of the losses going higher unless a sharp lesson be given upon the folly of fooling with a very keen and active buzz saw—and it was the determination of the outfit of the Bar-20 to teach that lesson, and as quickly as circumstances would permit.

It was common knowledge that there was a more or less organized band of shiftless malcontents making its headquarters in and near Perry's Bend, some distance up the river, and the deduction in this case was easy. The Bar-20 cared very little about what went on at Perry's Bend—

that was a matter which concerned only the ranches near that town—as long as no vexatious happenings sifted too far south. But they had so sifted, and Perry's Bend, or rather the undesirable class hanging out there, was due to receive a shock before long.

About a week after the finding of the first skinned cows, Pete Wilson tornadoed up to the bunkhouse with a perforated arm. Pete was on foot, having lost his horse at the first exchange of shots, which accounts for the expression describing his arrival. Pete hated to walk, he hated still more to get shot, and most of all he hated to have to admit that his rifle shooting was so far below par. He had seen the thief at work and, too eager to work up close to the cattle skinner before announcing his displeasure, had missed the first shot. When he dragged himself out from under his deceased horse the scenery was undisturbed save for a small cloud of dust hovering over a distant rise to the north of him. After delivering a short and bitter monologue he struck out for the ranch and arrived in a very hot and wrathful condition. It was contagious, that condition, and before long the entire outfit was in the saddle and pounding north, Pete overjoyed because his wound was so slight as not to bar him from the chase. The shock was on the way, and as events proved, was to be one long to linger in the minds of the inhabitants of Perry's Bend and the surrounding range.

• • •

The patrons of the Oasis liked their tobacco strong. The pungent smoke drifted in sluggish clouds along the low, black ceiling, following its upward slant toward the east wall and away from the high bar at the other end. This bar, rough and strong, ran from the north wall to within a scant two feet of the south wall, the opening bridged by a hinged board which served as an extension to the counter. Behind the bar was a rear door, low and double, the upper part barred securely—the lower part was used most. In front of and near the bar was a large round table, at which four men played cards silently, while two smaller tables were located along the north wall. Besides dilapidated chairs there were half a dozen low wooden boxes partly filled with sand, and attention was directed to the existence and purpose of these by a roughly lettered sign on the wall, reading: *Gents will look for a box first,* which the "gents" sometimes did. The majority of the "gents" preferred to aim at various knotholes in the floor and bet on the result, chancing the outpouring of the proprietor's wrath if they missed.

On the wall behind the bar was a smaller and neater request: *Leave your guns with the bartender—Edwards.* This, although a month old, still called forth caustic and profane remarks from the regular frequenters of the saloon, for hitherto restraint in the matter of carrying weapons had been unknown. They forthwith evaded the order in a manner consistent with their characteristics—by carrying smaller guns where they could not be seen. The majority had simply sawed off a generous part of the long barrels of their Colts and Remingtons, which did not improve their accuracy.

Edwards, the new marshal of Perry's Bend, had come direct from Kansas and his reputation as a fighter had preceded him. When he took up his first day's work he was kept busy proving that he was the rightful owner of it and that it had not been exaggerated in any manner or degree. With the exception of one instance the proof had been bloodless, for he reasoned that gunplay should give way, whenever possible, to a crushing right or left to the point of the jaw or the pit of the stomach. His proficiency in the manly art was polished and thorough and bespoke earnest application. The last doubting Thomas to be convinced came to five minutes after his diaphragm had been rudely and suddenly raised several inches by a low right hook, and as he groped for his bearings and got his wind back again he asked, very feebly, where "Kansas" was, and the name stuck.

When Harlan heard the nickname for the first time he stopped pulling the cork out of a whisky bottle long enough to remark casually, "I allus reckoned Kansas was purty close to hell," and said no more about it. Harlan was the proprietor and bartender of the Oasis and catered to the excessive and uncritical thirsts of the ruck of range society, and he had objected vigorously to the placing of the second sign in his place of business, but at the close of an incisive if inelegant reply from the marshal the sign went up, and stayed up. Edwards's language and delivery were as convincing as his fists.

The marshal did not like the Oasis; indeed, he went further and cordially hated it. Harlan's saloon was a thorn in his side and he was only waiting for a good excuse to wipe it off the local map. He was the Law, and behind him were the range riders, who would be only too glad to have the nest of rustlers wiped out and its gang of ne'er-do-wells scattered to the four winds. Indeed, he had been given to understand in a most polite and diplomatic way that if this were not done lawfully they would try to do it themselves, and they had great faith in their ability to handle the situation in a thorough and workmanlike manner. This would not do in a law-abiding community, as he called the town, and so he had replied that the work was his and that it would be performed as soon as he believed himself justified to act. Harlan and his friends were fully conversant with the feeling against them and had become a little more cautious, alertly watching out for trouble.

On the evening of the day which saw Pete Wilson's discomfiture most of the *habitués* had assembled in the Oasis where, besides the card-players already mentioned, eight men lounged against the bar. There was some laughter, much subdued talking, and a little whispering. More whispering went on under that roof than in all the other places in town put together, for here rustling was planned, wayfaring strangers were "trimmed" in frame-ups at cards, and a hunted man was certain to find assistance. Harlan had once boasted that no fugitive had ever been taken from his saloon, and he was behind the bar and standing on the trap door which led to the six-by-six cellar when he made the assertion. It was true, for only those in his confidence knew of the place of refuge under the floor: it had been dug at night and the dirt carefully disposed of.

It had not been dark very long before talking ceased and cardplaying was suspended while all looked up as the front door crashed open and two punchers entered, looking the crowd over with critical care.

"Stay here, Johnny," Hopalong told his youthful companion, and then walked forward, scrutinizing each scowling face in turn, while Johnny stood with his back to the door, keenly alert, his right hand resting lightly on his belt not far from the holster.

Harlan's thick neck grew crimson and his eyes

hard. "Lookin' fer something?" he asked with bitter sarcasm, his hands under the bar. Johnny grinned hopefully and a sudden tenseness took possession of him as he watched for the first hostile move.

"Yes," Hopalong replied coolly, appraising Harlan's attitude and look in one swift glance, "but it ain't here, now. Johnny, get out," he ordered, backing after his companion, and safely outside, the two walked toward Jackson's store, Johnny complaining about the little time spent in the Oasis.

As they entered the store they saw Edwards, whose eye asked a question.

"No, he ain't in there yet," Hopalong replied.

"Did you look all over? Behind th' bar?" Edwards asked slowly. "He can't get out of town through that cordon you've got strung around it, an' he ain't nowhere else. Leastwise, I couldn't find him."

"Come on back!" excitedly exclaimed Johnny, turning toward the door. "You didn't look behind th' bar! Come on—bet you ten dollars that's where he is!"

"Mebby yo're right, Kid," replied Hopalong, and the marshal's nodding head decided it.

In the saloon there was strong language, and Jack Quinn, expert skinner of other men's cows, looked inquiringly at the proprietor. "What's up now, Harlan?"

The proprietor laughed harshly but said nothing—taciturnity was his one redeeming trait. "Did you say cigars?" he asked, pushing a box across the bar to an impatient customer. Another beckoned to him and he leaned over to hear the whispered request, a frown struggling to show itself on his face. "Nix; you know my rule. No trust in here."

But the man at the far end of the line was unlike the proprietor and he prefaced his remarks with a curse. "*I* know what's up! They want Jerry Brown, that's what! An' I hopes they don't get him, th' bullies!"

"What did he do? Why do they want him?" asked the man who had wanted trust.

"Skinning. He was careless or crazy, working so close to their ranch houses. Nobody that had any sense would take a chance like that," replied Boston, adept at sleight-of-hand with cards and very much in demand when a frame-up was to be rung in on some unsuspecting stranger. His one great fault in the eyes of his partners was that he hated to divvy his winnings and at times had to be coerced into sharing equally.

"Aw, them big ranches make me mad," announced the first speaker. "Ten years ago there was a lot of little ranchers, an' every one of 'em had his own herd, an' plenty of free grass an' water for it. Where are th' little herds now? Where are th' cows that *we* used to own?" he cried, hotly.

"What happens to a maverickb hunter nowadays? By God, if a man helps hisself to a pore, sick dogie he's hunted down! It can't go on much longer, an' that's shore."

Cries of approbation arose on all sides, for his auditors ignored the fact that their kind, by avarice and thievery, had forever killed the occupation of maverick hunting. That belonged to the old days, before the demand for cows and their easy and cheap transportation had boosted the prices and made them valuable.

Slivers Lowe leaped up from his chair. "Yo're right, Harper! Dead right! *I* was a little cattle owner onct, so was you, an' Jerry, an' most of us!" Slivers found it convenient to forget that fully half of his small herd had perished in the bitter and long winter of five years before, and that the remainder had either flowed down his parched throat or been lost across the big round table near the bar. Not a few of his cows were banked in the east under Harlan's name.

The rear door opened slightly and one of the loungers looked up and nodded. "It's all right, Jerry. But get a move on!"

"Here, *you!*" called Harlan, quickly bending over the trap door. *"Lively!"*

Jerry was halfway to the proprietor when the front door swung open and Hopalong, closely followed by the marshal, leaped into the room, and immediately thereafter the back door banged open and admitted Johnny. Jerry's right hand was in his side coat pocket and Johnny, young and self-confident, and with a lot to learn, was certain that he could beat the fugitive on the draw.

"I reckon you won't blot no more brands!" he cried triumphantly, watching both Jerry and Harlan.

The cardplayers had leaped to their feet and at a signal from Harlan they surged forward to the bar and formed a barrier between Johnny and his friend, and as they did so that puncher jerked at his gun, twisting to half face the crowd. At that instant fire and smoke spurted from Jerry's side coat pocket and the odor of burning cloth arose. As Johnny fell, the rustler ducked low and sprang for the door. A gun roared twice in the front of the room and Jerry staggered a little and cursed as he gained the opening, but he plunged into the darkness and threw himself into the saddle on the first horse he found in the small corral.

When the crowd massed, Hopalong leaped at it and strove to tear his way to the opening at the end of the bar, while the marshal covered Harlan and the others. Finding that he could not get through, Hopalong sprang on the shoulder of the nearest man and succeeded in winging the fugitive at the first shot, the other going wild. Then, frantic with rage and anxiety, he beat his way through the crowd, hammering mercilessly at heads with the butt of his Colt, and knelt at his friend's side.

Edwards, angered almost to the point of killing, ordered the crowd to stand against the wall, and laughed viciously when he saw two men senseless on the floor. "Hope he beat in yore heads!" he gritted savagely. "Harlan, put yore paws up in sight or I'll drill you clean! Now climb over an' get in line—quick!"

Johnny moaned and opened his eyes. "Did—did I—get him?"

"No, but he gimleted you, all right," Hopalong replied. "You'll come 'round if you keep quiet." He arose, his face hard with the desire to kill. "I'm coming back for *you,* Harlan, after I get yore friend! An' all th' rest of you pups, too!"

"Get me out of here," whispered Johnny.

"Shore enough, Kid, but keep quiet," replied Hopalong, picking him up in his arms and moving carefully toward the door. "We'll get him, Johnny, an' all th' rest, too, when—" The voice died out in the direction of Jackson's and the marshal, backing to the front door, slipped out and to one side, running backward, his eyes on the saloon.

"Yore day's about over, Harlan," he muttered. "There's going to be some few funerals around here before many hours pass."

When he reached the store he found the owner and two Double-Arrow punchers taking care of Johnny. "Where's Hopalong?" he asked.

"Gone to tell his foreman," replied Jackson.

"Hey, youngster, you let them bandages alone! Hear me?"

"Hullo, Kansas," remarked John Bartlett, foreman of the Double-Arrow. "I come nigh getting yore man; somebody rode past me like a streak in th' dark, so I just ups an' lets drive for luck, an' so did he. I heard him cuss an' I emptied my gun after him."

"Th' rest was a-passing th' word along to ride in when I left th' line," remarked one of the other punchers. "How you feeling now, Johnny?"

Chapter Sixteen

The End of the Trail

THE rain slanted down in sheets and the broken plain, thoroughly saturated, held the water in pools or sent it down the steep sides of the arroyo, to feed the turbulent flood which swept along the bottom, foam-flecked and covered with swiftly moving driftwood. Around a bend in the arroyo, where the angry water flung itself against the ragged bulwark of rock and flashed away in a gleaming line of foam, a horseman appeared, bending low in the saddle for better protection against the storm. He rode along the edge of the stream on the farther bank, opposite the steep bluff on the northern side, forcing his wounded and jaded horse to keep fetlock-deep in the water which swirled and sucked about its legs. He was trying his hardest to hide his trail. Lower down the hard, rocky ground extended to the water's edge, and if he could delay his pursuers for an hour or so, he felt that, even with his tired horse, he would have more than an even chance.

But they had gained more than he knew. Suddenly above him on the top of the steep bluff across the torrent a man loomed up against the clouds, peered intently into the arroyo, and then waved his sombrero to an unseen companion. A puff of smoke flashed from his shoulder and streaked away, the report of the shot lost in the gale. The fugitive's horse reared and plunged into the deep water and with its rider was swept rapidly toward the bend, the way they had come.

"That makes th' fourth time I've missed that coyote!" angrily exclaimed Hopalong as Red Connors joined him.

The other quickly raised his rifle and fired, and the horse, spilling its rider out of the saddle, floated away tail first. The fugitive, gripping his rifle, bobbed and whirled at the whim of the greedy water as shots struck near him. Making a desperate effort, he staggered up the bank and fell exhausted behind a boulder.

"Well, th' coyote is afoot, anyhow," said Red with great satisfaction.

"Yes, but how are we going to get to him?" asked Hopalong. "We can't get th' cayuses down here, an' we can't swim *that* water without them. An' if we could, he'd pot us easy."

"There's a way out of it somewhere," Red replied, disappearing over the edge of the bluff to gamble with Fate.

"Hey! Come back here, you chump!" cried Hopalong, running forward. "He'll get you, shore!"

"That's a chance I've got to take if I get him," was the reply.

A puff of smoke sailed from behind the boulder

on the other bank and Hopalong, kneeling for steadier aim, fired and then followed his friend. Red was downstream casting at a rock across the torrent but the wind toyed with the heavy, water-soaked *reata* as though it were a string. As Hopalong reached his side a piece of driftwood ducked under the water and an angry humming sound died away downstream. As the report reached their ears a jet of water spurted up into Red's face and he stepped back involuntarily.

"He's so shaky," Hopalong remarked, looking back at the wreath of smoke above the boulder. "I reckon I must have hit him harder than I thought in Harlan's. Gee! he's wild as blazes!" he ejaculated as a bullet hummed high above his head and struck sharply against the rock wall.

"Yes," Red replied, coiling the rope. "I was trying to rope that rock over there. If I could anchor to that, th' current would push us over quick. But it's too far with this wind blowing."

"We can't do nothing here 'cept get plugged. He'll be getting steadier as he rests from his fight with th' water," Hopalong remarked, and added quickly, "Say, remember that meadow back there a ways? We can make her from there, all right."

"Yo're right, that's what we've got to do. He's sending 'em nearer every shot—gee! I could 'most feel th' wind of that one. An' blamed if it ain't stopped raining. Come on."

They clambered up the slippery, muddy bank to

where they had left their horses, and cantered back over their trail. Minute after minute passed before the cautious skulker among the rocks across the stream could believe in his good fortune. When he at last decided that he was alone again he left his shelter and started away, with slowly weakening stride, over cleanly washed rock where he left no trail.

It was late in the afternoon before the two irate punchers appeared upon the scene, and their comments, as they hunted slowly over the hard ground, were numerous and bitter. Deciding that it was hopeless in that vicinity, they began casting in great circles on the chance of crossing the trail farther back from the river. But they had little faith in their success. As Red remarked, snorting like a horse in his disgust, "I'll bet four dollars an' a match he's swum down th' river clean to hell just to have th' laugh on us." Red had long since given it up as a bad job, though continuing to search, when a shout from the distant Hopalong sent him forward on a run.

"Hey, Red!" cried Hopalong, pointing ahead of them. "Look there! Ain't that a house?"

"Naw, course not! It's a—it's a ship!" Red snorted sarcastically. "What did you think it might be?"

"G'wan!" retorted his companion. "It's a mission."

"Ah, g'wan yoreself! What's a mission doing up here?" Red snapped.

"What do you think they do? What do they do

anywhere?" hotly rejoined Hopalong, thinking about Johnny. "There! See th' cross?"

"Shore enough!"

"An' there's tracks at last—mighty wobbly, but tracks just th' same. Them rocks couldn't go on forever. Red, I'll bet he's cashed in by this time."

"Cashed nothing! Them fellers don't."

"Well, if he's in that joint we might as well go back home. We won't get him, not nohow," declared Hopalong.

"Huh! You wait an' see!" replied Red pugnaciously.

"Reckon you never run up agin' a mission real hard," Hopalong responded, his memory harking back to the time he had disagreed with a convent, and they both meant about the same to him as far as winning out was concerned.

"Think I'm a fool kid?" snapped Red aggressively.

"Well, you ain't no *kid*."

"You let *me* do th' talking; *I'll* get him."

"All right; an' I'll do th' laughing," snickered Hopalong, at the door. "Sic 'em, Red!"

The other boldly stepped into a small vestibule, Hopalong close at his heels. Red hitched his holster and walked heavily into a room at his left. With the exception of a bench, a table, and a small altar, the room was devoid of furnishings, and the effect of these was lost in the dim light from the narrow windows. The peculiar, not unpleasant odor of burning incense and the dim light awakened a latent reverence and awe in Hopalong, and he sneaked off his sombrero, an inexplicable feeling of guilt stealing over him. There were three doors in the walls, deeply shrouded in the dusk of the room, and it was very hard to watch all three at once.

Red was peering into the dark corners, his hand on the butt of his Colt, and hardly knew what he was looking for. "This joint must 'a' looked plumb good to that coyote, all right. He had a hell of a lot of luck, but he won't keep it for long, damn him!" he remarked.

"Quit cussing!" tersely ordered Hopalong. "An' for God's sake, throw out that damned cigarette! Ain't you got no manners?"

Red listened intently and then grinned. "Hear that? They're playing dominoes in there—come on!"

"Aw, you chump! 'Dominee' means 'mother' in Latin, which is what they speak."

"How do you know?"

"Hanged if I can tell—I've heard it somewhere, that's all."

"Well, I don't care what it means. This is a frame-up so that coyote can get away. I'll bet they gave him a cayuse an' started him off while we've been losing time in here. I'm going inside an' ask some questions."

Before he could put his plan into execution, Hopalong nudged him and he turned to see his friend staring at one of the doors. There had been no sound, but he would swear that a monk stood gravely regarding them, and he rubbed his eyes. He stepped back suspiciously and then started forward again.

"Look here, stranger," he remarked, with quiet emphasis, "we're after that cow-lifter, an' we mean to get him. Savvy?"

The monk did not appear to hear him, so he tried another tack. "*Habla Española?*" he asked experimentally.

"You have ridden far?" replied the monk in perfect English.

"All th' way from th' Bend," Red replied, relieved. "We're after Jerry Brown. He tried to kill Johnny, an' near made good. An' I reckon we've treed him, judgin' from th' tracks."

"And if you capture him?"

"He won't have no more use for no side-pocket shooting."

"I see; you will kill him."

"Shore's it's wet outside."

"I'm afraid you are doomed to disappointment."

"Ya-as?" asked Red with a rising inflection.

"You will not want him now," replied the monk.

Red laughed sarcastically and Hopalong smiled.

"There ain't a-going to be no argument about it. Trot him out," ordered Red, grimly.

The monk turned to Hopalong. "Do you, too, want him?"

Hopalong nodded.

"My friends, he is safe from your punishment."

Red wheeled instantly and ran outside, returning in a few moments, smiling triumphantly. "There are tracks coming in, but there ain't none going away. He's here. If you don't lead us to him we'll shore have to rummage around an' poke him out for ourselves: which is it?"

"You are right—he is here, and he is not here."

"We're waiting," Red replied, grinning.

"When I tell you that you will not want him, do you still insist on seeing him?"

"We'll see him, an' we'll want him, too."

As the rain poured down again the sound of approaching horses was heard, and Hopalong ran to the door in time to see Buck Peters swing off his mount and step forward to enter the building. Hopalong stopped him and briefly outlined the situation, begging him to keep the men outside. The monk met his return with a grateful smile and, stepping forward, opened the chapel door, saying, "Follow me."

The unpretentious chapel was small and nearly dark, for the usual dimness was increased by the lowering clouds outside. The deep, narrow window openings, fitted with stained glass, ran almost to the rough-hewn rafters supporting the steep-pitched roof, upon which the heavy rain beat again with a sound like that of distant drums. Gusts of rain and the water from the roof beat against the south windows, while the wailing wind played its mournful cadences about the eaves, and the stanch timbers added their creaking notes to swell the dirgelike chorus.

At the farther end of the room two figures knelt and moved before the white altar, the soft light of flickering candles playing fitfully upon them and glinting from the altar ornaments, while before a rough coffin, which rested upon two pedestals, stood a third, whose rich, sonorous Latin filled the chapel with impressive sadness: "Give eternal rest to them, O Lord"—the words seeming to become a part of the room. The ineffably sad, haunting melody of the mass whispered back from the roof between the assaults of the enraged wind, while from the altar came the responses in a low, Gregorian chant, and through it all the clinking of the censer chains added intermittent notes. Aloft streamed the vapor of the incense, wavering with the air currents, now lost in the deep twilight of the sanctuary, and now faintly revealed by the glow of the candles, perfuming the air with its aromatic odor.

As the last deep-toned words died away the celebrant moved slowly around the coffin, swinging the censer over it and then, sprinkling the body and making the sign of the cross above its head, solemnly withdrew.

From the shadows along the side walls other figures silently emerged and grouped around the coffin. Raising it they turned it slowly around and carried it down the dim aisle in measured tread, moving silently as ghosts.

"He is with God, Who will punish according to his sins," said a low voice, and Hopalong started, for he had forgotten the presence of the guide. "God be with you, and may you die as he died—repentant and in peace."

Buck chafed impatiently before the chapel door leading to a small, well-kept graveyard, wondering what it was that kept quiet for so long a time his two most assertive men, when he had momentarily expected to hear more or less turmoil and confusion.

C-r-e-a-k! He glanced up, gun in hand and raised as the door swung slowly open. His hand dropped suddenly and he took a short step forward; six black-robed figures shouldering a long box stepped slowly past him, and his nostrils were assailed by the pungent odor of the incense. Behind them came his fighting punchers, humble, awed, reverent, their sombreros in their hands, and their heads bowed.

"What in blazes!" exclaimed Buck, wonder and surprise struggling for the mastery as the others cantered up.

"He's cashed," Red replied, putting on his sombrero and nodding toward the procession.

Buck turned like a flash and spoke sharply: "Skinny! Lanky! Follow that glory-outfit, an' see what's in that box!"

Billy Williams grinned at Red. "Yo're shore pious, Red."

"Shut up!" snapped Red, anger glinting in his eyes, and Billy subsided.

Lanky and Skinny soon returned from accompanying the procession.

"I had to look twice to be shore it was him. His face was plumb happy, like a baby. But he's gone, all right," Lanky reported.

"Deader'n hell," remarked Skinny, looking around curiously. "This here is some shack, ain't it?" he finished.

"All right—he knowed how he'd finish when he began. Now for that dear Mr. Harlan," Buck replied, vaulting into the saddle. He turned and looked at Hopalong, and his wonder grew. "Hey, *you!* Yes, *you!* Come out of that an' put on yore lid! Straddle leather—we can't stay here all night."

Hopalong started, looked at his sombrero, and silently obeyed. As they rode down the trail and around a corner he turned in his saddle and looked back, and then rode on, buried in thought.

Billy, grinning, turned and playfully punched him in the ribs. "Gettin' glory, Hoppy?"

Hopalong raised his head and looked him steadily in the eyes; and Billy, losing his curiosity and the grin at the same instant, looked ahead, whistling softly.

CHAPTER SEVENTEEN

EDWARDS'S ULTIMATUM

EDWARDS slid off the counter in Jackson's store and glowered at the pelting rain outside, perturbed and grouchy. The wounded man in the corner stirred and looked at him without interest and forthwith renewed his profane monologue, while the proprietor, finishing his task, leaned back against the shelves and swore softly. It was a lovely atmosphere.

"Seems to me they've been gone a long time," grumbled the wounded man. "Reckon he led 'em a long chase—had six hours' start, th' toad." He paused and then as an afterthought said with conviction, "But they'll get him—they allus do when they make up their minds to it."

Edwards nodded moodily and Jackson replied with a monosyllable.

"Wish I could 'a' gone with 'em," Johnny growled. "I like to square my own accounts. It's allus that way. I get plugged an' my friends clean th' slate. There was that time Bye-an'-Bye went an' ambushed me—ah, th' devil! But I tell you one thing: when I get well I'm going down to Harlan's an' clean house proper."

"Yo're in hard luck again: that'll be done as soon as yore friends get back," Jackson replied, carefully selecting a dried apricot from a box on the counter and glancing at the marshal to see how he took the remark.

"That'll be done before then," Edwards said crisply, with the air of a man who has just settled a doubt. "They won't be back much before to-morrow if he headed for the country I think he did. I'm going down to th' Oasis an' tell that gang to clear out of this town. They've been here too long now. I never had 'em dead to rights before, but I've got it on 'em this time. I'd 'a' sent 'em packing yesterday only I sort of hated to take a man's business away from him an' make him lose his belongings. But I've wrastled it all out an' they've got to go." He buttoned his coat about him and pulled his sombrero more firmly on his head, starting for the door. "I'll be back soon," he said over his shoulder as he grasped the handle.

"You better wait till you get help—there's too many down there for one man to watch an' handle," Jackson hastily remarked. "Here, I'll go with you," he offered, looking for his hat.

Edwards laughed shortly. "You stay here. I do my own work by myself when I can—that's what I'm here for, an' I can do this, all right. If I took any help they'd reckon I was scared," and the door slammed shut behind him.

"He's got sand aplenty," Jackson remarked. "He'd try to push back a stampede by main strength if he reckoned it was his duty. It's his good luck that he wasn't killed long ago—*I'd 'a'* *been.*"

"They're a bunch of cowards," replied Johnny. "As long as you ain't afraid of 'em, none of 'em wants to start anything. Bunch of sheep!" he snorted. "Didn't Jerry shoot me through his pocket?"

"Yes, an' yo're another lucky dog," Jackson responded, having in mind that at first Johnny had been thought to be desperately wounded. "Why, yore friends have got th' worst of this game; they're worse off than you are—out all day an' night in this cussed storm."

While they talked Edwards made his way through the cold downpour to Harlan's saloon, alone and unafraid, and greatly pleased by the order he would give. At last he had proof enough to work on, to satisfy his conscience, for the inevitable had come as the culmination of continued and clever defiance of law and order.

He deliberately approached the front door of the Oasis and, opening it, stepped inside, his hands resting on his guns—he had packed two Colts for the last 24 hours. His appearance caused a ripple of excitement to run around the room. After what had taken place, a visit from him could mean only one thing—trouble. And it was entirely possible that he had others within call to help him out if necessary.

Harlan knew that he would be the one held

225

responsible and he ceased wiping a glass and held the cloth suspended in one hand and the glass in the other. "Well?" he snapped angrily, his eyes smouldering with fixed hatred.

"Mebby you think it's well, but it's going to be a blamed sight better before sundown tomorrow night," evenly replied the marshal. "I just dropped in sort of free-like to tell you to pack up an' get out of town before dark—load yore wagon an' vamoose, an' take yore friends with you, too. If you don't—" he did not finish in words, for his tightening lips made them unnecessary.

"*What!*" yelled Harlan, red with anger. He placed his hands on the bar and leaned over it as if to give emphasis to his words. "*Me* pack up an' git! *Me* leave this shack! Who's going to pay me for it, hey? *Me* leave town! You drop out again an' go back to Kansas where you come from—they're easier back there!"

"Well, so far I ain't found nothing very craggy 'round here," retorted Edwards, closely watching the muttering crowd by the bar. "Takes more than a loud voice an' a pack of sneaking coyotes to send me looking for something easier. An' let me tell you this: *you* stay away from Kansas—they hangs people like you back there. That's whatever. You pack up an' git out of this town or I'll start a burying-plot with you on yore own land."

The low, angry buzz of Harlan's friends and their savage, scowling faces would have deterred a less determined man, but Edwards knew they were afraid of him and the men on whom he could call to back him up. And he knew that there must always be a start, there must be one man to show the way; and each of the men he faced was waiting for someone else to lead.

"You all slip over th' horizon before dark to-night, an' it's dark early these days," he continued. *"Don't get restless with yore hands!"* he snapped ominously at the crowd. "I means what I say—you shake th' mud from this town off yore boots before dark—before that Bar-20 outfit get back," he finished meaningly.

Questions, imprecations, and threats filled the room, and the crowd began to spread out slowly. His guns came out like a flash and he laughed with the elation that comes with impending battle. "Th' first man to start it'll drop," he said evenly. "Who's going to be th' martyr?"

"I *won't* leave town!" shouted Harlan. "I'll stay here if I'm killed for it!"

"I admire yore loyalty to principle, but you've got damned little sense," retorted the marshal. "You ain't no practical man. *Keep yore hands where they are!"* His vibrant voice turned the shifting crowd to stonelike rigidity and he backed slowly toward the door, the poor light gleaming dully from the polished blue steel of his Colts. Rugged, lionlike, charged to the fingertips with reckless courage and daredevil self-confidence, his personality overflowed and dominated the room, almost hypnotic in its effect. He was but one against many, but he was the master, and they knew it; they had known it long enough to accept it without question, and the training now stood him in good stead.

For a moment he stood in the open doorway, keenly scrutinizing them for signs of danger, his unwavering guns charged with certain death and his strong face made stronger by the shadows in its hollows. "Before dark!"—and he was gone. He left behind him deep silence, which endured for several moments.

"By th' Lord, I *won't!*" cried Harlan, still staring at the door.

The spell was broken and a babel of voices filled the room, threats mingling with excuses, hot, vibrant, profane. These men were not cowards all the way through, but only when face to face with the master. They had flourished in a way by their wits alone on the same range with the outfits of the C-80 and the Double-Arrow, for individually they were "bad," and collectively they made a force of no mean strength. Edwards had landed among them like a thunderbolt and had proved his prowess, and they still held him in awesome respect. His reckless audacity and grim singleness of purpose had saved him on more than one occasion, for had he wavered once he would have been shot down without mercy. But gradually his enforcement of hampering laws became more and more intolerable, and their subordinated spirits were nearly on the point of revolt. When he faced them they resumed their former positions in relation to him—but once out of his sight they plotted to destroy him. Here was the crisis: it was now or never. They could not evade his ultimatum—it was obey or fight.

Submission was not to be thought of, for to flee would be to lose caste, and the story of such an act would follow them wherever they went, and brand them as cowards. Here they had lived, and here they would stay if possible, and to this end they discussed ways and means.

"Harlan's right!" emphatically announced Laramie Joe. "We can't pull out and have this foller us."

"We should have started it with a rush when he was in here," remarked Boston regretfully.

Harlan stopped his pacing and faced them, shoving out a bottle of whisky as an aid to his logic. "That chance is past, an' I don't know but what it is a good thing," he began. "He was primed an' looking fer trouble, an' he'd shore got a few of us afore he went under. What we want is strategy—that's th' game. You fellers have got as much brains as him, an' if we thrash this thing out we can find a way to call his play—an' get him! No use of any of us getting plugged 'less we have to. But whatever we do we've got to start it right quick an' have it over before that Bar-20 gang comes back. Harper, you an' Quinn go scouting—an' don't take no guns with you, either. Act like you was hitting th' long trail out, an' work back here on a circle. See how many of his friends are in town. While you are gone th' rest of us will hold a powwow an' take th' kinks out of this game. Chase along, an' don't waste no time."

"Good!" cried Slivers Lowe emphatically. "There's blamed few fellers in town now that have any use for him, for most of them are off on th' ranges. Bet we won't have more than six to fight, an' there's that many of us here."

The scouts departed at once and the remaining four drew close in consultation.

"One more drink around and then no more till this trouble is over," Harlan said, passing the bottle. The drinks, in view of the coming drouth and the thirsty work ahead, were long and deep, and new courage and vindictiveness crept through their veins.

"Now here's th' way it looks to me," Harlan continued, placing the bottle, untasted by himself, on the floor behind him. "We've got to work a surprise an' take Edwards an' his friends off their guard. That'll be easy if we're careful, because they think we ain't looking for fight. When we get them out of the way we can take Jackson's store an' use one of th' other shacks and wait for th'

Bar-20 to ride in. They'll canter right in, like they allus do, an' when they get close enough we'll open th' game with a volley an' make every shot tell. 'T won't last long, 'cause every one of us will have his man named before they get here. Then th' few straddlers in town, seeing how easy we've gone an' handled it, 'll join us. We've got four men to come in yet, an' by th' time th' C-80 an' Double-Arrow hear about it we'll be fixed to drive 'em back home. We ought to be over a dozen strong by dark."

"That sounds good, all right," remarked Slivers thoughtfully, "but can we do it that easy?"

"Course we can! We ain't fools, an' we all can shoot as well as them," snapped Laramie Joe, the most courageous of the lot. Laramie had taken only one drink, and that a small one, for he was wise enough to realize that he needed his wits as keen as he could have them.

"We can do it easy, if Edwards goes under first," hastily replied Harlan. "An' me an' Laramie will see to that part of it. If we don't get him, you=all can hit th' trail an' we won't be sore about it. That is, unless you are made of th' stuff that stands up an' fights 'stead of running away. I reckon I ain't none mistaken in any of you. You'll all be there when things get hot."

"You can bet th' shack *I* won't do no trail-hitting," growled Boston, glancing at Slivers, who squirmed a little under the hint.

"Well, I'm glued to th' crowd—you can't lose me, fellers," Slivers remarked, re-crossing his legs uneasily. "Are we going to begin it from here?"

"We ought to spread out cautious and surround Jackson's, or wherever Edwards is," Laramie Joe suggested. "That's my—"

"Yo're right! Now you've hit it plumb on th'head!" interrupted Harlan, slapping Laramie heartily across the back. "What did I tell you about our brains?" he cried enthusiastically. He had been on the point of suggesting that plan of operations when Laramie took the words out of his mouth. "I'd never thought of that, Laramie," he lied, his face beaming. "Why, we've got 'em licked to a finish right now!"

"This *is* a hummer of a game," laughed Slivers. "But how about th' Bar-20 crowd?"

"I've told you that already," replied the proprietor.

"You bet it's a hummer," cried Boston, reaching for the whisky bottle under cover of the excitement and enthusiasm.

Harlan pushed it away with his foot and raised his clenched fist. "Do you wonder I didn't think of that plan?" he demanded. "Ain't I been too mad to think at all? Hain't I seen my friends treated like dogs, an' made to swaller insults when I couldn't raise my hand to stop it? Didn't I see Jerry Brown chased out of my place like a wild beast? If we are what we've been called, then we'll sneak out of town with our tails atween our laigs; but if we're men we'll stay right here an' cram th' insults down th' throats of them that made 'em! If we're *men* let's prove it an' make them liars swaller our lead."

"My sentiments an' allus was!" roared Slivers, slapping Harlan's shoulder.

"We're men, all right, an' we'll show 'em it, too!"

At that instant the door opened and four guns covered it before it had swung a foot.

"Put 'em down—it's Quinn!" exclaimed the man in the doorway, flinching a bit. "All right, Jed," he called over his shoulder to the man who crowded him. After Quinn came Big Jed, and Harper brought up the rear. They had no more than shaken the water from their sombreros when the back door let in Charley Rich and his two companions, Frank and Tom Nolan. While greetings were being exchanged and the existing conditions explained to the newcomers, Harper and Quinn led Harlan to one side and reported, the proprietor smiling and nodding his head wisely. And while he listened, Slivers surreptitiously corralled the whisky bottle and when the last man finished with it there was nothing in it but air.

"Well, boys," exclaimed Harlan, "things are our way. Quinn, here, met Joe Barr, of th' C-80, who said Converse an' four other fellers, all friends of

Edwards, stopped at th' ranch an' won't be back home till th' storm stops. Harper saw Fred Neal going back to his ranch, so all we've got to figger on is th' marshal, Barr, an' Jackson, an' they're all in Jackson's store. Lacey might cut in, since he'd sell more liquor if I went under, but he can't do very much if he does take a hand. Now we'll get right at it." The whole thing was gone over thoroughly and in detail, positions assigned, and a signal agreed upon. Seeing that weapons were in good condition after their long storage in the cellar, and that cartridge belts were full, the ten men left the room one at a time or in pairs, Harlan and Laramie Joe being the last. And both Harlan and Laramie delayed long enough to take the precaution of placing horses where they would be handy in case of need.

CHAPTER EIGHTEEN

HARLAN STRIKES

JOE BARR laughingly replied to Johnny Nelson's growled remarks about the condition of things in general and tried to soothe him, but Johnny was unsoothable.

"An' I've been telling him right along that he's got th' best of it," complained Jackson in a weary voice. "Got a measly hole through his shoulder—good Lord! if it had gone a little lower!" he finished with a show of exasperation.

"An' ain't I been telling you all along that it ain't th' measly hole in my shoulder that's got me on th' prod?" retorted Johnny with more earnestness than politeness. "But why couldn't I go with my friends after Jerry an' get shot later if I had to get it at all? Look what I'm missing, roped an' throwed in this cussed ten-by-ten shack while they're having a little excitement."

"Yo're missing some blamed nasty weather, Kid," replied the marshal. "You ain't got no kick coming at all. Why, I got soaked clean through just going down to th' Oasis."

"Well, I'm kicking, just th' same," snapped Johnny. "An' furthermore, I don't see nobody big enough to stop me, neither—did you all get that?"

The rear door opened and Fred Neal looked

in. "Hey, Barr, come out an' gimme a hand in th' corral. Busted my cinch all to pieces half a mile out—an' how th' devil it ever busted like that is—" the door slammed shut and softened his monologue.

"Would you listen to that!" snorted Barr in an injured tone. "Didn't I go an' tell him near a month ago that his cussed cinch wouldn't hold no better'n a piece of wet paper?" His complaint added materially to the atmosphere of sullen discontent pervading the room. "An' now I gotter go out in this rain an'—" the slam of the door surpassed anything yet attempted in that line of endeavor. Jackson grabbed a can of corn as it jarred off the shelf behind him and directed a pleasing phrase after the peevish Barr.

"Say, won't somebody please smile?" gravely asked Edwards. "I never saw such a happy, cheerful bunch before."

"I might smile if I wasn't so blamed hungry," retorted Johnny. "Doesn't anybody ever eat in this town?" he asked in great sarcasm. "Mebby a good feed won't do me no good, but I'm going to fill myself regardless. An' after that, if th' grub don't shock me to death, I'm shore going to trim somebody at Ol' Sledge—for two bits a hand."

"If I could play you enough hands at that price I could sell out an' live high without working," grinned Jackson, preparing to give the reckless invalid all he could eat. "That's purty high, Kid,

236

but I just feel real devilish, an' I'm coming in."

"An' I'll go over to my shack, get some money, an' bust th' pair of you," laughed Edwards, again buttoning his coat and going toward the door. "Holy cats! A log must 'a' got jammed in th' sluice gate up there," he muttered, scowling at the black sky. "It's coming down harder'n ever, but here goes," and he stepped quickly into the storm.

Jackson paused with a frying pan in his hands and looked through the window after the departing marshal, and saw him stagger, stumble forward, then jerk out his guns and begin firing. Hard firing now burst out in front and Jackson, cursing angrily, dropped the pan and reached for his rifle—to drop it also and sink down, struck by the bullet which drilled through the window. Johnny let out a yell of rage, grabbed his Colt, and ran to the door in time to see Edwards slowly raise up on one elbow, fire his last shot, and fall back riddled by bullets.

Jackson crawled to his rifle and then to the side window, where he propped his back against a box and prepared to do his best. "It was shore a surprise," he swore. "An' they went an' got Edwards before he could do anything."

"They did not!" retorted Johnny. "He—" the glass in the door vibrated sharply and the speaker, stepping to one side out of sight, with a new and superficial wound, opened fire on the building down the street. Two men were lying on the ground across the street—these Edwards had shot—and another was trying to drag himself to the shelter of a building. A man sprinted from an old corral close by in a brave and foolhardy attempt to save his friend, and Johnny swore because he had to fire twice at the same mark.

The rear door crashed open and shut as Barr, closely followed by Neal, ran in. They had been caught in the corral but, thanks to Harlan's whisky, had managed to hold their own until they had a chance to make a rush for the store.

"Where's th' marshal?" cried Barr, catching sight of Jackson. "Are you plugged bad?" he asked anxiously.

"Well, I ain't plugged a whole lot *good!*" snapped Jackson. "An' Edwards is dead. They shot him down without warning. We're going to get ours, too—these walls don't stop them bullets. How many out there?"

"Must be a dozen," hastily replied Neal, who had not remained idle. Both he and Barr were working like mad men moving boxes and barrels against the walls to make a breastwork capable of stopping the bullets which came through the boards.

"I reckon—I'm bleeding inside," Jackson muttered, wearily and without hope. "Wonder how—long we—can hold out?"

"We'll hold out till we're good an' dead!" replied Johnny hotly. "They ain't got us yet an' they'll pay for it before they do. If we can hold

238

'em off till Buck an' th' rest come back we'll have th' pleasure of seein' 'em buried."

"Oh, I'll get you next time!" assured Barr to an enemy, slipping a fresh cartridge into the Sharps and peering intently at a slight rise on the muddy plain. "You shoot like yo're drunk," he mumbled.

"But what is it all about, anyhow?" asked Neal, finding time for an immaterial question. "Who are they?—can't see nothing but blurs through this rain."

"Yes, what's th' game?" asked Barr, mildly surprised that he had not thought of it before.

"It's that Oasis gang," Johnny responded. He fired, and growled with disappointment. "Harlan's at th' head of it," he added.

"Edwards—told Harlan to—get out of—town," Jackson began.

"An' to take his gang with him," Johnny interposed quickly to save Jackson from the strain. "They had till dark. Guess th' rest. Oh, you *coyote!*" he shouted, staggering back. There was a report farther down the barricade and Neal called out, "I got him, Nelson; he's done. How are you?"

"Mad! Mad!" yelled Johnny, touching his twice-wounded shoulder and dancing with rage and pain. "Right in th' same place! Oh, wait! *Wait!* Hey, gimme a rifle—I can't do nothing with a Colt at this range—my name ain't Hopalong," and he went slamming around the room in hot search of what he wanted.

"There ain't—no more—Johnny," feebly called Jackson, raising slightly to ease himself. "You can have—my gun purty—soon. I won't be able—to use it—much longer."

"Why don't Buck an' Hoppy hurry up!" snarled Johnny.

"Be a long time—mebby," mumbled Jackson, his trembling hands trying to steady the rifle. "They're all—around us. *Ah,* missed!" he intoned hoarsely, trying to pump the lever with unobeying hands. "I can't last—much—" the words ceased abruptly and the clatter of the rifle on the floor told the story.

Johnny stumbled over to him and dragged him aside, covering the upturned face with his own sombrero, and picked up the rifle. Rolling a barrel of flour against the wall below the window, he fixed himself as comfortably as possible and threw a shell into the chamber.

"Now, you coyotes, you pay *me* for *that!*" he gritted, resting the gun on the window sill and holding it so he could work it with one hand and shoulder.

"Wonder how them pups ever pumped up enough courage to cut loose like this?" queried Neal from behind his flour barrel.

"Whisky," hazarded Barr. "Harlan must 'a' got 'em drunk. An' that's three times I've missed that snake. Wish it would stop raining so I could see better."

"Why don't you wish they'd all drop dead? Wish good when you wish at all: got as much chance of having it come true," responded Neal sarcastically. He smothered a curse and looked curiously at his left arm, and from it to the new, yellow-splintered hole in the wall, which was already turning dark from the water soaking into it. "Hey, Joe, we need some more boxes!" he exclaimed, again looking at his arm.

"Yes," came Johnny's voice. "Three of 'em—five of 'em, an' about six feet long an' a foot deep. But if my outfit gets here in time we'll want more'n a dozen."

"Say! Lacey's firing now!" suddenly cried Barr. "He's shooting out of his windy. That'll stop 'em from rushing us! Good boy, Lacey!" he shouted, but Lacey did not hear him in the uproar.

"An' he's worse off than we are, being alone," commented Neal. "Hey! One of us better make a break for help—my ranch's th' nearest. What d'ye say?"

"It's suicide; they'll get you before you get ten feet," Barr replied with conviction.

"No; they won't—th' corral hides th' back door, an' all th' firing is on this side. I can sneak along th' back wall an' by keeping th' buildings atween me an' them, get a long ways off before they know anything about it. Then it's a dash—an' they can't catch me. But can you fellers hold out if I do?"

"Two can hold out as good as three—go ahead," Johnny replied. "Leave me some of yore Colt cartridges, though. You can't use 'em all before you get home."

"Don't stop fer that; there's all kinds behind th' counter," Barr interposed.

"Well, so long an' good luck," and the rear door closed, and softly this time.

"Two hours is some wait under th' present circumstances," Barr muttered, shifting his position behind his barricade. "He can't do it in less, nohow."

Johnny ducked and looked foolish. "Missed me by a foot," he explained. "He can't do it in two— not there an' back," he replied. "Th' trail is mud over th' fetlocks. Give him three at th' least."

"They ain't shooting as much as they was before."

"Waiting till they gets sober, I reckon," Johnny replied.

"If we don't hear no ruction in a few minutes we'll know he got away all right," Barr soliloquized. "An' he's got a fine cayuse for mud, too."

"Hey, why can't you do th' same thing if he makes it?" Johnny suddenly asked. "I can hold her alone, all right."

"Yo're a cheerful liar, you are," laughed Barr. "But can *you* ride?"

"Reckon so, but I ain't a-going to."

"Why, we *both* can go—it's a cinch!" Barr cried. "Come on!"

"Lord—an' I never even thought of that! Reckon I was too mad," Johnny replied. "But I sort of hates to leave Jackson an' Edwards," he added sullenly.

"But they're gone! You can't do them no good by staying."

"Yes; I know. An' how about Lacey chipping in on our fight?" demanded Johnny. "I ain't a-going to leave him to take it all. You go, Barr; it wasn't yore fight, nohow. You didn't even know what you was fighting for!"

"Huh! When anybody shoots at me it's my fight, all right," replied Barr, seating himself on the floor behind the breastwork. "I forgot all about Lacey," he apologized. At that instant a tomato can went *spang!* and fell off the shelf. "An' it's too late, anyhow; they ain't a-going to let nobody else get away on that side."

"An' they're tuning up again, too," Johnny replied, preparing for trouble. "Look out for a rush, Barr."

CHAPTER NINETEEN

THE BAR-20 RETURNS

HOPALONG CASSIDY stopped swearing at the weather and looked up and along the trail in front of him, seeing a hard-riding man approach. He turned his head and spoke to Buck Peters, who rode close behind him. "Somebody's shore in a hurry—why, it's Fred Neal."

It was. Mr. Neal was making his arms move and was also shouting something at the top of his voice. The noise of the rain and of the horses' hoofs splashing in the mud and water at first made his words unintelligible, but it was not long before Hopalong heard something which made him sit up even straighter. In a moment Neal was near enough to be heard distinctly and the outfit shook itself out of its weariness and physical misery and followed its leader at reckless speed. As they rode, bunched close together, Neal briefly and graphically outlined the relative positions of the combatants, and while Buck's more cautious mind was debating the best way to proceed against the enemy, Hopalong cried out the plan to be followed. There would be no strategy—Johnny, wounded and desperate, was fighting for his life. The simplest way was the best—a dash regardless of consequences to those making it, for time was a big factor to the two men in Jackson's store.

"Ride right at 'em!" Hopalong cried. "I know that bunch. They'll be too scared to shoot straight. Paralyze 'em! Three or four are gone now—an' th' whole crowd wasn't worth one of th' men they went out to get. Th' quicker it's over th' better."

"Right you are," came from the rear.

"Ride up th' arroyo as close as we can get, an' then over th' edge an' straight at 'em," Buck ordered. "Their shooting an' th' rain will cover what noise we make on th' soft ground. An' boys, *no quarter!*"

"Reckon *not!*" gritted Red savagely. "Not with Edwards an' Jackson dead, an' th' Kid fighting for his life!"

"They're still at it!" cried Lanky Smith, as the faint and intermittent sound of firing was heard; the driving wind was blowing from the town, and this also would deaden the noise of their approach.

"Thank th' Lord! That means that there's somebody left to fight 'em," exclaimed Red. "Hope it's th' Kid," he muttered.

"They can't rush th' store till they get Lacey, an' they can't rush him till they get th' store," shouted Neal over his shoulder. "They'd be in a cross fire if they tried either—an' that's what licks 'em."

"They'll be in a cross fire purty soon," promised Pete grimly.

Hopalong and Red reached the edge of the

arroyo first and plunged over the bank into the yellow storm water swirling along the bottom like a miniature flood. After them came Buck, Neal, and the others, the water shooting up in sheets as each successive horse plunged in. Out again on the farther side they strung out into single file along the narrow foothold between water and bank and raced toward the sharp bend some hundreds of yards ahead, the point in the arroyo's course nearest the town. The dripping horses scrambled up the slippery incline and then, under the goading of spurs and quirts, leaped forward as fast as they could go across the level, soggy plain.

A quarter of a mile ahead of them lay the scattered shacks of the town, and as they drew nearer to it the riders could see the flashes of guns and the smoke-fog lying close to the ground. Fire spat from Jackson's store and a cloud of smoke still lingered around a window in Lacey's saloon. Then a yell reached their ears—a yell of rage, consternation, and warning. Figures scurried to seek cover and the firing from Jackson's and Lacey's grew more rapid.

A mounted man emerged from a corral and tore away, others following his example, and the outfit separated to take up the chase individually. Harlan, wounded hard, was trying to run to where he had left his horse, and after him fled Slivers Lowe. Hopalong was gaining on them when he saw Slivers raise his arm and fire deliberately into the back of the proprietor of the Oasis, leap over the falling body, vault into the saddle of Harlan's horse and gallop for safety. Hopalong's shots went wide and the last view any one had of Slivers in that part of the country was when he dropped into an arroyo to follow it for safety. Laramie Joe fled before Red Connors and Red's rage was so great that it spoiled his accuracy, and he had the sorrow of seeing the pursued grow faint in the mist and fog. Pursuit was tried until the pursuers realized that their mounts were too worn out to stand a show against the fresh animals ridden by the survivors of the Oasis crowd.

Red circled and joined Hopalong. "Blasted coyotes," he growled. "Killed Jackson an' Edwards, an' wanted th' Kid! He's shore showed 'em what fighting is, all right. But I wonder what got into 'em all at once to give 'em nerve enough to start things?"

"Edwards paid his way, all right," replied Hopalong. "If I do as well when my time comes I won't do no kicking."

"Yore time ain't coming that way," responded Red, grinning. "You'll die a natural death in bed, unless you get to cussing me."

"Shore there ain't no more, Buck?" Hopalong called.

"Yes. There was only five, I reckon, an' they was purty well shot up when we took a hand. You know, Johnny was in it all th' time," replied the foreman, smiling. "This town's had th' cleaning-up it's needed for some time," he added.

They were at Jackson's store now, and hurriedly dismounted and ran in to see Johnny. They found him lying across some boxes, which brought him almost to the level of a window sill. He was too weak to stand, while near him in similar condition lay Barr, too weak from loss of blood to do more than look his welcome.

"How are you, Kid?" cried Buck anxiously, bending over him, while others looked to Barr's injuries.

"Tired, Buck, awful tired, an' all shot up," Johnny slowly replied. "When I saw you fellers—streak past this windy—I sort of went flat—something seemed to break inside me," he said faintly and with an effort, and the foreman ordered him not to talk. Deft fingers, schooled by practice in rough and ready surgery, were busy over him and in half an hour he lay on Jackson's cot, covered with bandages.

"Why, hullo, Lacey!" exclaimed Hopalong, leaping forward to shake hands with the man Red and Billy had gone to help. "Purty well scratched up, but lively yet, hey?"

"I'm able to hobble over here an' shake han's with these scrappers—they're shore wonders," Lacey replied. "Fought like a whole regiment! Hullo, Johnny!" and his handclasp told much.

"Yore cross fire did it, Lacey; that was th' whole thing," Johnny smiled. "Yo're all right!"

Red turned and looked out of the window toward the Oasis and then glanced at Buck. "Reckon we better burn Harlan's place—it's all that's left of that gang now," he suggested.

"Why, yes, I reckon so," replied the foreman. "That's as—"

"No, we won't!" Hopalong interposed quickly. "That stands till Johnny sets it off. It's th' Kid's celebration—he was shot in it."

Johnny smiled.

CHAPTER TWENTY

BARB WIRE

AFTER the flurry at Perry's Bend the Bar-20 settled down to the calm routine work and sent several drive herds to their destination without any unusual incidents. Buck thought that the last herd had been driven when, late in the summer, he received an order that he made haste to fill. The outfit was told to get busy and soon rounded up the necessary number of three-year-olds. Then came the road branding, the final step except inspection, and this was done not far from the ranch house, where the facilities were best for speedy work.

Entirely recovered from all ill effects of his afternoon in Jackson's store up in Perry's bend, Johnny Nelson waited with Red Connors on the platform of the branding-chute and growled petulantly at the sun, the dust, but most of all at the choking, smarting odor of burned hair which filled their throats and caused them to rub the backs of grimy hands across their eyes. Chute-branding robbed them of the excitement, the leaven of fun and frolic, which they always took from open or corral branding—and the work of a day in the corral or open was condensed into an hour or two by the chute. This was one cow wide, narrow at the bottom and flared out as it went up, so the animal could not turn, and when filled was, to use Johnny's graphic phrase, "like a chain of cows in a ditch." Eight of the wondering and crowded animals, guided into the pen by men who knew their work to the smallest detail and lost no time in its performance, filed into the pen after those branded had filed out. As the first to enter reached the farther end a stout bar dropped into place, just missing the animal's nose; and as the last cow discovered that it could go no farther and made up its mind to back out, it was stopped by another bar, which fell behind it. The iron heaters tossed a hot iron each to Red and Johnny and the eight were marked in short order, making about 250 they had branded in three hours. This number compared very favorably with that of the second chute where Lanky Smith and Frenchy McAlister waved cold irons and sarcastically asked their iron men if the sun was supposed to provide the heat; whereat the down-trodden heaters provided heat with great generosity in their caustic retorts.

"Oh, Susanna, don't you cry for me," sang Billy Williams, one of the feeders. "But why in Jericho don't you fellers get a move on you? You ain't no good on th' platform—you ought to be mixin' biscuits for cookie. Frenchy an' Lanky are th' boys to turn 'em out," he offered, gratis.

Red's weary air bespoke a vast and settled contempt for such inanities and his iron descended with exaggerated slowness and exactitude against the side of the victim below him—he would not deign to reply. Not so with Johnny, who could not refrain from hot retort.

"Don't be a fool *all* th' time," snapped Johnny. "Mind yore own business, you shorthorn. Big-mouthed old woman, that's what—" his tone dropped and the words sank into vague mutterings which a strangling cough cut short. "Blasted idiot," he whispered, tears coming into his eyes at the effort. Burning hair is bad for throat and temper alike.

Red deftly knocked his companion's iron up and spoke sharply. "You mind yourn better—that makes th' third you've tried to brand twice. Why don't you look what yo're doin'? Hot iron! Hot iron! What're you fellers doin'?" he shouted down at the heaters. "This ain't no time to go to sleep. How d' y' expect us to do any work when you ain't doin' any yoreselves!" Red's temper was also on the ragged edge.

"You've got one in your other hand, you sheep!" snorted one of the iron heaters with restless pugnacity. "Go tearin' into us when you—" he growled the rest and kicked viciously at the fire.

"Lovely bunch," grinned Billy, who, followed by Pete Wilson, mounted the platform to relieve the branders. "Chase yoreselves—me an' Pete are shore going to show you cranky bugs how to do a hundred an hour. Ain't we, Pete? An' look here, you," he remarked to the heaters, "don't you fellers keep *us* waitin' for hot irons!"

"That's right! Make a fool out of yoreself first thing!" snapped one of the pair on the ground.

"Billy, I never loved you as much as I do this minute," grinned Johnny wearily. "Wish you'd 'a' come along to show us how to do it an hour ago."

"I would, only—"

"Quit chinning an' get busy," remarked Red, climbing down. "Th' chute's full an' it's all yourn."

Billy caught the iron, gave it a preliminary flourish, and started to work with a speed that would not endure for long. He branded five out of the eight and jeered at his companion for being so slow.

"Have your fun now, Billy," Pete replied with placid good nature. "Before we're through with this job you'll be lucky if you can do two of th' string, if you keep up that pace."

"He'll be missing every other one," growled his heater with overflowing malice. "That iron ain't cold, you fool!"

"Too cold for me—don't miss none," chuckled Billy sweetly. "Fill th' chute! Fill th' chute! Don't keep us waitin'!" he cried to the guiders, hopping around with feigned eagerness and impatience.

Hopalong Cassidy rode up and stopped as Red returned to take the place of one of the iron heaters. "How they coming, Red?" he inquired.

"Fast. You can sic that inspector on 'em th' first thing tomorrow mornin', if he gets here on time. Bet he's off som'ers gettin' full of redeye. Who're goin' with you on this drive?"

"Th' inspector is all right—he's here now an' is going to spend th' night with us so as to be on hand th' first thing tomorrow," replied Hopalong, grinning at the hard-working pair on the platform. "Why, I reckon I'll take you, Johnny, Lanky, Billy, Pete, an' Skinny, an' we'll have two hoss wranglers an' a cook, of course. We'll drive up th' right-hand trail through West Valley this time. It's longer, but there'll be more water that way at this time of th' year. Besides, I don't want no more footsore cattle to nurse along. Even th' West Valley trail will be dry enough before we strike Bennett's Creek."

"Yes, we'll have to drive 'em purty hard till we reach th' creek," replied Red thoughtfully. "Say, we're going to have three thousand of th' finest three-year-old steers ever sent north out of these parts. An' we ought to do it in a month an' deliver 'em fat an' frisky. We can feed 'em good for th' last week."

"I just sent some of th' boys out to drive in th' cayuses," Hopalong remarked, "an' when they get here you fellers match for choice an' pick yore remuda. No use takin' too few. About eight apiece'll do us nice. I shore like a good cavvieyeh."

"Hullo, Hoppy!" came from the platform as Billy grinned his welcome through the dust on his face. "Want a job?"

"Hullo yoreself," growled Pete. "Stick yore iron on that fourth steer before he gets out, an' talk less with yore mouth."

"Pete's still rabid," called Billy, performing the duty Pete suggested.

"That may be th' polite name for it," snorted one of the iron heaters, testing an iron, "but that ain't what I'd say. Might as well cover th' subject thoroughly while yo're on it."

"Yea, verily," endorsed his companion.

"Here comes th' last of 'em," smiled Pete, watching several cattle being driven toward the chute. "We'll have to brand 'em on th' move, Billy; there ain't enough ta fill th' chute."

"All right; hot iron, you!"

Early the next morning the inspector looked them over and made his count, the herd was started north and at nightfall had covered 12 miles. For the next week everything went smoothly, but after that, water began to be scarce and the herd was pushed harder, and became harder to handle.

On the night of the 12th day out four men sat around the fire in West Valley at a point a dozen miles south of Bennett's Creek, and ate heartily. The night was black—not a star could be seen and the south wind hardly stirred the trampled and burned grass. They were thoroughly tired out and their tempers were not in the sweetest state imaginable, for the heat during the last four days had been almost unbearable even to them and they had had their hands full with the cranky herd. They ate silently, hungrily—there would be time enough for the few words they had to say when the pipes were going for a short smoke before turning in.

"I feel like hell," growled Red, reaching for another cup of coffee, but there was no reply; he had voiced the feelings of all.

Hopalong listened intently and looked up, staring into the darkness, and soon a horseman was seen approaching the fire. Hopalong nodded welcome and waved his hand toward the food, and the stranger, dismounting, picketed his horse and joined the circle. When the pipes were lighted he sighed with satisfaction and looked around the group. "Drivin' north, I see."

"Yes, an' blamed glad to get off this dry range," Hopalong replied. "Th' herd's getting cranky an' hard to hold—but when we pass th' creek everything'll be all right again. An' ain't it hot! When you hear us kick about th' heat it means something."

"I'm going yore way," remarked the stranger. "I came down this trail about two weeks ago. Reckon I was th' last to ride through before th' fence went up. Damned outrage, says I, an' I told 'em so, too. They couldn't see it that way an' we had a little disagreement about it. They said as how they was going to patrol it."

"Fence! What fence?" exclaimed Red.

"Where's there any fence?" demanded Hopalong sharply.

"Twenty mile north of th' creek," replied the stranger, carefully packing his pipe.

"What? Twenty miles north of th' creek?" cried Hopalong. "What creek?"

"Bennett's. Th' 4X has strung three strands of barb wire from Coyote Pass to th' North Arm. Thirty mile long, without a gate, so they says."

"But it don't close this trail!" cried Hopalong in blank astonishment.

"It shore does. They say they owns that range an' can fence it in all they wants. I told 'em different, but naturally they didn't listen to me. An' they'll fight about it, too."

"But they *can't* shut off this trail!" ejaculated Billy with angry emphasis. "They don't own it no more'n we do!"

"I know all about that—you heard me tell you what they said."

"But how can we get past it?" demanded Hopalong.

"Around it, over th' hills. You'll lose about three days doin' it, too."

"I can't take no sand-range herd over them rocks, an' I ain't going to drive 'round no North

Arm or Coyote Pass if I could," Hopalong replied with quiet emphasis. "There's poison springs on th' east an' nothing but rocks on th' west. We go straight through."

"I'm afraid that you'll have to fight if you do," remarked the stranger.

"Then we'll fight!" cried Johnny, leaning forward. "Blasted coyotes! What right have they got to block a drive trail that's as old as cattle-raising in these parts! That trail was here before I was born, it's allus been open, an' it's going to stay open! You watch us go through!"

"Yo're dead right, Kid, we'll cut that fence an' stick to this trail, an' fight if we has to," endorsed Red. "Th' Bar-20 ain't crawlin' out of no hole that it can walk out of. They're bluffing, that's all."

"I don't think they are, an' there's twelve men in that outfit," suggested the stranger, offhand.

"We ain't got time to count odds; we never do down our way when we know we're right. An' we're right enough in this game," retorted Hopalong quickly. "For th' last twelve days we've had good luck, barrin' th' few on this dry range, an' now we're in for th' other kind. By th' Lord, I wish we was here without th' cows to take care of—we'd show 'em something about blockin' drive trails that ain't in their little book!"

"Blast it all! Wire fences coming down this way now," mused Johnny sullenly. He hated them by training as much as he hated horse thieves and sheep, and his companions had been brought up in the same school. Barb wire, the death knell to the old-time punching, the bar to riding at will, a steel insult to fire the blood—it had come at last.

"We've shore got to cut it, Red—" began Hopalong, but the cook had to rid himself of some of his indignation and interrupted with heat.

"Shore we have!" came explosively from the tail-board of the chuck wagon. "Got to lay it agin my li'l ax an' swat it with my big ol' monkey wrench! An' won't them posts save me a lot of trouble huntin' chips an' firewood!"

"We've shore got to cut it, Red," Hopalong repeated slowly. "You an' Johnny an' me'll ride ahead after we cross th' creek tomorrow an' do it. I don't hanker after no fight with all these cows on my han's, but we've got to risk one."

"Shore!" cried Johnny hotly. "I can't get over th' gall of them fellers closing up th' West Valley drive trail. Why, I never heard tell of such a thing afore!"

"We're short-handed; we ought to have more'n we have to guard th' herd if there's a fight. If it stampedes—oh, well, that'll work out tomorrow. Th' creek's only about twelve miles away an' we'll start at daylight, so tumble in," Hopalong said as he arose. "Red, I'm going out to take my shift—I'll send Pete in. Stranger," he added, turning, "I'm much obliged to you for th' warning. They might 'a' caught us with our hands tied."

"Oh, that's all right," hastily replied the stranger, who was in hearty accord with the plans, such as they were. "My name's Hawkins, an' I don't like range fences no more'n you do. I used to hunt buffalo all over this part of th' country before they was all killed off, an' I allus rode where I pleased. I'm purty old, but I c'n still see an' shoot, an' I'm going to stick right along with you fellers an' see it through. Every man counts in this game."

"Well, that's blamed white of you," Hopalong replied, greatly pleased by the other's offer. "But I can't let you do it. I don't want to drag you into no trouble, an'—"

"You ain't draggin' me none; I'm doing it myself. I'm about as mad as you are over it. I ain't good for much no more, an' if I shuffles off fightin' barb wire I'll be doing my duty. First it was nesters, then railroads an' more nesters, then sheep, an' now it's wire—won't it never stop? By th' Lord, it's got to stop, or this country will go to th' devil an' won't be fit to live in. Besides, I've heard of your fellers before—I'll tie to th' Bar-20 any day."

"Well, I reckon you must if you must; yo're welcome enough," laughed Hopalong, and he strode off to his picketed horse, leaving the others to discuss the fence, with the assistance of the cook, until Pete rode in.

CHAPTER TWENTY-ONE

THE FENCE

WHEN Hopalong rode in at midnight to arouse the others and send them out to relieve Skinny and his two companions, the cattle were quieter than he had expected to leave them, and he could see no change of weather threatening. He was asleep when the others turned in, or he would have been further assured in that direction.

Out on the plain where the herd was being held, Red and the three other guards had been optimistic until half of their shift was over and it was only then that they began to worry. The knowledge that running water was only 12 miles away had the opposite effect than the one expected, for instead of making them cheerful, it caused them to be beset with worry and fear. Water was all right, and they could not have got along without it for another day, but it was, in this case, filled with the possibility of grave danger.

Johnny was thinking hard about it as he rode around the now restless herd, and then pulled up suddenly, peered into the darkness and went on again. "Damn that disreputable li'l rounder! Why th' devil can't he behave, 'stead of stirring things up when they're ticklish?" he muttered, but he had to grin despite himself. A lumbering form had blundered past him from the direction of the camp and was swallowed up by the night as it sought the herd, annoying and arousing the thirsty and irritable cattle along its trail, throwing challenges right and left and stirring up trouble as it passed. The fact that the challenges were bluffs made no difference to the pawing steers, for they were anxious to have things out with the rounder.

This frisky disturber of bovine peace was a yearling that had slipped into the herd before it left the ranch and had kept quiet and respectable and out of sight in the middle of the mass for the first few days and nights. But keeping quiet and respectable had been an awful strain, and his mischievous deviltry grew constantly harder to hold in check. Finally he could stand the repression no longer, and when he gave way to his accumulated energy it had the snap and ginger of a tightly stretched rubber band recoiling on itself. On the fourth night out he had thrown off his mask and announced his presence in his true light by butting a sleepy steer out of its bed, which bed he straightway proceeded to appropriate for himself. This was folly, for the ground was not cold and he had no excuse for stealing a body-warmed place to lie down; it was pure cussedness, and retribution followed hard upon the act. In about half a minute he had discovered the great difference between bullying poor, miserable, defenseless dogies and trying to bully a healthy, fully developed, and pugnacious steer. After assimilating the preliminary punishment of what promised to be the most thorough and workmanlike thrashing he had ever known, the indignant and frightened bummer wheeled and fled incontinently with the aroused steer in angry pursuit. The best way out was the one most puzzling to the vengeful steer, so the bummer cavorted recklessly through the herd, turning and twisting and doubling, stepping on any steer that happened to be lying down in his path, butting others, and leavening things with great success. Under other conditions he would have relished the effect of his efforts, for the herd had arisen as one animal and seemed to be debating the advisability of stampeding, but he was in no mood to relish anything and thought only of getting away. Finally escaping from his pursuer, that had paused to fight with a belligerent brother, he rambled off into the darkness to figure it all out and to maintain a sullen and chastened demeanor for the rest of the night. This was the first time a brick had been under the hat.

But the spirits of youth recover quickly—his recovered so quickly that he was banished from the herd the very next night, which banishment, not being at all to his liking, was enforced only by rigid watchfulness and hard riding, and he was roundly cursed from dark to dawn by the worried men, most of whom disliked the bumming youngster less than they pretended. He was only a cub, a wild youth having his fling, and there was something irresistibly likable and comical in his awkward antics and eternal persistence, even though he was a pest. Johnny saw more in him than his companions could find, and had quite a little sport with him: he made fine practice for roping, for he was about as elusive as a grasshopper and uncertain as a flea. Johnny was in the same general class and he could sympathize with the irrepressible nuisance in its efforts to stir up a little life and excitement in so dull a crowd; Johnny hoped to be as successful in his mischievous deviltry when he reached the town at the end of the drive.

But tonight it was dark, and the bummer gained his coveted goal with ridiculous ease, after which he started right in to work off the high pressure of the energy he had accumulated during the last two nights. He had desisted in his efforts to gain the herd early in the evening and had rambled off and rested during the first part of the night, and the herders breathed softly lest they should stir him to renewed trials. But now he had succeeded, and although only Johnny had seen him lumber past, the other three guards were aware of it immediately by the results and swore in their throats, for the cattle were now on their feet, snorting and moving about restlessly, and the rattling of horns grew slowly louder.

"Ain't he having a devil of a good time!" grinned Johnny. But it was not long before he realized the possibilities of the bummer's efforts and he lost his grin. "If we get through th' night without trouble I'll see that you are picketed if it takes me all day to get you," he muttered. "Fun is fun, but it's getting a little too serious for comfort."

Sometime after the middle of the second shift the herd, already irritable, nervous, and cranky because of the thirst they were enduring, and worked up to the fever pitch by the devilish maneuvers of the exuberant and hard-working bummer, wanted only the flimsiest kind of an excuse to stampede, and they might go without an excuse. A flash of lightning, a crash of thunder, a wind-blown paper, a flapping wagon cover, the sudden and unheralded approach of a careless rider, the cracking and flare of a match, or the scent of a wolf or coyote—or water, would send an avalanche of 3000 crazed steers crashing its irresistible way over a pitch-black plain.

Red had warned Pete and Billy, and now he rode to find Johnny and send him to camp for the others. As he got halfway around the circle he heard Johnny singing a mournful lay, and soon a black bulk loomed up in the dark ahead of him. "That you, Kid?" he asked. "That you, Johnny?" he repeated, a little louder.

The song stopped abruptly. "Shore," replied

Johnny. "We're going to have trouble aplenty to-night. Glad daylight ain't so very far off. That cussed li'l rake of a bummer got by me an' into th' herd. He's shore raising Ned tonight, the li'l monkey: it's getting serious, Red."

"I'll shoot that yearling at daylight, damn him!" retorted Red. "I should 'a' done it a week ago. He's picked th' worst time for his cussed devilment! You ride right in an' get th' boys, an' get 'em out here quick. Th' whole herd's on its toes waitin' for th' signal, an' th' wink of an eye'll send 'em off. God only knows what'll happen between now and daylight! If th' wind should change an' blow down from th' north, they'll be off as shore as shootin'. One whiff of Bennett's Creek is all that's needed, Kid, an'—"

"Oh, pshaw!" interposed Johnny. "There ain't no wind at all now. It's been quiet for an hour."

"Yes, an' that's one of th' things that's worrying me. It means a change, shore."

"Not always; we'll come out of this all right," assured Johnny, but he spoke without his usual confidence. "There ain't no use—" he paused as he felt the air stir, and he was conscious of Red's heavy breathing. There was a peculiar hush in the air that he did not like, a closeness that sent his heart up in his throat, and as he was about to continue a sudden gust snapped his neckerchief out straight. He felt that refreshing coolness which so often precedes a storm and as he

268

weighed it in his mind a low rumble of thunder rolled in the north and sent a chill down his back.

"Good God! Get th' boys!" cried Red, wheeling. "It's *changed!* An' Pete an' Billy out there in front of—*there they go!*" he shouted as a sudden tremor shook the earth and a roaring sound filled the air. He was instantly lost to ear and eye, swallowed by the oppressive darkness as he spurred and quirted into a great, choking cloud of dust which swept down from the north, unseen in the night. The deep thunder of hoofs and the faint and occasional flash of a six-shooter told him the direction, and he hurled his mount after the uproar with no thought of the death which lurked in every hole and rock and gully on the uneven and unseen plain beneath him. His mouth and nose were lined with dust, his throat choked with it, and he opened his burning eyes only at intervals, and then only to a slit, to catch a fleeting glance of—nothing. He realized vaguely that he was riding north, because the cattle would head for water, but that was all, save that he was animated by a desperate eagerness to gain the firing line, to join Pete and Billy, the two men who rode before that crazed mass of horns and hoofs and who were pleading and swearing and yelling in vain only a few feet ahead of annihilation—if they were still alive. A stumble, a moment's indecision, and the avalanche would roll over them as if they were straws and trample them flat beneath the pounding hoofs, a modern Juggernaut. If he, or they, managed to escape with life, it would make a good tale for the bunkhouse some night; if they were killed it was in doing their duty—it was all in a day's work.

Johnny shouted after him and then wheeled and raced toward the camp, emptying his Colt in the air as a warning. He saw figures scurrying across the lighted place, and before he had gained it his friends raced past him and gave him hard work catching up to them. And just behind him rode the stranger, to do what he could for his new friends, and as reckless of consequences as they.

It seemed an age before they caught up to the stragglers, and when they realized how true they had ridden in the dark they believed that at last their luck was turning for the better, and pushed on with renewed hope. Hopalong shouted to those nearest him that Bennett's Creek could not be far away and hazarded the belief that the steers would slow up and stop when they found the water they craved, but his words were lost to all but himself.

Suddenly the punchers were almost trapped and their escape made miraculous, for without warning the herd swerved and turned sharply to the right, crossing the path of the riders and forcing them to the east, showing Hopalong their silhouettes against the streak of pale gray low down in the eastern sky. When free from the sudden press of cattle they slowed perceptibly, and Hopalong did likewise to avoid running them down. At that instant the uproar took on a new note and increased three-fold. He could hear the shock of impact, whiplike reports, the bellowing of cattle in pain, and he arose in his stirrups to peer ahead for the reason, seeing, as he did so, the silhouettes of his friends arise and then drop from his sight. Without additional warning his horse pitched forward and crashed to the earth, sending him over its head. Slight as was the warning it served to ease his fall, for instinct freed his feet from the stirrups, and when he struck the ground it was feet first, and although he fell flat at the next instant, the shock had been broken. Even as it was, he was partly stunned, and groped as he arose on his hands and knees. Arising painfully, he took a short step forward, tripped and fell again, and felt a sharp pain shoot through his hand as it went first to break the fall. Perhaps it was ten seconds before he knew what it was that had thrown him, and when he learned that he also learned the reason for the whole calamity—in his torn and bleeding hand he held a piece of barb wire.

"Barb wire!" he muttered, amazed. "Barb wire! Why, what th'—*Damn that ranch!*" he shouted, sudden rage sweeping over him as the situation flashed through his mind and banished all the mental effects of the fall. "They've gone an' strung it south of th' creek as well! Red! Johnny! Lanky!" he shouted at the top of his voice, hoping to be heard over the groaning of injured cattle and the general confusion. "Good Lord! *are they killed?*"

They were not, thanks to the forced slowing up and to the pool of water and mud which formed an arm of the creek, a backwater away from the pull of the current. They had pitched into the mud and water up to their waists, some headfirst, some feet-first, and others as they would go into a chair. Those who had been fortunate enough to strike feetfirst pulled out the divers, and the others gained their feet as best they might and with varying degrees of haste, but all mixed profanity and thankfulness equally well, and were equally and effectually disguised.

Hopalong, expecting the silence of death or at least the groaning of injured and dying, was taken aback by the fluent stream of profanity which greeted his ears. But all efforts in that line were eclipsed when the drive foreman tersely explained about the wire, and the providential mud bath was forgotten in the new idea. They forthwith clamored for war, and the sooner it came the better they would like it.

"Not now, boys, we've got work to do first," replied Hopalong, who, nevertheless, was troubled grievously by the same itching trigger finger. They subsided—as a steel spring subsides when held down by a weight—and went off in search of their mounts. Daylight had won the skirmish in the east and was now attacking in force, and revealed a sight which, stilling the profanity for the moment, caused it to flow again with renewed energy. The plain was a shambles near the creek, and dead and dying steers showed where the fence had stood. The rest of the herd had passed over these. The wounded cattle and three horses were put out of their misery as the first duty. The horse that Hopalong had ridden had a broken back, the other two, broken legs. When this work was out of the way the bruised and shaken men gave their attention to the scattered cattle on the other side of the creek, and when Hawkins rode up after wasting time in hunting for the trail in the dark, he saw four men with the herd, which was still scattered, four others near the creek, of whom only Johnny was mounted, and a group of six strangers riding toward them from the west and along the fence, or what was left of that portion of it.

"That's awful!" he cried, stopping his limping horse near Hopalong. "An' here come th' fools that done it."

"Yes," replied Johnny, his voice breaking from rage, "but they won't go back again! I don't care if I'm killed if I can get one or two of that crowd—"

"Shut up, Kid!" snapped Hopalong as the 4X

outfit drew near. "I know just how you feel about it; feel that way myself. But there ain't a-goin' to be no fightin' while I've got these cows on my han's. That gang'll be here when we come back, all right."

"Mebby one or two of 'em won't," remarked Hawkins as he looked again over the carnage along the fence. "I never did much pot-shootin', 'cept agin Injuns; but I dunno—" He did not finish, for the strangers were almost at his elbow.

Cranky Joe led the 4X contingent and he did the talking for it without waste of time. "Who th' hell busted that fence?" he demanded belligerently, looking around savagely. Johnny's hand twitched at the words and the way they were spoken.

"I did; did you think somebody leaned agin it?" replied Hopalong, very calmly—so calmly that it was about one step short of an explosion.

"Well, why didn't you go around?"

"Three thousand stampedin' cattle don't go 'round wire fences in th' dark."

"Well, that's not our fault. Reckon you better dig down an' settle up for th' damages, an' half a cent a head for water, an' then go 'round. You can't stampede through th' other fence."

"That so?" asked Hopalong.

"Reckon it is."

"Yo're real shore it is?"

"Well there's only six of us here, but there's six

more that we can get blamed quick if we need 'em. It's so, all right."

"Well, comin' down to figures, there's eight here, with two hoss wranglers an' a cook to come," retorted Hopalong, kicking the belligerent Johnny on the shins. "We're just about mad enough to tackle anything—ever feel that way?"

"Oh, no use gettin' all het up," rejoined Cranky Joe. "We ain't a-goin' to fight 'less we has to. Better pay up."

"Send yore bills to th' ranch—if they're O. K., Buck'll pay 'em."

"Nix, I take it when I can get it."

"I ain't got no money with me that I can spare."

"Then you can leave enough cows to buy back again."

"I'm not going to pay you one damned cent, an' th' only cows I'll leave are th' dead ones—an' if I could take them with me I'd do it. An' I'm not going around th' fence, neither."

"Oh, yes, you are. An' you're goin' to pay," snapped Cranky Joe.

"Take it out of th' price of two hundred dead cows an' gimme what's left," Hopalong retorted. "It'll cost you nine of them twelve men to pry it out'n me."

"You won't pay?" demanded the other coldly.

"Not a plugged *peso*."

"Well, as I said before, I don't want to fight nobody 'less I has to," replied Cranky Joe. "I'll

275

give you a chance to change yore mind. We'll be out here after it t'morrow, cash or cows. That'll give you twenty-four hours to rest yore herd an' get ready to drive. Then you pay, an' go back, 'round th' fence."

"All right, tomorrow suits me," responded Hopalong, who was boiling with rage and felt constrained to hold it back. If it wasn't for the cows—!

Red and three companions swept up and stopped in a swirl of dust and asked questions until Hopalong shut them up. Their arrival and the manner of their speech riled Cranky Joe, who turned around and loosed one more remark, and he never knew how near to death he was at that moment.

"You fellers must own th' earth, th' way you act," he said to Red and his three companions.

"We ain't fencin' it in to prove it," rejoined Hopalong, his hand on Red's arm.

Cranky Joe wheeled to rejoin his friends. "T'morrow," he said, significantly.

Hopalong and his men watched the six ride away, too enraged to speak for a moment. Then the drive foreman mastered himself and turned to Hawkins. "Where's their ranch house?" he demanded sharply. "There must be some way out of this, an' we've got to find it—an' before to-morrow."

"West, three hours' ride along th' fence. I could

find 'em th' darkest night what ever happened; I was out there onct," Hawkins replied.

"Describe 'em as exact as you can," demanded Hopalong, and when Hawkins had done so the Bar-20 drive foreman slapped his thigh and laughed nastily. "One house with one door an' only two windows—are you shore? Good! Where's th' corrals? Good again! So they'll take pay for their blasted fence, eh? Cash or cows, hey! Don't want no fight 'less it's necessary, but they're going to make us pay for th' fence that killed two hundred head, an' blamed nigh got us, too. An' half a cent a head for drinkin' water! I've paid that more'n once—some of th' poor devils squattin' on th' range ain't got nothin' to sell but water, but I don't buy none out of Bennett's Creek! Pete, you mounted fellers round up a little—bunch th' herd a little closer, an' drive straight along th' trail toward that other fence. We'll all help you as soon as th' wranglers bring us up somethin' to ride. Push 'em hard, limp or no limp, till dark. They'll be too tired to go crow-hopping 'round any in th' dark tonight. An' say! When you see that bummer if he wasn't got by th' fence, drop him clean. So they've got twelve men, hey! Huh!"

"What you goin' to do?" asked Red, beginning to cool down, and very curious.

"Yes, tell us," urged Johnny.

"Why, I'm going to cut that fence, an' cut it all

to hell. Then I'm going to push th' herd through it an' as far out of danger as I can. When they're all right cookie an' th' hoss wranglers will have to hold 'em during th' night while we do th' rest."

"What's th' rest?" demanded Johnny.

"Oh, I'll tell you that later; it can wait," replied Hopalong. "Meanwhile, you get out there with Pete an' help get th' herd in shape. We'll be with you soon—here comes th' wranglers an' th' cavvieyeh. 'Bout time, too."

Chapter Twenty-Two

Mr. Boggs Is Disgusted

THE herd gained 12 miles by dark and would pass through the northern fence by noon of the next day, for Cook's ax and monkey wrench had been put to good use. For quite a distance there was no fence: about a mile of barb wire had been pulled loose and was tangled up into several large piles, while rings of burned grass and ashes surrounded what was left of the posts. The cook had embraced this opportunity to lay in a good supply of firewood and was the happiest man in the outfit.

At ten o'clock that night eight figures loped westward along the southern fence and three hours later dismounted near the first corral of the 4X ranch. They put their horses in a depression on the plain and then hastened to seek cover, being careful to make no noise.

At dawn the door of the bunkhouse opened quickly and as quickly slammed shut again, three bullets in it being the reason. An uproar ensued and guns spat from the two windows in the general direction of the unseen besiegers, who did not bother about replying; they had given notification of their presence and until it was necessary to shoot there was no earthly use of wasting ammunition. Besides, the drive outfit had cooled down rapidly when it found that its herd was in no immediate danger and was not anxious to kill anyone unless there was need. The situation was conducive to humor rather than anger. But every time the door moved it collected more lead, and it finally remained shut. The noise in the bunkhouse continued and finally a sombrero was waved frantically at the south window and a moment later Nat Boggs, foreman of the incarcerated 4X outfit, stuck his head out very cautiously and yelled questions which bore directly on the situation and were to the point. He appeared to be excited and unduly heated, if one might judge from his words and voice. There was no reply, which still further added to his heat and excitement. Becoming bolder and a little angrier he allowed his impetuous nature to get the upper hand and forthwith attempted the feat of getting through that same window, but a sharp *pat!* sounded on a board not a foot from him, and he reconsidered hastily. His sombrero again waved to insist on a truce, and collected two holes, causing him much mental anguish and threatening the loss of his worthy soul. He danced up and down with great agility and no grace and made remarks, thereby leading a full-voiced chorus.

"Ain't that a hell of a note?" he demanded plaintively as he paused for breath. "Stick *yore* hat out, Cranky, an' see what *you* can do," he suggested irritably.

Cranky Joe regarded him with pity and reproach and moved back towards the other end of the room, muttering softly to himself. "I know it ain't much of a bonnet, but he needn't rub it in," he growled peevishly.

"Try again; mebby they didn't see you," suggested Jim Larkin, who had a reputation for never making a joke. He escaped with his life and checked himself at the side of Cranky Joe, with whom he conferred on the harshness of the world toward unfortunates.

The rest of the morning was spent in snipe-shooting at random, trusting to luck to hit some one, and trusting in vain. At noon Cranky Joe could stand the strain no longer and opened the door just a little to relieve the monotony. He succeeded, being blessed with a smashed shoulder, and immediately became a general nuisance, adding greatly to the prevailing atmosphere. Boggs called him a few kinds of fools and hastened to nail the door shut; he hit his thumb and his heart became filled with venom.

"*Now* look at what they went an' done!" he yelled, running around in a circle. "Damned outrage!"

"Huh!" snorted Cranky Joe with maddening superiority. "That ain't nothing—just look at me!"

Boggs looked, very fixedly, and showed signs of apoplexy, and Cranky Joe returned to his end of the room to resume his soliloquy.

"Why don't you come out an' take them cows?" inquired an unkind voice from without. "Ain't changed yore mind, have you?"

"We'll give you a drink for half a cent a head— that's th' regular price for waterin' cows," called another.

The faint ripple of mirth which ran around the plain was lost in opinions loudly expressed within the room; and Boggs, tears of rage in his eyes, flung himself down on a chair and invented new terms for describing human beings.

John Terry was observing. He had been fluttering around the north window, constantly getting bolder, and had not been disturbed. When he withdrew his sombrero and found that it was intact he smiled to himself and leaned his elbows on the sill, looking carefully around the plain. The discovery that there was no cover on the north side cheered him greatly and he called to Boggs, outlining a plan of action.

Boggs listened intently and then smiled for the first time since dawn. "Bully for you, Terry!" he enthused. "Wait till dark—we'll fool 'em."

A bullet chipped the 'dobe at Terry's side and he ducked as he leaped back. "From an angle— what did I tell you?" he laughed. "We'll drop out here an' sneak behind th' house after dark. They'll be watching th' door—an' they won't be able to see us, anyhow."

Boggs sucked his thumb tenderly and grinned. "After which—" he elated.

"After which—" gravely repeated Terry, the others echoing it with unrestrained joy.

"Then, mebby, I can get a drink," chuckled Larkin, brightening under the thought.

"Th' moon comes up at ten," warned a voice. "It'll be full tonight—an' there ain't many clouds in sight."

"Ol' King Cole was a merry ol' soul," hummed McQuade lightly.

"An'—a—merry—ol'—soul—was—he! was— he!" thundered the chorus, deep-toned and strong. *"He had a wife for ev-'ery toe, an' some toes coun-ted three!"*

"Listen!" cried Meade, holding up his hand.

"An' ev-ery wife had sixteen dogs, an' ev-ery dog a flea!" shouted a voice from the besiegers, followed by a roar of laughter.

The hilarity continued until dark, only stopping when John Terry slipped out of the window, dropped to all fours and stuck his head around the corner of the rear wall. He saw many stars and was silently handed to Pete Wilson.

"What was that noise?" exclaimed Boggs in a low tone. "Are you all right, Terry?" he asked anxiously.

Three knocks on the wall replied to his question

and then McQuade went out, and three more knocks were heard.

"Wonder why they make that funny noise," muttered Boggs.

"Bumped inter somethin', I reckon," replied Jim Larkin. "Get out of my way—I'm next."

Boggs listened intently and then pushed Duke Lane back. "Don't like that—sounds like a crack on th' head. Hey, Jim! *Say* something!" he called softly. The three knocks were repeated, but Boggs was suspicious and he shook his head decisively. "T'ell with th' knockin'—*say* something!"

"Still got them twelve men?" asked a strange voice, pleasantly.

"An' ev-ery dog a flea," hummed another around the corner.

"Hell!" shouted Boggs. "To th' door, fellers! to th' door—quick!"

A whistle shrilled from behind the house and a leaden tattoo began on the door. "Other window!" whispered O'Neill. The foreman got there before him and, shoving his Colt out first to clear the way, yelled with rage and pain as a pole hit his wrist and knocked the weapon out of his hand. He was still commenting when Duke Lane pried open the door and, dropping quickly on his stomach, wriggled out, followed closely by Charley Beal and Tim. At that instant the tattoo drummed with greater vigor and such a hail of lead poured in through the opening that the door was promptly closed, leaving the three men outside to shift for themselves, with the darkness their only cover.

Duke and his companions whispered together as they lay flat and agreed upon a plan of action. Going around the ends of the house was suicide and no better than waiting for the rising moon to show them to the enemy, but there was no reason why the roof could not be utilized. Tim and Charley boosted Duke up, then Tim followed, and the pair on the roof pulled Charley to their side. Flat roofs were great institutions, they decided as they crawled cautiously toward the other side. This roof was of hard, sun-baked adobe, over two feet thick, and they did not care if their friends shot up on a gamble.

"Fine place, all right," thought Charley, grinning broadly. Then he turned an agonized face to Tim, his chest rising. *"Hitch! Hitch!"* he choked, fighting with all his will to master it. *"Hitch-chew! Hitch-chew! Hitch-chew!"* he sneezed loudly. There was a scramble below and a ripple of mirth floated up to them.

"Hitch-chew!" jeered a voice. "What do we want to hit you for?"

"Look us over, children," invited another.

"Wait until th' moon comes up," chuckled the third. "Be like knockin' th' nigger baby down for Red an' th' others. Ladies an' gents: we'll now have a little sketch entitled 'Shootin' snipe by moonlight.'"

"Jack-snipe, too," laughed Pete. "Will somebody please hold th' bag?"

The silence on the roof was profound and the three on the ground tried again.

"Let me call yore attention to th' trained coyotes, ladies an' gents," remarked Johnny in a deep, solemn voice. "Coyotes are not birds; they do not roost on roofs as a general thing, but they are some intelligent an' can be trained to do lots of foolish tricks. These ani-mules were—"

"Step this way, people; on-ly ten cents, two nickels," interrupted Pete. "They bark like dogs, an' howl like hell."

"Shut up!" snapped Tim angrily.

"After th' moon comes up," said Hopalong, "when you fellers get tired dodgin', you can chuck us yore guns an' come down. An' don't forget that this side of th' house is much th' safest," he warned.

"Go to hell!" snarled Duke bitterly.

"Won't, they're laying for me down there."

Johnny crawled to the north end of the wall and, looking cautiously around the corner, funneled his hands: "On th' roof, Red! On th' roof!"

"Yes, dear," was the reply, followed by gunshots.

"Hey! Move over!" snapped Tim, working toward the edge farthest from the cheerful Red, whose bullets were not as accurate in the dark as they promised to become in a few minutes when the moon should come up.

"Want to shove me off?" snarled Charley angrily. "For God's sake, Duke, do you want th' whole earth?" he demanded of his second companion.

"You just bet yore shirt I do! An' I want a hole in it, too!"

"Ain't you got no sense?"

"Would I be up here if I had?"

"It's going to be hot as blazes up here when th' sun gets high," cheerfully prophesied Tim; "an' dry, too," he added for a finishing touch.

"We'll be lucky if we're live enough to worry about th' sun's heat—*say*, that was a *close* one!" exclaimed Duke, frantically trying to flatten a little more. "Ah, thought so—there's that blamed moon!"

"Wish I'd gone out th' window instead," growled Charley, worming behind Duke, to the latter's prompt displeasure.

"You fellers better come down, one at a time," came from below. "Send yore guns down first, too. Red's a blamed good shot."

"Hope he croaks," muttered Duke. "*That's* closer yet!"

Tim's hand raised and a flash of fire singed Charley's hair. "Got to do somethin', anyhow," he explained, lowering the Colt and peering across the plain.

"You damned near succeeded!" shouted Charley, grabbing at his head. "Why, they're three hundred, an' you trying for 'em with a—*oh!*" he moaned, writhing.

"Locoed fool!" swore Duke, "showin' 'em where we are! They're doing good enough as it is! You ought—got *you,* too!"

"*I'm* going down—that blamed fool out there ain't caring what he hits," mumbled Charley, clenching his hands from pain. He slid over the edge and Pete grabbed him.

"Next," suggested Pete expectantly.

Tim tossed his Colt over the edge. "Here's another," he swore, following the weapon. He was grabbed and bound in a trice.

"When may we expect you, Mr. Duke?" asked Johnny, looking up.

"Presently, friend, presently. I want to—*wow!*" he finished, and lost no time in his descent, which was meteoric. "That feller'll *kill* somebody if he ain't careful!" he complained as Pete tied his hands behind his back.

"You wait till daylight an' see," cheerily replied Pete as the three were led off to join their friends in the corral.

There was no further action until the sun arose and then Hopalong hailed the house and demanded a parley, and soon he and Boggs met midway between the shack and the line.

"What d'you want?" asked Boggs sullenly.

"Want you to stop this farce so I can go on with my drive."

"Well, I ain't holding you!" exploded the 4X foreman.

"Oh, yes, but you are. I can't let you an' yore men out to hang on our flanks an' worry us, an' I don't want to hold you in that shack till you all die of thirst, or come out to be all shot up. Besides, I can't fool around here for a week; I got business to look after."

"Don't you worry about us dying with thirst; that ain't worrying us none."

"I heard different," replied Hopalong, smiling. "Them fellers in th' corral drank a quart apiece. See here, Boggs: you can't win, an' you know it. Yo're not buckin' me, but th' whole range, th' whole country. It's a fight between conditions— th' fence idea agin' th' open-range idea an' open trails. Th' fence will lose. You closed a drive trail that's 'most as old as cow-raising. Will th' punchers of this part of th' country stand for it? Suppose you lick us—which you won't—can you lick all th' rest of us, th' JD, Wallace's, Double-Arrow, C-80, Cross-O-Cross, an' th' others! That's just what it amounts to, an' you better stop right now, before somebody gets killed. You know what that means in this section. Yo're six to our eight, you ain't got a drink in that shack, an' you dasn't try to get one. You can't do a thing agin' us, an' you know it."

Boggs rested his hands on his hips and considered, Hopalong waiting for him to reply. He knew that the Bar-20 man was right but he hated to admit it, he hated to say he was whipped.

"Are any of them six hurt?" he finally asked.

"Only scratches an' sore heads," responded Hopalong, smiling. "We ain't tried to kill anybody, yet. I'm putting that up to you."

Boggs made no reply and Hopalong continued: "I got six of yore twelve men prisoners, an' all yore cayuses are in my han's. I'll shoot every animal before I'll leave 'em for you to use against me, an' I'll take enough of yore cows to make up for what I lost by that fence. You've got to pay for them dead cows, anyhow. If I do let you out you'll have to road-brand me two hundred, or pay cash. My herd ain't worrying me—it's moving all th' time. It's through that other fence by now. An' if I have to keep my outfit here to pen you in or shoot you off I can send to th' JD for a gang to push th' herd. Don't make no mistake: yo're getting off easy. Suppose one of my men had been killed at th' fence—what then?"

"Well, what do you want me to do?"

"Stop this foolishness an' take down them fences for a mile each side of th' trail. If Buck has to come up here th' whole thing'll go down. Road-brand me two hundred of yore three-year-olds. Now as soon as you agree, an' say that th' fight's over, it will be. You can't win out, an' what's th' use of having yore men killed off?"

"I hate to quit," replied the other gloomily.

"I know how that is, but yo're wrong on this question, dead wrong. You don't own this range or th' trail. You ain't got no right to close that old drive trail—honest, now, have you?"

"You say them six ain't hurt?"

"No more 'n I said."

"An' if I give in will you treat my men right?"

"Shore."

"When will you leave?"

"Just as soon as I get them two hundred three-year-olds."

"Well, I hate a quitter, but I can't do nothing, nohow," mused the 4X foreman. He cleared his throat and turned to look at the house. "All right, when you get them cows you get out of here, an' don't never come back!"

Hopalong flung his arm with a shout to his men and the other kicked savagely at an inoffensive stick and slouched back to his bunkhouse, a beaten man.

CHAPTER TWENTY-THREE

TEX EWALT HUNTS TROUBLE

NOT more than a few weeks after the Bar-20 drive outfit returned to the ranch a solitary horseman pushed on toward the trail they had followed, bound for Buckskin and the Bar-20 range. His name was Tex Ewalt and he cordially hated all of the Bar-20 outfit and Hopalong in particular. He had nursed a grudge for several years and now, as he rode south to rid himself of it and to pay a long-standing debt, it grew stronger until he thrilled with anticipation and the sauce of danger. This grudge had been acquired when he and Slim Travennes had enjoyed a duel with Hopalong Cassidy up in Santa Fe, and had been worsted; it had increased when he learned of Slim's death at Cactus Springs at the hands of Hopalong; and, some time later, hearing that two friends of his, "Slippery" Trendley and "Deacon" Rankin, with their gang, had "gone out" in the Panhandle with the same man and his friends responsible for it, Tex hastened to Muddy Wells to even the score and clean his slate. Even now his face burned when he remembered his experiences on that never-to-be-forgotten occasion. He had been played with, ridiculed, and shamed, until he fled from the town as a place accursed, hating everything and everybody. It galled him to think that he had allowed Buck Peters's momentary sympathy to turn him from his purpose, even though he was convinced that the foreman's action had saved his life. And now Tex was returning, not to Muddy Wells, but to the range where the Bar-20 outfit held sway.

Several years of clean living had improved Tex, morally and physically. The liquor he had once been in the habit of consuming had been reduced to a negligible quantity; he spent the money on cartridges instead, and his pistol work showed the results of careful and dogged practice, particularly in the quickness of the draw. Punching cows on a remote northern range had repaid him in health far more than his old game of living on his wits and other people's lack of them, as proved by his clear eye and the pink showing through the tan above his beard; while his somber, steady gaze, due to long-held fixity of purpose, indicated the resourcefulness of a perfectly reliable set of nerves. His low-hung holster tied securely to his trousers leg to assure smoothness in drawing, the restrained swing of his right hand, never far from the well-worn scabbard which sheathed a triggerless Colt's "Frontier"—these showed the confident and ready gunman, the man who seldom missed. "Frontiers" left the factory with triggers attached, but the absence of that part did not always incapacitate a weapon. Some men found that the regular method was too slow, and painstakingly cultivated the art of thumbing the hammer. Thumbing was believed to save the split second so valuable to a man in argument with his peers. Tex was riding with the set purpose of picking a fair fight with the best six-shooter expert it had ever been his misfortune to meet, and he needed that split second. He knew that he needed it and the knowledge thrilled him with a peculiar elation; he had changed greatly in the past year and now he wanted an even break where once he would have called all his wits into play to avoid it. He had found himself and now he acknowledged no superior in anything.

On his way south he met and talked with men who had known him, the old Tex, in the days when he had made his living precariously. They did not recognize him behind his beard, and he was content to let the oversight pass. But from these few he learned what he wished to know, and he was glad that Hopalong Cassidy was where he had always been, and that his gun work had improved rather than depreciated with the passing of time. He wished to prove himself master of The Master, and to be hailed as such by those who had jeered and laughed at his ignominy several years before. So he rode on day after day, smiling and content, neither underrating nor overrating his enemy's ability with one weapon, but trying to think of him as he really was. He knew that if there was any difference between Hopalong Cassidy and himself that it must be very slight— perhaps so slight as to result fatally to both; but if that were so then it would have to work out as it saw fit—he at least would have accomplished what many, many others had failed in.

In the little town of Buckskin, known hardly more than locally, and never thought of by outsiders except as the place where the Bar-20 spent their spare time and money, and neutral ground for the surrounding ranches, was Cowan's saloon, in the dozen years of its existence the scene of good stories, boisterous fun, and quick deaths. Put together roughly, of crude materials, sticking up in inartistic prominence on the dusty edge of a dustier street, warped, bleached by the sun, and patched with boards ripped from packing-cases and with the flattened sides of tin cans, low of ceiling, the floor one huge brown discoloration of springy, creaking boards, knotted and split and worn into hollows, the unpretentious building offered its hospitality to all who might be tempted by the scrawled, sprawled lettering of its sign. The walls were smoke-blackened, pitted with numerous small and clear-cut holes, and decorated with initials carelessly cut by men who had come and gone.

Such was Cowan's, the best patronized place in many hot and dusty miles and the Mecca of the cowboys from the surrounding ranches. Often at night these riders of the range gathered in the humble building and told tales of exceeding interest, and on these occasions one might see a row of ponies standing before the building, heads down and quiet. It is strange how alike cow ponies look in the dim light of the stars. On the south side of the saloon, weak, yellow lamplight filtered through the dirt on the windowpanes and fell in distorted patches on the plain, blotched in places by the shadows of the wooden substitutes for glass.

It was a moonlight night late in the fall, after the last beef roundup was over and the last drive outfit home again, that two cow ponies stood in front of Cowan's while their owners lolled against the bar and talked over the latest sensation—the fencing in of the West Valley range, and the way Hopalong Cassidy and his trail outfit had opened up the old drive trail across it. The news was a month old, but it was the last event of any importance and was still good to laugh over.

"Boys," remarked the proprietor, "I want you to meet Mr. Elkins. He came down that trail last week, an' he didn't see no fence across it." The man at the table arose slowly. "Mr. Elkins, this is Sandy Lucas an' Wood Wright, of th' C-80. Mr. Elkins here has been a-lookin' over th' country, sizin' up what th' beef prospects will be for next year, an' he knows all about wire fences. Here's how," he smiled, treating on the house.

Mr. Elkins touched the glass to his bearded lips and set it down untasted while he joked over the sharp rebuff so lately administered to wire fences in that part of the country. While he was an ex-cowpuncher he believed that he was above allowing prejudice to sway his judgment, and it was his opinion, after careful thought, that barb wire was harmful to the best interests of the range. He had ridden over a great part of the cattle country in the last few yeas, and after reviewing the existing conditions as he understood them, his verdict must go as stated, and emphatically. He launched gracefully into a slowly delivered and lengthy discourse upon the subject, which proved to be so entertaining that his companions were content to listen and nod with comprehension. They had never met anyone who was so well qualified to discuss the pros and cons of the barb-wire-fence question, and they learned many things which they had never heard before. This was very gratifying to Mr. Elkins, who drew largely upon hearsay, his own vivid imagination, and a healthy logic. He was very glad to talk to men who had the welfare of the range at heart, and he hoped soon to meet the man who had taken the initiative in giving barb wire its first serious setback on that rich and magnificent southern range.

"You shore ought to meet Cassidy—he's a fine

man," remarked Lucas with enthusiasm. "You'll not find any better, no matter where you look. But you ain't touched yore liquor," he finished with surprise.

"You'll have to excuse me, gentlemen," replied Mr. Elkins, smiling deprecatingly. "When a man likes it as much as I do it ain't very easy to foller instructions an' let it alone. Sometimes I almost break loose an' indulge, regardless of whether it kills me or not. I reckon it'll get me yet." He struck the bar a resounding blow with his clenched hand. "But I ain't going to cave in till I has to!"

"That's purty tough," sympathized Wood Wright reflectively. "I ain't so very much taken with it, but I know I would be if I knowed I couldn't have any."

"Yes, that's human nature, all right," laughed Lucas. "That reminds me of a little thing that happened to me once—"

"Listen!" exclaimed Cowan, holding up his hand for silence. "I reckon that's th' Bar-20 now, or some of it—sounds like them when they're feelin' frisky. There's allus something happening when them fellers are around."

The proprietor was right, as proved a moment later when Johnny Nelson, continuing his argument, pushed open the door and entered the room. "I didn't neither, an' you know it!" he flung over his shoulder.

"Then who did?" demanded Hopalong, chuckling. "Why, hullo, boys," he said, nodding to his friends at the bar. "Nobody else would do a fool thing like that—nobody but you, Kid," he added, turning to Johnny.

"I don't care a hang what you think; I say I didn't an'—"

"He shore did, all right; I seen him just afterward," laughed Billy Williams, pressing close upon Hopalong's heels. "Howdy, Lucas, an' there's that ol' coyote, Wood Wright! How's everybody feeling?"

"Where's th' rest of you fellows?" inquired Cowan.

"Stayed home tonight," replied Hopalong.

"Got any loose money, you two?" asked Billy, grinning at Lucas and Wright.

"I reckon we have—an' our credit's good if we ain't. We're good for a dollar or two, ain't we, Cowan?" replied Lucas.

"Two dollars an' four bits," corrected Cowan. "I'll raise it to three dollars even when you pay me that 'leven cents you owe me."

" 'Leven cents? What 'leven cents?"

"Postage stamps an' envelope for that love letter you writ."

"Go to blazes, that wasn't no love letter!" snorted Lucas indignantly. "That was my quarterly report. I never did write no love letters, nohow."

"We'll trim you fellers tonight, if you've got th' nerve to play us," grinned Johnny expectantly.

"Yes, an' we've got that, too. Give us th' cards, Cowan," requested Wood Wright, turning. "They won't give us no peace till we take all their money away from 'em."

"Open game," prompted Cowan, glancing meaningly at Elkins, who stood by idly looking on, and without showing much interest in the scene.

"Shore! Everybody can come in what wants to," replied Lucas heartily, leading the others to the table. "I allus did like a six-handed game best—all th' cards are out an' there's some excitement in it."

When the deal began Elkins was seated across the table from Hopalong, facing him for the first time since that day over in Muddy Wells, and studying him closely. He found no change, for the few years had left no trace of their passing on the Bar-20 puncher. The sensation of facing the man he had come south expressly to kill did not interfere with Elkins's cardplaying ability, for he played a good game; and as if the Fates were with him it was Hopalong's night off as far as poker was concerned, for his customary good luck was not in evidence. That instinctive feeling which singles out two duellists in a card game was soon experienced by the others, who were careful, as became good players, to avoid being caught between them; in consequence, when the game broke up, Elkins had most of Hopalong's money. At one period of his life Elkins had lived on poker for five years, and lived well. But he gained more than money in this game, for he had made friends with the players and placed the first wire of his trap. Of those in the room Hopalong alone treated him with reserve, and this was cleverly swung so that it appeared to be caused by a temporary grouch due to the sting of defeat. As the Bar-20 man was known to be given to moods at times, this was accepted as the true explanation and gave promise of hotly contested games for revenge later on. The banter which the defeated puncher had to endure stirred him and strengthened the reserve, although he was careful not to show it.

When the last man rode off, Elkins and the proprietor sought their bunks without delay, the former to lie awake a long time, thinking deeply. He was vexed at himself for failing to work out an acceptable plan of action, one that would show him to be in the right. He would gain nothing more than glory, and pay too dearly for it, if he killed Hopalong and was in turn killed by the dead man's friends—and he believed that he had become acquainted with the quality of the friendship which bound the units of the Bar-20 outfit into a smooth, firm whole. They were like brothers, like one man. Cassidy must do the forcing as far as appearances went, and be clearly in the wrong before the matter could be settled.

The next week was a busy one for Elkins, every day finding him in the saddle and riding over some one of the surrounding ranches with one or more of its punchers for company. In this way he became acquainted with the men who might be called on to act as his jury when the showdown came, and he proceeded to make friends of them in a manner that promised success. And some of his suggestions for the improvement of certain conditions on the range, while they might not work out right in the long run, compelled thought and showed his interest. His remarks on the condition and numbers of cattle were the same in substance in all cases and showed that he knew what he was talking about, for the punchers were all very optimistic about the next year's showing in cattle.

"If you fellers don't break all records for drive herds of quality next year I don't know nothing about cows—an' I shore don't know nothing else," he told the foreman of the Bar-20, as they rode homeward after an inspection of that ranch. "There'll be more dust hangin' over th' drive trails leading from this section next year when spring drops th' barriers than ever before. You needn't fear for th' market, neither—prices will stand. Th' north an' central ranges ain't doing what they ought to this year—it'll be up to you fellers down south here to make that up, an' you can do it."

This was not a guess, but the result of thought and study based on the observations he had made on his ride south, and from what he had learned from others along the way. It paralleled Buck's own private opinion, especially in regard to the southern range, and the vague suspicions in the foreman's mind disappeared for good and all.

Needless to say, Elkins was a welcome visitor at the ranch houses and was regarded as a good fellow. At the Bar-20 he found only two men who would not thaw to him, and he was possessed of too much tact to try any persuasive measures. One was Hopalong, whose original cold reserve seemed to be growing steadily, the Bar-20 puncher finding in Elkins a personality that charged the atmosphere with hostility and quietly rubbed him the wrong way. Whenever he was in the presence of the newcomer he felt the tugging of an irritating and insistent antagonism and he did not always fully conceal it. John Bartlett, Lucas, and one or two of the more observing had noticed it and they began to prophesy future trouble between the two. The other man who disliked Elkins was Red Connors, but what was more natural? Red, being Hopalong's closest companion, would be very apt to share his friend's antipathy. On the other hand, as if to prove Hopalong's dislike to be unwarranted, Johnny Nelson swung far to the other extreme and was frankly enthusiastic in his liking for the cattle scout. And Johnny did not pour oil on the waters when he laughingly twitted Hopalong for allowing "a lickin' at cards to make him sore." This was the idea that Elkins was quietly striving to have generally accepted.

The affair thus hung fire, Elkins chafing at the delay and cautiously working for an opening, which at last presented itself, to be promptly seized. By a sort of mutual, unspoken agreement, the men in Cowan's that night passed up the cards and sat swapping stories. Cowan, swearing at a smoking lamp, looked up with a grin and burned his fingers as a roar of laughter marked the point of a droll reminiscence told by Bartlett.

"That's a good story, Bartlett," Elkins remarked, slowing refilling his pipe. "Reminds me of th' lame Greaser, Hippy Joe, an' th' canned oysters. They was both bad, an' neither of 'em knew it till they came together. It was like this—" The malicious side glance went unseen by all but Hopalong, who stiffened with the raging suspicion of being twitted on his own deformity. The humor of the tale failed to appeal to him, and when his full senses returned Lucas was in the midst of the story of the deadly game of tag played in a ten-acre lot of dense underbrush by two of his old-time friends. It was a tale of gripping interest and his auditors were leaning forward in their eagerness not to miss a word. "An' Pierce won," finished Lucas; "some shot up, but able to get about. He was all right in a couple of weeks. But he was bound to win: he could shoot all around Sam Hopkins."

"But th' best shot won't allus win in that game," commented Elkins. "That's one of th' minor factors."

"Yes, sir! It's *luck* that counts there," endorsed Bartlett quickly. "Luck, nine times out of ten."

"Best shot ought to win," declared Skinny Thompson. "It ain't all luck, nohow. Where'd I be against Hoppy, there?"

"Won't neither!" cried Johnny excitedly. "Th' man who sees th' other first wins out. That's woodcraft, an' brains."

"Aw! What do you know about it, anyhow?" demanded Lucas. "If he can't shoot so good what chance has he got—if he misses th' first try, what then?"

"What chance has he got! First chance, miss or no miss. If he can't see th' other first, where th' devil does his good shootin' come in?"

"Huh!" snorted Wood Wright belligerently. "Any fool can *see,* but he can't *shoot!* An' it's as much luck as woodcraft, too, an' don't you forget it!"

"Th' first shot don't win, Johnny, not in a game like that, with all th' dodgin' an' duckin'," remarked Red. "You can't put one where you want it when a feller's slippin' around in th' brush. It's th' most that counts, an' th' best shot gets in th' most. I wouldn't want to have to stand up against Hoppy an' a short gun, not in that game, no, sir!" and Red shook his head with decision.

The argument waxed hot. With the exception of Hopalong, who sat silently watchful, everyone spoke his opinion and repeated it without regard to the others. It appeared that in this game, the man with the strongest lungs would eventually win out, and each man tried to show his superiority in that line. Finally, above the uproar, Cowan's bellow was heard, and he kept it up until some notice was taken of it. "Shut up! *Shut up! For God's sake, quit!* Never saw such a bunch of tinder—let somebody drop a cold, burned-out match in this gang, an' hell's to pay. Here, *all* of you, play cards an' forget about cross-tag in th' scrub. You'll be arguin' about playin' marbles in th' dark purty soon!"

"All right," muttered Johnny, "but just the same, th' man who—"

"Never mind about th' man who! Did you hear *me?*" yelled Cowan, swiftly reaching for a bucket of water. "*This* is a game where *I* gets th' most in, an' don't forget it!"

"Come on, play cards," growled Lucas, who did not relish having his decision questioned on his own story. Undoubtedly somewhere in the wide, wide world there was such a thing as common courtesy, but none of it had ever strayed onto that range.

The chairs scraped on the rough floor as the men pulled up to a table. "I don't care a hang," came Elkins's final comment as he shuffled the cards with careful attention. "I'm not any fancy Colt expert, but I'm damned if I won't take a chance in that game with any man as totes a gun. Leastawise, of *course,* I wouldn't take no such advantage of a lame man."

The effect would have been ludicrous but for its deadly significance. Cowan, stooping to go under the bar, remained in that hunched-up attitude, his every faculty concentrated in his ears; the match on its way to the cigarette between Red's lips was held until it burned his fingers, when it was dropped from mere reflex action, the hand still stiffly aloft; Lucas, half in and half out of his chair, seemed to have got just where he intended, making no effort to seat himself. Skinny Thompson, his hand on his gun, seemed paralyzed; his mouth was open to frame a reply that never was uttered and he stared through narrowed eyelids at the blunderer. The sole movement in the room was the slow rising of Hopalong and the markedly innocent shuffling of the cards by Elkins, who appeared to be entirely ignorant of the weight and effect of his words. He dropped the pack for the cut and then looked up and around as if surprised by the silence and the expressions he saw.

Hopalong stood facing him, leaning over with

both hands on the table. His voice, when he spoke, rumbled up from his chest in a low growl. "You won't *have* no advantage, Elkins. Take it from me, you've had yore last fling. I'm glad you made it plain, this time, so it's something I can take hold of." He straightened slowly and walked to the door, and an audible sigh sounded through the room as it was realized that trouble was not immediately imminent. At the door he paused and turned half around, looking back over his shoulder. "At noon tomorrow I'm going to hoof it north through th' brush between th' river an' th' river trail, startin' at th' old ford a mile down th' river." He waited expectantly.

"Me too—only the other way," was the instant rejoinder. "Have it yore own way."

Hopalong nodded and the closing door shut him out into the night. Without a word the Bar-20 men arose and followed him, the only hesitant being Johnny, who was torn between loyalty and new-found friendship, but with a sorrowful shake of the head, he turned away and passed out, not far behind the others.

"Clannish, ain't they?" remarked Elkins gravely.

Those remaining were regarding him sternly, questioningly, Cowan with a deep frown darkening his face. "You hadn't ought to 'a' said that, Elkins." The reproof was almost an accusation.

Elkins looked steadily at the speaker. "You hadn't ought to 'a' let me say it," he replied. "How did I know he was so touchy?" His gaze left Cowan and lingered in turn on each of the others. "Some of you ought to 'a' told me. I wouldn't 'a' said it only for what I said just before, an' I didn't want him to think I was challenging him to no duel in th' brush. So I says so, an' then he goes an' takes it up that I *am* challenging him. I ain't got no call to fight with nobody. Ain't I tried to keep out of trouble with him ever since I've been here? Ain't I kept out of th' poker games on his account? Ain't I?" The grave, even tones were dispassionate, without a trace of animus and serenely sure of justice.

The faces around him cleared gradually and heads began to nod in comprehending consent.

"Yes, I reckon you have," agreed Cowan slowly, but the frown was not entirely gone. "Yes, I reckon—mebby—you have."

CHAPTER TWENTY-FOUR

THE MASTER

IT was noon by the sun when Hopalong and Red shook hands south of the old ford and the former turned to enter the brush. Hopalong was cool and ominously calm while his companion was the opposite. Red was frankly suspicious of the whole affair and nursed the private opinion that Mr. Elkins would lay in ambush and shoot his enemy down like a dog. And Red had promised himself a dozen times that he would study the signs around the scene of action if Hopalong should not come back and take a keen delight, if warranted, in shooting Mr. Elkins full of holes with no regard for an even break. He was thinking the matter over as his friend breasted the first line of brush and could not refrain from giving a slight warning. "Get him, Hoppy," he called, earnestly, "get him good. Let *him* do some of th' moving about. I'll be here waiting for you."

Hopalong smiled in reply and sprang forward, the leaves and branches quickly shutting him from Red's sight. He had worked out his plan of action the night before when he was alone and the world was still, and as soon as he had it to his satisfaction he had dropped off to sleep as easily as a child—it took more than gunplay to disturb his nerves. He glanced about him to make sure of his bearings and then struck on a curving line for the river. The first hundred yards were covered with speed and then he began to move more slowly and with greater regard for caution, keeping close to the earth and showing a marked preference for low ground. Sky lines were all right in times of peace, but under the present conditions they promised to become unhealthy. His eyes and ears told him nothing for a quarter of an hour, and then he suddenly stopped short and crouched as he saw the plain trail of a man crossing his own direction at a right angle. From the bottom of one of the heel prints a crushed leaf was slowly rising back towards its original position, telling him how new the trail was, and as if this were not enough for his trained mind he heard a twig snap sharply as he glanced along the line of prints. It sounded very close, and he dropped instantly to one knee and thought quickly. Why had the other left so plain a trail, why had he reached up and broken twigs that projected above his head as he passed? Why had he kicked aside a small stone, leaving a patch of moist, bleached grass to tell where it had lain? Elkins had stumbled here, but there were no toe marks to tell of it. Hopalong would not track, for he was no assassin; but he knew what he would do if he were, and careless.

The answer leaped to his suspicious mind like a flash, and he did not care to waste any time in trying to determine whether or not Elkins was capable of such a trick. He acted on the presumption that the trail had been made plain for a good reason, and that not far ahead at some suitable place—and there were any number of such within 100 yards, the maker of the plain trail lay in wait. Smiling savagely he worked backward and turning, struck off in a circle. He had no compunctions whatever now about shooting the other player of the game. It was not long before he came upon the same trail again and he started another circle. A bullet *zipped* past his ear and cut a twig not two inches from his head. He fired at the smoke as he dropped, and then wriggled rapidly backward, keeping as flat to the earth as he could. Elkins had taken up his position in a thicket which stood in the center of a level patch of sand in the old bed of the river—the bed it had used five years before and forsaken at the time of the big flood when it cut itself a new channel and made the U-bend which now surrounded this piece of land on three sides. Even now, during the rainy season, the thicket which sheltered Mr. Elkins was frequently an island in a sluggish, shallow overflow.

"Hole up, blast you!" jeered Hopalong, hugging the ground. The second bullet from Mr. Elkins's gun cut another twig, this one just over his head, and he laughed insolently. "I ain't a-scared to do th' movin', even if you are. Judging from th' way you keep out o' sight th' canned oysters are in th' can again. *I* never did no ambushin', you coyote."

"You can't make remarks like that an' get away with 'em—I've knowed you too long," retorted Elkins, shifting quickly and none too soon. "You went an' got Slim afore he was wide awake. I know *you,* all right."

Hopalong's surprise was but momentary, and his mind raced back over the years. Who was this man Elkins, that he knew Slim Travennes? "Yo're a liar, Elkins, an' so was th' man who told you that!"

"Call me Ewalt," jeered the other nastily. "Nobody'll hear it, an' you'll not live to tell it. Ewalt, Tex Ewalt; call me that."

"So you've come back after all this time to make me get you, have you? Well, I ain't a-goin' to shoot no buttons off you *this* time. I allus reckoned you learned something at Muddy Wells—but you'll learn it here," Hopalong rejoined, sliding into a depression and working with great caution towards the dry river bed, where fallen trees and hillocks of sand provided good cover in plenty. Everything was clear now and despite the seriousness of the situation he could not repress a smile as he remembered vividly that day at the carnival when Tex Ewalt came to town with the determination to kill him and show him up as an imitation. His grievance against Elkins was petty when compared to that against Ewalt, and he began to force the issue. As he peered over a stranded log he caught sight of his enemy disappearing into another part of the thicket, and two of his three shots went home. Elkins groaned with pain and fear as he realized that his right kneecap was broken and would make him slow in his movements. He was lamed for life, even if he did come out of the duel alive; lamed in the same way that Hopalong was —the affliction he had made cruel sport of had come to him. But he had plenty of courage and he returned the fire with remarkable quickness, his two shots sounding almost as one.

Hopalong wiped the blood from his cheek and wormed his way to a new place; when halfway there he called out again: "How's yore health— Tex?" in mock sympathy.

Elkins lied manfully and when he looked to get in another shot his enemy was on the farther bank, moving up to get behind him. He did not know Hopalong's new position until he raised his head to glance down over the dried river bed, and was informed by a bullet that nicked his ear. As he ducked, another grazed his head, the third going wild. He hazarded a return shot, and heard Hopalong's laugh ring out again.

"Like th' story Lucas told, th' best shot is going to win out this time, too," the Bar-20 man remarked grimly. "You thought a game like this would give you some chance against a better shot, didn't you? You are a fool."

"It ain't over yet, not by a damned sight!" came the retort.

"An' you thought you had a little th' best of it if you stayed still an' let me do th' movin', didn't you? You'll learn something before I get through with you, but it'll be too late to do you any good," Hopalong called, crouched below a hillock of sand so the other could not take advantage of the words and single him out for a shot.

"You can't learn me nothing, you assassin; I've got my eyes open this time." He knew that he had had them open before, and that Hopalong was in no way an assassin, but if he could enrage his enemy and sting him into some reflex carelessness he might have the last laugh.

Elkins's retort was wasted, for the sudden and unusual, although a familiar sound, had caught Hopalong's ear and he was giving all his attention to it. While he weighed it, his incredulity holding back the decision his common sense was striving to give him, the noise grew louder rapidly and common sense won out in a cry of warning an instant before a five-foot wall of brown water burst upon his sight, sweeping swiftly down the old, dry river bed; and behind it towered another and greater wall. Tree trunks were dancing end over end in it as if they were straws.

"Cloudburst!" he yelled. "Run, Tex! Run for yore life! Cloudburst up th' valley! Run, you fool, *run!*"

Tex's sarcastic retort was cut short as he instinctively glanced north, and his agonized curse lashed Hopalong forward. "Can't run—kneecap's busted! Can't swim, can't do—ah, hell—!"

Hopalong saw him torn from his shelter and whisked down the raging torrent like an arrow from a bow. The Bar-20 puncher leaped from the bank, shot under the yellow flood and rose, gasping and choking, many yards downstream, fighting madly to get the muddy water out of his throat and eyes. As he struck out with all his strength down the current, he caught sight of Tex being torn from a jutting tree limb, and he shouted encouragement and swam all the harder, if such a thing were possible. Tex's course was checked for a moment by a boiling back-current and as he again felt the pull of the rushing stream Hopalong's hand gripped his collar and the fight for safety began. Whirled against logs and stumps, drawn down by the weight of his clothes and the frantic efforts of Tex to grasp him— fighting the water and the man he was trying to save at the same time, his head under water as often as it was out of it, and Tex's viselike fingers threatening him—he headed for the west shore against powerful crosscurrents that made his efforts seem useless. He seemed to get the worst of every break. Once, when caught by a friendly current, they were swung under an overhanging branch, but as Hopalong's hand shot up to grasp it a submerged bush caught his feet and pulled him under, and Tex's steel-like arms around his throat almost suffocated him before he managed to beat the other into insensibility and break the hold.

"I'll let you go!" he threatened, but his hand grasped the other's collar all the tighter and his fighting jaw was set with greater determination than ever.

They shot out into the main stream, where the U-bend channel joined the short cut, and it looked miles wide to the exhausted puncher. He was fighting only on his will now. He would not give up, though he scarce could lift an arm and his lungs seemed on fire. He did not know whether Tex was dead or alive, but he would get the body ashore with him, or go down trying. He bumped into a log and instinctively grasped it. It turned, and when he came up again it was bobbing five feet ahead of him. Ages seemed to pass before he flung his numb arm over it and floated with it. He was not alone in the flood; a coyote was pushing steadily across his path toward the nearer bank, and on a gliding treetrunk crouched a frightened cougar, its ears flattened and its sharp claws dug solidly through the bark. Here and there were cattle, and a snake wriggled smoothly past him, apparently as much at home in the water as out of it. The log turned again and he just managed to catch hold of it as he came up for the second time.

Things were growing black before his eyes and strange, weird ideas and images floated through his brain. When he regained some part of his senses he saw ahead of him a long, curling crest of yellow water and foam, and he knew, vaguely, that it was pouring over a bar. The next instant his feet struck bottom and he fought his way blindly and slowly, with the stubborn determination of his kind, towards the brush-covered point 20 feet away.

When he opened his eyes and looked around he became conscious of excruciating pains and he closed them again to rest. His outflung hand struck something that made him look around again, and he saw Tex Ewalt, face-down at his side. He released his grasp on the other's collar and slowly the whole thing came to him, and then the necessity for action, unless he wished to lose what he had fought so hard to save.

Anything short of the iron man Tex had become would have been dead before this or have been finished by the mauling he now got from Hopalong. But Tex groaned, gurgled a curse, and finally opened his eyes upon his rescuer, who sank back with a grunt of satisfaction. Slowly his intelligence returned as he looked steadily into Hopalong's eyes, and with it came the realization of a strange truth: he did not hate this man at all. Months of right living, days and nights of honest labor shoulder to shoulder with men who respected him for his ability and accepted him as one of themselves, had made a new man of him, although the legacy of hatred from the old Tex had disguised him from himself until now; but the new Tex, battered, shot-up, nearly drowned, looked at his old enemy and saw him for the man he really was. He smiled faintly and reached out his hand.

"Cassidy, yo're the boss," he said. "Shake."
They shook.

Center Point Publishing
600 Brooks Road • PO Box 1
Thorndike ME 04986-0001 USA

(207) 568-3717

US & Canada:
1 800 929-9108
www.centerpointlargeprint.com